Thirteen tales of a weird and uncontrollable universe where a woman can be terrorized by her own unborn child —where an innocent little girl can be trapped alone in an unpeopled world of echoes—where a prize fight features a killer robot.

THE SHORES OF SPACE

STRANGE AND STARTLING STORIES
OF HORRIBLE HIDDEN DIMENSIONS THAT
SURROUND A WORLD . . . AS SANE AS OURS!

Books by Richard Matheson

THE SHORES OF SPACE
THE BEARDLESS WARRIORS
THIRD FROM THE SUN
THE SHRINKING MAN
EARTHBOUND
I AM A LEGEND

Published by Bantam Books, Inc.

THE SHORES OF SPACE

BY RICHARD MATHESON

BANTAM BOOKS · TORONTO · NEW YORK · LONDON

THE SHORES OF SPACE
A Bantam Book / published February 1957
2nd printing ...... January 1969

Table of Contents

Being ••

IN darkness hovering. A soundless shell of metals glistening pale—held aloft by threads of anti-gravity. Below, the planet, shrouded with night, turning from the moon. On its black-swept face, an animal staring up with bright-eyed panic at the dully phosphorescent globe suspended overhead. A twitch of muscle. The hard earth drums delicately beneath fleeing pawbeats. Silence again, wind-soughed and lone. Hours. Black hours passing into grey, then mottled pink. Sunlight sprays across the metal globe. It shimmers with unearthly light.

It was like putting his hand into a scorching oven.

"Oh my God, it's hot," he said, grimacing, jerking back his hand and closing it once more, gingerly, over the sweat-stained steering wheel.

"It's your imagination." Marian lay slumped against the warm, plastic-covered seat. A mile behind, she'd stuck her sandaled feet out the window. Her eyes were closed, breath fell in fitful gasps from her drying lips. Across her face, the hot wind fanned bluntly, ruffling the short blond hair.

"It's not hot," she said, squirming uncomfortably, tugging at the narrow belt on her shorts. "It's cool. As a cucumber."

"Ha," Les grunted. He leaned forward a little and clenched his teeth at the feel of his sport shirt clinging damply to his back. "What a month for driving," he growled.

They'd left Los Angeles three days before on their way to visit Marian's family in New York. The weather had been equatorial from the start, three days of blazing sun that had drained them of energy.

The schedule they were attempting to maintain made things even worse. On paper, four hundred miles a day didn't seem like much. Converted into practical traveling it was brutalizing. Traveling over dirt cutoffs that sent up spinning, choking dust clouds. Traveling over rut-pocked stretches of highway under repair; afraid to hit more than twenty miles an hour on them for fear of snapping an axle or shaking their brains loose.

Worst of all, traveling up twenty to thirty mile grades that sent the radiator into boiling frenzies every half hour or so. Then sitting for long, sweltering minutes, waiting for the motor to cool off, pouring in fresh water from the water bag, sitting and waiting in the middle of an oven.

"I'm done on one side," Les said, breathlessly. "Turn me."

"And ha to you," Marian sotto voiced.

"Any water left?"

Marian reached down her left hand and tugged off the heavy top of the portable ice box. Feeling inside its coolish interior, she pulled up the thermos bottle. She shook it.

"Empty," she said, shaking her head.

"As my *head*," he finished in a disgusted voice, "For ever letting you talk me into driving to New York in August."

"Now, now," she said, her cajoling a trifle worn, "Don't get heated up."

"*Damn!*" he snapped irritably, "When is this damn cutoff going to get back to the damn highway?"

"Damn," she muttered lightly, "Damn damn."

He said no more. His hands gripped tighter on the wheel. Hwy. 66, *alt. rte.*—they'd been on the damn thing for hours now, shunted aside by a section of the main highway undergoing repair. For that matter, he wasn't even sure they were on the alternate route. There had been five crossroads in the past two hours. In speeding along to get out of the desert, he hadn't looked too carefully at the crossroad signs.

"Honey, there's a station," Marian said, "let's see if we can get some water."

"And some gas," he added, glancing at the gauge, "And some instructions on how to get back to the highway."

"The damn highway," she said.

A faint smile tugged at Les's mouth corners as he pulled the Ford off the road and braked up beside the two paint-chipped pumps that stood before an old sagging shack.

"This is a hot looking spot," he said dispassionately. "Ripe for development."

"For the right party." Marian's eyes closed again. She drew in a heavy breath through her open mouth.

No one came out of the shack.

"Oh, don't tell me it's deserted," Les said disgustedly, looking around.

Marian drew down her long legs. "Isn't there anybody here?" she asked, opening her eyes.

"Doesn't look like it."

Les pushed open the door and slid out. As he stood, an involuntary grunt twitched his body and his knees almost buckled. It felt as if someone had dropped a mountain of heat on his head.

"*God!*" He blinked away the waves of blackness lapping at his ankles.

"What is it?"

"This *heat*." He stepped between the two rusty handled pumps and crunched over the hot, flaky ground for the doorway of the shack.

"And we're not even a third of the way," he muttered grimly to himself. Behind him, he heard the car door slam on Marian's side and her loose sandals flopping on the ground.

Dimness gave the illusion of coolness only for a second. Then the muggy, sodden air in the shack pressed down on Les and he hissed in displeasure.

There was no one in the shack. He looked around its small confines at the uneven-legged table with the scarred surface, the backless chair, the cobwebbed coke machine, the price lists and calendars on the wall, the threadbare shade on the small window, drawn down to the sill, shafts of burnished light impaling the many rents.

The wooden floor creaked as he stepped back out into the heavy sunlight.

"No one?" Marian asked and he shook his head. They looked at each other without expression a moment and she patted at her forehead with a damp handkerchief.

"Well, onward," she said wryly.

That was when they heard the car come rattling down the rutted lane that led off the road into the desert. They walked to the edge of the shack and watched the old, home-made tow truck make its wobbling, noisy approach toward the station. Far back from the road was the low form of the house it had come from.

"To the rescue," Marian said. "I hope he has water."

As the truck groaned to a halt beside the shack, they could see the heavily-tanned face of the man behind the wheel. He was somewhere in his thirties, a dour looking individual in a tee shirt and patched and faded blue overalls. Lank hair protruded from beneath the brim of his grease-stained Stetson.

It wasn't a smile he gave them as he slid out of the truck. It was more like a reflex twitching of his lean, humorless mouth. He moved up to them with jerky boot strides, his dark eyes moving from one to the other of them.

"You want gas?" he asked Les in a hard, thick-throated voice.

"Please."

The man looked at Les a moment as if he didn't understand. Then he grunted and headed for the Ford, reaching into his back overall pocket for the pump key. As he walked past the front bumper, he glanced down at the license plate.

He stood looking dumbly at the tank cap for a moment, his calloused fingers trying vainly to unscrew it.

"It locks," Les told him, walking over hurriedly with the keys. The man took them without a word and unlocked the cap. He put the cap on top of the trunk door.

"You want ethyl?" he asked, glancing up, his eyes shadowed by the wide hat brim.

"Please," Les told him.

"How much?"

"You can fill it."

The hood was burning hot. Les jerked back his fingers with a gasp. He took out his handkerchief, wrapped it around his hand and pulled up the hood. When he unscrewed the radiator cap, boiling water frothed out and splashed down smoking onto the parched ground.

"Oh, fine," he muttered to himself.

The water from the hose was almost as hot. Marian came over and put one finger in the slow gush as Les held it over the radiator.

"Oh . . . gee," she said in disappointment. She looked over at the overalled man. "Have you got any cool water?" she asked.

The man kept his head down, his mouth pressed into a thin, drooping line. She asked again, without result.

"The hair-triggered Arizonian," she muttered to Les as she started back toward the man.

"I beg your pardon," she said.

The man jerked up his head, startled, the pupils of his dark eyes flaring. "Ma'm?" he said quickly.

"Can we get some cool drinking water?"

The man's rough-skinned throat moved once. "Not here, ma'm," he said, "but . . ."

His voice broke off and he looked at her blankly.

"You . . . you're from California, ain't you?" he said.

"That's right."

"Goin' . . . far?"

"New York," she said impatiently. "But what about—"

The man's bleached eyebrows moved together. "New York," he repeated. "Pretty far."

"What about the water?" Marian asked him.

"Well," the man said, his lips twitching into the outline of a smile, "I ain't got none here but if you want to drive back to the house, my wife'll get you some."

"Oh." Marian shrugged slightly. "All right."

"You can look at my zoo while my wife gets the water," the man offered, then crouched down quickly beside the fender to listen and hear if the tank were filling up.

"We have to go back to his house to get water," Marian told Les as he unscrewed one of the battery caps.

"Oh? Okay."

The man turned off the pump and replaced the cap.

"New York, haah?" he said, looking at them. Marian smiled politely and nodded.

After Les had pushed the hood back down, they got into the car to follow the man's truck back to the house.

"He has a zoo," Marian said, expressionlessly.

"How nice," Les said as he let up the clutch and the car rolled down off the slight rise on which the gas pumps stood.

"They make me mad," Marian said.

They'd seen dozens of the zoos since they'd left Los Angeles. They were usually located beside gas stations—designed to lure extra customers. Invariably, they were pitiful collections—barren little cages in which gaunt foxes cringed, staring out with sick, glazed eyes, rattlesnakes coiled lethargically, maybe a feather-molted eagle glowered from a dark cage corner. And, usually, in the middle of the so-called zoo would be a chained-up wolf or coyote; a straggly woe-be-gone crea-ture who paced constantly in a circle whose radius was the length of the chain; who never looked at the people but stared straight ahead with red-rimmed eyes, pacing endlessly on thin stalks of legs.

"I hate them," Marian said bitterly.

"I know, baby," Les said.

"If we didn't need water, I'd never go back to his damned old house."

Les smiled. "Okay ma," he said quietly, trying to avoid the holes in the lane. "*Oh.*" He snapped two fingers. "I for-got to ask him how to get back to the highway."

"Ask him when we get to his house," she said.

The house was faded brown, a two-story wooden structure that looked a hundred years old. Behind it stood a row of low, squarish huts.

"The zoo," Les said, "Lions 'n tigers 'n everything."

"Nuts," she said.

He pulled up in front of the quiet house and saw the man in the Stetson slide off the dusty seat of his truck and jump down off the running board.

"Get you the water," he said quickly and started for the house. He stopped a moment and looked back. "Zoo's in the back," he said, gesturing with his head.

They watched him move up the steps of the old house. Then Les stretched and blinked at the glaring sunlight.

"Shall we look at the zoo?" he asked, trying not to smile.

"No."

"Oh, come on."

"No, I don't want to see *that.*"

"I'm going to take a look."

"Well . . . all right," she said, "but it's going to make me mad."

They walked around the edge of the house and moved along its side in the shade.

"Oh, does that feel good," Marian said.

"Hey, he forgot to ask for his money."

"He will," she said.

They approached the first cage and looked into the dim interior through the two-foot-square window that was barred with thick doweling.

"Empty," Les said.

"Good."

"Some zoo."

They walked slowly toward the next cage. "Look how small they are," Marian said unhappily, "How would he like to be cooped up in one of them?"

She stopped walking.

"No, I'm not going to look," she said angrily, "I don't want to see how the poor things are suffering."

"I'll just take a look," he said.

"You're a fiend."

She heard him chuckle as she stood watching him walk up to the second of the cages. He looked in.

"*Marian!*" His cry made her body twitch.

"What is it?" she asked, running to him anxiously.

"*Look.*"

He stared with shocked eyes into the cage.

Her whisper trembled. "*Oh my God.*"

There was a man in the cage.

She looked at him with unbelieving eyes, unconscious of the large drops of sweat trickling across her brow and down her temples.

The man was lying on the floor, sprawled like a broken doll across a dirty army blanket. His eyes were open but the man saw nothing. His pupils were dilated, he looked doped. His grimy hands rested limply on the thinly-strawed floor, motionless twists of flesh and bone. His mouth hung open like a yellow-toothed wound, edged with dry, cracking lips.

When Les turned, he saw that Marian was already looking at him, her face blank, the skin drawn tautly over her paling cheeks.

"What is this?" she asked in a faint tremor of voice.

"I don't know."

He glanced once more into the cage as if he already doubted what he'd seen. Then he was looking at Marian again. "I don't know," he repeated, feeling the heartbeats throb heavily in his chest.

Another moment they looked at each other, their eyes stark with uncomprehending shock.

"What are we going to do?" Marian asked, almost whispering the words.

Les swallowed the hard lump in his throat. He looked into

the cage again. "Hello," he heard himself say, "Can you—"

He broke off abruptly, throat moving again. The man was comatose.

"Les, what if—"

He looked at her. And, suddenly, his scalp was crawling because Marian was looking in wordless apprehension at the next cage.

His running footsteps thudded over the dry earth, raising the dust.

"No," he murmured, looking into the next cage. He felt himself shudder uncontrollably as Marian ran up to him.

"Oh my God, this is *hideous*," she cried, staring with sick fright at the second caged man.

They both started as the man looked up at them with glazed, lifeless eyes. For a moment, his slack body lurched up a few inches and his dry lips fluttered as though he were trying to speak. A thread of saliva ran from one corner of his mouth and dribbled down across his beard-blackened chin. For a moment his sweaty, dirt-lined face was a mask of impotent entreaty.

Then his head rolled to one side and his eyes rolled back.

Marian backed away from the cage, shaking hand pressed to her cheek.

"The man's *insane*," she muttered and looked around abruptly at the silent house.

Then Les had turned too and both of them were suddenly aware of the man in the house who had told them to go and look at his zoo.

"Les, what are we going to do?" Marian's voice shook with rising hysteria.

Les felt numb, devoured by the impact of what they'd seen. For a long moment he could only stand shivering and stare at his wife, feeling immersed in some fantastic dream.

Then his lips jammed together and the heat seemed to flood over him.

"Let's get out of here," he snapped and grabbed her hand.

The only sound was their harsh panting and the quick slap of Marian's sandals on the hard ground. The air throbbed with intense heat, smothering their breath, making perspiration break out heavily across their faces and bodies.

"Faster," Les gasped, tugging at her hand.

Then, as they turned the edge of the house, they both recoiled with a violent contracting of muscles.

"No!" Marian's cry contorted her face into a twisted mask of terror.

The man stood between them and their car, a long double-barreled shotgun leveled at them.

Les didn't know why the idea flooded through his brain. But, suddenly, he realized that no one knew where he and Marian were, no one could even know where to begin searching for them. In rising panic, he thought of the man asking them where they were going, he thought of the man looking down at their California license plate.

And he heard the man, the hard, emotionless voice of the man.

"Now go on back," the man said, "to the zoo."

After he'd locked the couple in one of the cages, Merv Ketter walked slowly back to the house, the heavy shotgun pulling down his right arm. He'd felt no pleasure in the act, only a draining relief that had, for a moment, loosened the tightness in his body. But, already, the tightness was returning. It never went away for more than the few minutes it took him to trap another person and cage him.

If anything, the tightness was worse now. This was the first time he'd ever put a woman in one of his cages. The knowledge twisted a cold knot of despair in his chest. A woman—he'd put a woman in his cage. His chest shuddered with harsh breath as he ascended the rickety steps of the back porch.

Then, as the screen door slapped shut behind him, his long mouth tightened. Well, what was he supposed to do? He slammed the shotgun down on the yellow oil-clothed surface of the kitchen table, another forced breath wracking his chest. What else could I do—he argued with himself. His boots clacked sharply across the worn linoleum as he walked to the quiet, sun-lanced livingroom.

Dust rose from the old arm chair as he dropped down heavily, spiritlessly. What was he supposed to do? He'd had no choice.

For the thousandth time, he looked down at his left forearm, at the slight reddish bulge just under the elbow joint.

Inside his flesh, the tiny metal cone was still humming delicately. He knew it without listening. It never stopped.

He slumped back exhaustedly with a groan and lay his head on the high back of the chair. His eyes stared dully across the room, through the long slanting bar of sunlight quivering with dust motes. At the mantelpiece.

The Mauser rifle—he stared at it. The Luger, the bazooka shell, the hand grenade, all of them still active. Vaguely, through his tormented brain, curled the idea of putting the Luger to his temple, holding the Mauser against his side, even of pulling out the pin and holding the grenade against his stomach.

War hero. The phrase scraped cruelly at his mind. It had long lost its meaning, its comfort. Once, it had meant something to him to be a medaled warrior, ribboned, lauded, admired.

Then Elsie had died, then the battles and the pride were gone. He was alone in the desert with his trophies and with nothing else.

And then one day he'd gone into that desert to hunt.

His eyes shut, his leathery throat moved convulsively. What was the use of thinking, of regretting? The will to live was still in him. Maybe it was a stupid, a pointless will but it was there just the same; he couldn't rid himself of it. Not after two men were gone, not after five, no, not even after seven men were gone.

The dirt-filled nails dug remorselessly into his palms until they broke the skin. But a woman, a woman. The thought knifed at him. He'd never planned on caging a woman.

One tight fist drove down in futile rage on his leg. He couldn't help it. Sure, he'd seen the California plate. But he wasn't going to do it. Then the woman had asked for water and he suddenly had known that he had no choice, he had to do it.

There were only two men left.

And he'd found out that the couple were going to New York and the tension had come and gone, loosened and tightened in a spastic rhythm as he knew, in his very flesh, that he was going to tell them to come and look at his zoo.

I should have given them an injection, he thought. They might start screaming. It didn't matter about the man, he was used to men screaming. But a woman . . .

Merv Ketter opened his eyes and stared with hopeless eyes at the mantelpiece, at the picture of his dead wife, at the weapons which had been his glory and now were meaningless —steel and wood without worth, without substance.

Hero.

The word made his stomach turn.

The glutinous pulsing slowed, paused a moment's fraction, then began again, filling the inner shell with its hissing, spumous sound. A flaccid wave of agitation rippled down along the rows of muscle coils. The being stirred. It was time.

Thought. The shapeless, gauzelike airbubble coalesced; surrounded. The being moved, an undulation, a gelatinous worming within the shimmering bubble. A bumping, a slithering, a rocking flow of viscous tissues.

Thought again—a wave directing. The hiss of entering atmosphere, the soundless swinging of metal. Open. Shutting with a click. Sunset's blood edged the horizon. A slow and noiseless sinking in the air, a colorless balloon filled with something formless, something alive.

Earth, cooling. The being touched it, settled. It moved across the ground and every living thing fled its scouring approach. In its ropy wake, the ground was left a green and yellow iridescence.

"Look out."

Marian's sudden whisper almost made him drop the nail file. He jerked back his hand, his sweat-grimed cheek twitching and drew back quickly into the shadows. The sun was almost down.

"Is he coming this way?" Marian asked, her voice husky with dryness.

"I don't know." He stood tensely, watching the overalled man approach, hearing the fast crunch of his boot heels on the baked ground. He tried to swallow but all the moisture in him had been blotted up by the afternoon heat and only a futile clicking sounded in his throat. He was thinking about the man seeing the deeply-filed slit in the window bar.

The man in the Stetson walked quickly, his face blank and hard, his hands swinging in tense little arcs at his sides.

"What's he going to do?" Marian's voice rasped nervously, her physical discomfort forgotten in the sudden return of fear.

Les only shook his head. All afternoon he'd been asking himself the same question. After they'd been locked up, after the man had gone back to his house, during the first terrifying minutes and for the rest of the time when Marian had found the nail file in the pocket of her shorts and shapeless panic had gained the form of hoping for escape. All during that time the question had plagued him endlessly. *What was the man going to do with them?*

But it wasn't their cage the man was headed for. A loosening of relief made them both go slack. The man hadn't even looked toward the cage they were in. He seemed to avoid looking toward it.

Then the man had passed out of their sight and they heard the sound of him unlocking one of the cages. The squeaking rasp of the rusty door hinges made Les's stomach muscles draw taut.

The man appeared again.

Marian caught her breath. They both stared at the unconscious man being dragged across the ground, his heels raking narrow gouges in the dust.

After a few feet, the man let go of the limp arms and the body fell with a heavy thud. The man in the overalls looked behind him then, his head jerking around suddenly. They saw his throat move with a convulsive swallow. The man's eyes moved quickly, looking in all directions.

"What's he *looking* for?" Marian asked in a shaking whisper.

"Marian, I don't know."

"He's *leaving* him there!" She almost whimpered the word.

Their eyes filled with confused fear, they watched the overalled man move for the house again, his long legs pumping rapidly, his head moving jerkily as he looked from side to side. *Dear God, what is he looking for?*—Les thought in rising dread.

The man suddenly twitched in mid-stride and clutched at his left arm. Then, abruptly, he broke into a frightened run and leaped up the porch steps two at a time. The screen door slapped shut behind him with a loud report and then everything was deadly still.

A sob caught in Marian's throat. "I'm afraid," she said in a thin, shuddering voice.

He was afraid too; he didn't know of what but he was terribly afraid. Chilling uneasiness crawled up his back and rippled coldly on his neck. He kept staring at the body of the man sprawled on the ground, at the still, white face looking up sightlessly at the darkening sky.

He jolted once as, across the yard, he heard the back door of the house being slammed shut and locked.

Silence. A great hanging pall of it that pressed down on them like lead. The man slumped motionless on the ground. Their breaths quick, labored. Their lips trembling, their eyes fastened almost hypnotically on the man.

Marian drew up one fist and dug her teeth into the knuckles. Sunlight rimmed the horizon with a scarlet ribbon. Soundlessness. Heavy soundlessness.

Soundlessness.

Sound.

Their breath stopped. They stood there, mouths open, ears straining at the sound they'd never heard before. Their bodies went rigid as they listened to—

A bumping, a slithering, a rocking flow of—

"Oh, God!" Her voice was a gasping of breathless horror as she spun away, shaking hands flung over her eyes.

It was getting dark and he couldn't be sure of what he saw. He stood paralyzed and numb in the fetid air of the cage, staring with blood-drained face at the thing that moved across the ground toward the man's body; the thing that had shape yet not shape, that crept like a current of shimmering jellies.

A terrified gagging filled his throat. He tried to move back but he couldn't. He didn't want to see. He didn't want to hear the hideous gurgling sound like water being sucked into a great drain, the turbid bubbling that was like vats of boiling tallow.

No, his mind kept repeating, unable to accept, no, no, no, *no!*

Then the scream made them both jerk like boneless things and drove Marian against one of the cage walls, shaking with nauseous shock.

And the man was gone from the earth. Les stared at the place where he had been, stared at the luminous mass that pulsated there like a great mound of balloon-encased plankton undulating palely in their fluids.

He stared at it until the man had been completely eaten.

Then he turned away on deadened legs and stumbled to Marian's side. Her shaking fingers clutched like talons at his back and he felt her tear-streaked, twisted face press into his shoulder. Unfeelingly, he slid his arms around her, his face stiff with spent horror. Vaguely, through the body-clutching horror, he felt the need to comfort her, to ease her fright.

But he couldn't. He felt as if a pair of invisible claws had reached into his chest and ripped out all his insides. There wasn't anything left, just a cold, frost-edged hollow in him. And, in the hollow, a knife jabbing its razor tip each time he realized again why they were there.

When the scream came, Merv slammed both hands across his ears so hard it made his head ache.

He couldn't seem to cut off the sound anymore. Doors wouldn't shut tightly enough, windows wouldn't seal away the world, walls were too porous—the screams always reached him.

Maybe it was because they were really in his mind where there were no doors to lock, no windows to shut and close away the screaming of terror. Yes, maybe they were in his mind. It would explain why he still heard them in his sleep.

And, when it was over and Merv knew that the thing had gone, he trudged slowly into the kitchen and opened the door. Then, like a robot driven by remorseless gears, he went to the calendar and circled the date. Sunday, August 22nd.

The eighth man.

The pencil dropped from his slack fingers and rolled across the linoleum. Sixteen days—one man each two days for sixteen days. The mathematics of it were simple. The truth was not.

He paced the living room, passing in and out of the lamplight aura which cast a buttery glow across his exhausted features, then melted away as he moved into shadow again. Sixteen days. It seemed like sixteen years since he'd gone out into the desert to hunt for jackrabbits. Had it only been sixteen days ago?

Once again he saw the scene within his mind; it never left. Him scuffing across late afternoon sands, shotgun cradled against his hip, head slowly turning, eyes searching beneath the brim of his hat.

Then, moving over the crest of a scrub-grown dune,

stopping with a gasp, his eyes staring up at the globe which shimmered like a light immersed in water. His heartbeat jolting, every muscle tensing abruptly at the sight.

Approaching then, standing almost below the luminescent sphere that caught the lowering sun rays redly.

A gasp tearing back his lips at the circular cavity appearing on the surface of the globe. And out of the cavity floating—

He'd spun then and run, his breath whistling as he scrambled frantically up the rise again, his boot heels gouging at the sand. Topping the rise, he'd started to run in long, panic-driven strides, the gun held tautly in his right hand, banging against his leg.

Then the sound overhead—like the noise of gas escaping. Wild-eyed, he'd looked up over his shoulder. A terrified cry had wrenched his face into a mask of horror.

Ten feet over his head, the bulbous glow floated.

Merv lunged forward, his legs rising high as he fled. A fetid heat blew across his back. He looked up again with terrified eyes to see the thing descending on him. Seven feet above him—six—five—

Merv Ketter skidded to his knees, twisted around, jerked up the shotgun. The silence of the desert was shattered by the blast.

A gagging scream ripped from his throat as shot sprayed off the lucent bubble like pebbles off a rubber ball. He felt some of it burrow into his shoulder and arm as he flung over to one side, the gun falling from his nerveless grip. Four feet—three—the heat surrounded him, the choking odor made the air swim before his eyes.

His arms flung up. "NO!"

Once he had jumped into a water hole without looking and been mired on the shallow bottom by hot slime. It felt like that now, only this time the ooze was jumping onto him. His screams were lost in the crawling sheath of gasses and his flailing limbs caught fast in glutinous tissue. Around his terror-frozen eyes, he saw an agitating gelatine filled with gyrating spangles. Horror pressed at his skull, he felt death sucking at his life.

But he didn't die.

He inhaled and there was air even though the air was grumous with a stomach-wrenching stench. His lungs labored, he gagged as he breathed.

Then something moved in his brain.

He tried to twist and tried to scream but he couldn't. It felt like vipers threading through his brain, gnawing with poisoned teeth on tissues of his thought.

The serpents coiled and tightened. *I could kill you now*—the words scalded like acid. The muscle cords beneath his face tensed but even they couldn't move in the putrescent glue.

And then more words had formed and were burning, were branding themselves indelibly into his mind.

You will get me food.

He was still shuddering now, standing before the calendar, staring at the penciled circles.

What else could he have done? The question pleaded like a groveling suppliant. The being had picked his mind clean. It knew about his home, his station, his wife, his past. It told him what to do, it left no choice. He had to do it. Would anyone have let themselves die like that if they had an alternative; would anyone? Wouldn't anyone have promised the world itself to be freed of that horror?

Grim-faced, trembling, he went up the stairs on feeble legs, knowing there would be no sleep, but going anyway.

Slumped down on the bed, one shoe off, he stared with lifeless eyes at the floor, at the hooked rug that Elsie had made so long ago.

Yes, he'd promised to do what the being had ordered. And the being had sunk the tiny, whirring cone deep into his arm so that he could only escape by cutting open his own flesh and dying.

And then the hideous gruel had vomited him onto the desert sands and he had lain there, mute and palsied while the being had raised slowly from the earth. And he had heard in his brain the last warning—

In two days . . .

And it had started, the endless, enervating round of trapping innocent people in order to preserve himself from the fate he knew awaited them.

And the horrible thing, the truly horrible thing was that he knew he would do it again. He knew he'd do anything to keep the being away from him. Even if it meant that the woman must—

His mouth tightened. His eyes shut and he sat trembling without control on the bed.

What would he do when the couple were gone? What would he do if no one else came to the station? What would he do if the police came checking on the disappearances of eleven people?

His shoulders twisted and an anguished sobbing pulsed in his throat.

Before he lay down he took a long swallow from the dwindling whiskey bottle. He lay in the darkness, a nerve-scraped coil, waiting, the small pool of heat in his stomach unable to warm the coldness and the emptiness of him.

In his arm the cone whirled.

Les jerked out the last bar and stood there for a moment, head slumped forward on his chest, panting through clenched teeth, his body heaving with exhausted breath. Every muscle in his back and shoulders and arms ached with throbbing pain.

Then he sucked in a rasping breath. "Let's go," he gasped.

His arms vibrated as he helped Marian clamber through the window.

"Don't make any noise." He could hardly speak he was so tired from the combination of thirst, hunger, heat exhaustion and seemingly endless, muscle-cramped filing.

He couldn't get his leg up, he had to go through the rough-edged opening head first, pushing and squirming, feeling splinters jab into his sweat-greased flesh. When he thudded down, the pain of impact ran jaggedly along his extended arms and, for a second, the darkness swam with needles of light.

Marian helped him up.

"Let's go," he said again, breathlessly and they started to run across the ground toward the front of the house.

Abruptly, he grabbed her wrist and jerked her to a halt.

"Get those sandals off," he ordered hoarsely. She bent over quickly and unbuckled them.

The house was dark as they hurried around the back corner of it and dashed along the side beneath the moon-reflecting windows. Marian winced as her right foot jarred down on a sharp pebble.

"Thank God," Les gasped to himself as they reached the front of the house.

The car was still there. As they ran toward it, he felt into his back pocket and took out his wallet. His shaking fingers reached into the small change purse and felt the coolness of the extra ignition key. He was sure the other keys wouldn't be in the car.

They reached it.

"*Quick,*" he gasped and they pulled open the doors and slid in. Les suddenly realized that he was shivering in the chilly night air. He took out the key and fumbled for the ignition slot. They'd left the doors open, planning to close them when the motor started.

Les found the slot and slid in the key, then drew in a tense, shuddering breath. If the man had done anything to the motor, they were lost.

"Here goes," he murmured and jabbed at the starter button.

The motor coughed and turned over once with a groan. Les's throat clicked convulsively, he jerked back his hand and threw an apprehensive look at the dark house.

"Oh God, won't it start?" Marian whispered, feeling her legs and arms break out in gooseflesh.

"I don't know, I hope it's just cold," he said hurriedly. He caught his breath, then pushed in the button again, pumping at the choke.

The motor turned again lethargically. Oh God, he *has* done something to it!—the words exploded in Les's mind. He jammed in the button feverishly, his body tense with fear. Why didn't we *push* it to the main road!—the new thought came, deepening the lines on his face.

"*Les!*"

He felt her hand clutch at his arm and, almost instinctively, his gaze jerked over to the house.

A light had flared up at a second story window.

"Oh Jesus, *start!*" he cried in a broken frenzy and pushed at the button with a rigid thumb.

The motor coughed into life and a wave of relief covered him. Simultaneously, he and Marian pulled at the doors and slammed them shut while he gunned the engine strongly to get it warm.

As he threw the gears into first, the head and trunk of the man appeared in the window. He shouted something but neither of them heard it over the roar of the motor.

The car jerked forward and stalled.

Les hissed in impotent fury as he jabbed in the button again. The motor caught and he eased up the clutch. The tires bumped over the uneven ground. Upstairs, the man was gone from the window and Marian, her eyes fastened to the house, saw a downstairs light go on.

"Hurry!" she begged.

The car picked up speed and Les, shoving the gears into second, jerked the car into a tight semicircle. The tires skidded on the hard earth and, as the car headed for the lane, Les threw it into third and jerked at the knob that sent the two headlights splaying out brightly into the darkness.

Behind them, something exploded and they both jerked their shoulders forward convulsively as something gouged across the roof with a grating shriek. Les shoved the accelerator to the floor and the car leaped forward, plunging and rocking into the rutted lane.

Another shotgun blast tore open the night and half of the back window exploded in a shower of glass splinters. Again, their shoulders twitched violently and Les grunted as a sliver gouged its razor edge across the side of his neck.

His hands jerked on the wheel, the car hit a small ditch and almost veered into a bank on the left side of the lane. His fingers tightened convulsively and, with arms braced, he pulled the car back into the center of the lane, crying to Marian,

"Where *is* he?"

Her white face twisted around.

"I can't see him!"

His throat moved quickly as the car bucked and lurched over the holes, the headlights jerking wildly with each motion.

Get to the next town, he thought wildly, tell the sheriff, try and save that other poor devil. His foot pressed down on the pedal as the lane smoothed out. Get to the next town and—

She screamed it. "*Look out!*"

He couldn't stop in time. The hood of the Ford drove splintering into the heavy gate across the lane and the car jolted to a neck-jerking halt. Marian went flailing forward against the dashboard, the side of her head snapping against the windshield. The engine stalled and both headlights smashed out in an instant.

Les shoved away from the steering wheel, knocked breathless by the impact.

"Honey, *quick*," he gasped.

A choking sob shook in Marian's throat. "My head, my

head." Les sat in stunned muteness a moment, staring at her as she twisted her head around in an agony of pain, one hand pressed rigidly to her forehead.

Then he shoved open the door at his side and grabbed for her free hand. "Marian, we have to get out of here!"

She kept crying helplessly as he almost dragged her from the car and threw his arm around her waist to support her. Behind him, he heard the sound of heavy boots running down the lane and saw, over his shoulder, a bright flashlight eye bobbing as it bore down on them.

Marian collapsed at the gate. Les stood there holding her, trembling impotently as the man came running up, a forty-five clutched in his right hand, a flashlight in his left. Les winced at the beam flaring into his eyes.

"Back," was all the man said, panting heavily and Les saw the barrel of the gun wave once toward the house.

"But my wife is hurt!" he said, "She hit her head against the windshield. You can't just put her back in a cage!"

"I said get back!" The man's shout made Les start.

"But she can't walk, she's unconscious!"

He heard a rasping breath shudder through the man's body and saw that he was stripped to the waist and shivering.

"Carry her then," the man said.

"But—"

"Shall I blast ya where ya stand!" the man yelled in a frenzied anger.

"No. No." Les shook nervously as he lifted up Marian's slack body. The man stepped aside and Les started back up the lane, trying to watch Marian's face and his footing at the same time.

"Honey," he whispered, "Marian?"

Her head hung limply over his left forearm, the short blond hair ruffling against her temples and brow as he walked. Tension kept building up in him until he felt like screaming.

"Why are you doing this?" he suddenly blurted out over his shoulder.

No answer, just the rhythmic slogging of the man's boots over the pocked ground.

"How can you do this to anyone?" Les asked brokenly. "Trapping your own kind and giving them to that—that God only knows what it is!"

"*Shut* up!" But there was more defeat than anger in the man's voice.

"Look," Les said suddenly, impulsively, "Let my wife go. Keep me here if you have to but . . . but let her go. *Please!*"

The man said nothing and Les bit his lips in frustrated anguish. He looked down at Marian with sick, frightened eyes.

"Marian," he said, "Marian." He shivered violently in the cold night air.

The house loomed up bleakly out of the flat darkness of the desert.

"For God's sake, don't put her in a cage!" he cried out desperately.

"*Get back.*" The man's voice was flat, there was nothing in it, neither promise nor emotion.

Les stiffened. If it had been just him, he would have whirled and leaped at the man, he knew it. He wouldn't, willingly, walk back past the edge of the house again, back toward the cages, toward that *thing*.

But there was Marian.

He stepped over the thrown-down shotgun on the ground and heard, behind him, the grunt of the man as he bent over and picked it up. I have to get her out of here, he thought, I *have* to!

It happened before he could do anything. He heard the man step up suddenly behind him and then felt a pinprick on his right shoulder. He caught his breath at the sudden sting and turned as quickly as he could, weighed down by Marian's dead limpness.

"What are you—"

He couldn't even finish the sentence. It seemed suddenly as if hot, numbing liquors were being hosed through his veins. An immense lassitude covered his limbs and he hardly felt it when the man took Marian from his arms.

He stumbled forward a step, the night alive with glittering pinpoints of light. The earth ran like water beneath his feet, his legs turned to rubber.

"No." He said it in a lethargic grumble.

Then he toppled. And didn't even feel the impact of the ground against his falling body.

The belly of the globe was warm. It undulated with a thick and vaporous heat. In the humid dimness, the being rested, its shapeless body quivering with monotonous pulsations of sleep. The being was comfortable, it was content, coiled grotesquely like some cosmic cat before a hearth.

For two days.

Piercing screams woke him. He stirred fitfully and moved his lips as though to speak. But his lips were made of iron. They sagged inertly and he couldn't move them. Only a great forcing of will would raise his leaden eyelids.

The cage air fluttered and shimmered with strange convections. His eyes blinked slowly; glazed, uncomprehending eyes. His hands flopped weakly at his sides like dying fish.

It was the man in the other cage screaming. The poor devil had come out of his drugged state and was hysterical because he knew.

Les's sweat-grimed brow wrinkled slowly, evenly. *He could think.* His body was like a massive stone, unwieldy and helpless. But, behind its flint, immobile surface, his brain was just as sure.

His eyes fell shut. That made it all the more horrible. To know what was coming. To lie there helpless and know what was going to happen to him.

He thought he shuddered, but he wasn't sure. That thing, what was it? There was nothing in knowledge to construct from, no foundation of rational acceptance to build upon. What he'd seen that night was something beyond all—

What day was it? Where was—

Marian!

It was like rolling a boulder to turn his head. Clicking filled his throat, saliva dribbled unnoticed from the corners of his mouth. Again, he forced his eyes open with a great straining of will.

Panic drove knife blades into his brain even though his face changed not at all.

Marian wasn't there.

She lay, limply drugged, on the bed. He'd laid another cool, wet cloth across her brow, across the welt on her right temple.

Now he stood silently, looking down at her. He'd just gotten back from the cages where he'd injected the screaming man again to quiet him. He wondered what was in the drug that being had given him, he wondered what it did to the man. He hoped it made him completely insensible.

It was the man's last day.

No, it's dumb imagination, he told himself suddenly. She didn't look like Elsie, she didn't look at all like Elsie.

It was his mind. He *wanted* her to look like Elsie, that was what it was. His throat twitched as he swallowed. Stupid. The word slapped dully at his brain. She *didn't* look like Elsie.

For a moment, he let his gaze move once more over the woman's body, at the smooth rise of her bust, the willowy hips, the long, well-formed legs. Marian. That was what the man had called her. Marian.

It was a nice name.

With an angry twist of his shoulders, he turned away from the bed and strode quickly from the room. What was the *matter* with him anyway? What did he think he was going to do—let her go? There had been no sense in taking her into the house the night before last, in putting her in the spare bedroom. No sense in it at all. He couldn't let himself feel sympathy for her, for anyone. If he did, he was lost. That was obvious.

As he moved down the steps, he tried to remind himself once more of the horror of being absorbed into that gelatinous mass. He tried to remember the brain-searing terror of it. But, somehow, the memory kept disappearing like wind-blown cloud and he kept thinking instead of the woman. Marian. She did look like Elsie; the same color hair, the same mouth. *No!*

He'd leave her in the bedroom until the drug wore off. Then he'd put her back in the cage again. *It's me or them!*— he argued furiously with himself. I ain't going to die like *that!* Not for anyone.

He kept arguing with himself all the way down to the station.

I must be crazy, he thought, taking her in the house like that, feeling sorry for her. I can't afford it, I *can't*. She's just two days to me, that's all, just a two-day reprieve from—

The station was empty, silent. Merv braked the truck and got out.

His boots crunched over the hot earth as he paced restlessly around the pumps. *I can't let her go!* he lashed out at himself, his face taut with fury. He shuddered then at the realization that he had been entertaining the thought for two days now.

"Why wasn't she a man?" he muttered to himself, fists tight and blood-drained at his sides. He raised his left arm and looked at the reddish lump. Why couldn't he tear it out of his flesh? Why?

The car came then. A salesman's car, dusty and hot.

As Merv pumped gas in, as he checked the oil and water, he kept glancing from under his hat brim at the hot-faced little man in the linen suit and panama hat. *Replace her.* Merv wouldn't let the thought out yet he knew it was there. He found himself glancing down at the license plate.

Arizona.

His face tightened. No. No, he'd always gotten out-of-state cars, it was safer that way. I'll have to let him go, he thought miserably, I'll *have* to. I can't afford to . . .

But when the little man was reaching into his wallet, Merv felt his hand slide back to his back overall pocket, he felt his fingers tighten over the warm butt of the forty-five.

The little man stared, slack-jawed, at the big gun.

"What *is* this?" he asked weakly. Merv didn't tell him.

Night brushed its black iced fingers across the moving bubble. Earth flowed beneath its liquid coming.

Why was the air so faint with nourishment, why did the atmosphere press so feebly in? This land, it was a weak, a dying land, its life-administering gasses almost spent.

Amidst slithering, amidst scouring approach, the being thought of escape.

How long now had it been here in this barren place? There was no way of telling for the planet's sun appeared and disappeared with insane rapidity, darkness and light flickering in alternation like the wink of an eye.

And, on the ship, the instruments of chronometry were shattered, they were irreparable. There was no context any more, no customed metric to adjust by. The being was lost upon this tenuous void of living rock, unable to do more than forage for its sustenance.

Off in the black distance, the dwelling of the planet's animal appeared, grotesquely angular and peaked. It was a stupid animal, this brainless beast incapable of rationality, able only to emit wild squawking cries and flap its tendrils

like the night plants of his own world. And its body—it was
too hard with calciumed rigidity, providing scant nutriment,
making it necessary for the being to eat twice as often so
violent an energy did digestion take.

Closer. The clicking grew louder,

The animal was there, as usual, lying still upon the ground,
its tendrils curled and limp. The being shot out threads of
thought and sapped the sluggish juices of thought from the
animal. It was a barbaric place if this was its intelligence. The
being heaved closer, swelling and sucking along the wind-
swept earth.

The animal stirred and deep revulsion quivered in the being's mind. If it were not starving and helpless it could never
force itself to absorb this twitching, stiff-ribbed beast.

Bubble touched tendril. The being flowed across the animal
form and trembled to a stop. Visual cells revealed the animal
looking up, distended eyed. Audial cells transferred the wild
and strangling noise the dying animal made. Tactile cells absorbed the flimsy agitations of its body.

And, in its deepest center, the being sensed the tireless
clicking that emanated from the dark lair where, hidden and
shaking, the first animal was—the animal in whose flaccid
tendril was imbedded the location cone.

The being ate. And, eating, wondered if there would ever
be enough food to keep it alive—

—for the thousand earth years of its life.

He lay slumped across the cage floor, his heartbeat jolting
as the man looked in at him.

He'd been testing the walls when he heard the slap of the
screen door and the sound of the man's boots descending the
porch steps. He'd lunged down and rolled over quickly onto
his back, trying desperately to remember what position he'd
been in while he was still drugged, arranging his hands limply at his sides, drawing up his right leg a little, closing his
eyes. The man mustn't know that he was conscious. The man
had to open the door without caution.

Les forced himself to breathe slowly and evenly even though
it made his stomach hurt. The man made no sound as he
gazed in. When he opens the lock, Les kept telling himself—
as soon as I hear the door pulled open, I'll jump.

His throat moved once as a nervous shudder rippled

through him. Could the man tell he was faking? His muscles tensed, waiting for the sound of the door opening. He *had* to get away now.

There would be no other time. *It* was coming tonight.

Then the sound of the man's boots started away. Abruptly, Les opened his eyes, a look of shocked disbelief contorting his features. The man wasn't going to open the cage!

For a long time he lay there, shivering, staring up mutely at the barred window where the man had stood. He felt like crying aloud and beating his fists against the door until they were bruised and bleeding.

"No . . . no." His voice was a lifeless mumble.

Finally, he pushed up and got on his knees. Cautiously, he looked over the rim of the window. The man was gone.

He crouched back down and went through his pockets again.

His wallet—nothing there to help him. His handkerchief, the stub of pencil, forty-seven cents, his comb.

Nothing else.

He held the articles in his palms and stared down at them for long moments as if, somehow, they held the answer to his terrible need. There *had* to be an answer, it was inconceivable that he should actually end up out there on the ground like that other man, put there for that thing to—

"*No!*"

With a spasmodic twitch of his hands, he flung the articles onto the dirt floor of the cage, his lips drawn back in a dull cry of frightened outrage. It can't be real, it has to be a dream!

He fell to his knees desperately and once more began running shaking fingers over the sides of the cage, looking for a crack, a weak board, anything.

And, while he searched in vain, he tried not to think about the night coming and what the night was going to bring.

But that was all he could think about.

She sat up, gasping, as the man's calloused fingers stroked at her hair. Her widened eyes stared at him in horror as he jerked back his hand.

"Elsie," he muttered.

The whiskey-heavy cloud of his breath poured across her face and she drew back, grimacing, her hands clutching tensely at the bedspread.

"Elsie." He said it again, thick voiced, his glazed eyes looking at her drunkenly.

The bedspread rustled beneath her as she pushed back further until her back bumped against the wooden headboard.

"Elsie, I didn't mean to," the man said, dark blades of hair hanging down over his temples, breath falling hotly from his open mouth, "Elsie, don't . . . don't be scared of me."

"W-where's my husband?"

"Elsie, you look like Elsie," the man slurred the words, his blood-streaked eyes pleading, "You look like Elsie, oh . . . God, you look like Elsie."

"Where's my husband!"

His hand clamped over her wrist and she felt herself jerked like a flimsy doll against the man's chest. His stale breath surrounded her.

"No," she gasped, her hands pushing at his shoulders.

"I love ya, Elsie, I *love* ya!"

"*Les!*" Her scream rang out in the small room.

Her head snapped to the side as the man's big palm drove across her cheek.

"He's *dead!*" the man shouted hoarsely, "It ate him, it *ate* him! You *hear!*"

She fell back against the headboard, her eyes stark with horror. "No." She didn't even know she'd spoken.

The man struggled up to his feet and stood there weaving, looking down at her blank face.

"You think I wanted to?" he asked brokenly, a tear dribbling down his beard-darkened cheek, "You think I *liked* to do it?" A sob shuddered in his chest. "I *didn't* like to do it. But you don't know, y-you don't *know*. I was in it, I was *in* it! Oh God . . . you don't know what it was like. You don't *know!*"

He sank down heavily on the bed, his head slumped forward, his chest racked with helpless sobs.

"I didn't want to. God, do you think I w-*wanted* to?"

Her left fist was pressed rigidly against her lips. She couldn't seem to breathe. No. Her mind struggled to disbelieve. No, it's not true, it isn't true.

Suddenly, she threw her legs over the side of the bed and stood. Outside, the sun was going down. It doesn't come till dark, her mind argued desperately, not until dark. But how long had she been unconscious?

The man looked up with red-rimmed eyes. "What are ya doing?"

She started running for the door.

As she jerked open the door, the man collided with her and the two of them went crashing against the wall. Breath was driven from her body and the ache in her head flared up again. The man clutched at her; she felt his hands running wildly over her chest and shoulders.

"Elsie, Elsie . . ." the man gasped, trying to kiss her again.

That was when she saw the heavy pitcher on the table beside them. She hardly felt his tightening fingers, his hard, brutal mouth crushed against hers. Her stretching fingers closed over the pitcher handle, she lifted . . .

Great chunks of the white pottery showered on the floor as the man's cry of pain filled the room.

Then Marian was leaning against the wall, gasping for breath and looking down at his crumpled body, at his thick fingers still twitching on the rug.

Suddenly her eyes fled to the window. Almost sunset.

Abruptly, she ran back to the man and bent over his motionless body. Her shaking fingers felt through his overall pockets until they found the ring of keys.

As she fled from the room, she heard the man groan and saw, over her shoulder, the fleeting sight of him turning slowly onto his back.

She ran down the hall and jerked open the front door. Dying sunlight flooded the sky with its blood.

With a choking gasp, she jumped down the porch steps and ran in desperate, erratic strides around the house, not even feeling the pebbles her feet ran over. She kept looking at the silent row of cages she was running toward. It's not true, it's not true—the words kept running through her brain—he lied to me. A sob pulled back her lips. He *lied!*

Darkness was falling like a rapid curtain as she dashed up to the first cage on trembling legs.

Empty.

Another sob pulsed in her throat. She ran to the next cage. He was lying!

Empty.

"No."

"Les!"

"Marian!" He leaped across the cage floor, a sudden wild hope flashing across his face.

"Oh, *darling*." Her voice was a shaking, strengthless murmur, "He told me—"

"Marian, open the cage. Hurry! It's coming."

Dread fell over her again, a wave of numbing cold. Her head jerked to the side instinctively, her shocked gaze fled out across the darkening desert.

"Marian!"

Her hands shook uncontrollably as she tried one of the keys in the lock. It didn't fit. She bit her lip until pain flared up. She tried another key. It didn't fit.

"*Hurry*."

"Oh God." She whimpered as her palsied hands inserted another key. That didn't fit.

"I can't find the—"

Suddenly, her voice choked off, her breath congealed. In a second, she felt her limbs petrify.

In the silence, faintly, a sound of something huge grating, and hissing over the earth.

"Oh, *no*." She looked aside hurriedly, then back at Les again.

"It's all right, baby," he said. "All right, don't get excited. There's plenty of time." He drew in a heavy breath. "Try the next key. That's right. No, no, the other one. It's *all* right now. There. No, that doesn't work. Try the next one." His stomach kept contracting into a tighter, harder knot.

The skin of Marian's lower lip broke beneath her teeth. She winced and dropped the key ring. With a gagging whimper, she bent over and snatched it up. Across the desert, the wheezing, squashing sound grew louder.

"Oh, Les, I can't, I *can't!*"

"All right, baby," he heard himself say suddenly, "Never mind. Run for the highway."

She looked up at him, suddenly expressionless. "What?"

"Honey, don't stand there for God's sake!" he cried, "*Run!*"

She caught the breath that shook in her and dug her teeth again into the jagged break on her lip. Her hands stopped shaking and, almost numbed, she tried the next key, the next, while Les stood watching her with terrified eyes, looking over her shoulder toward the desert.

"Honey, don't—"

The lock sprang open. With a breathless grunt, Les shoved open the door and grabbed Marian's hand as the lathing sibilance shook in the twilight air.

"Run!" he gasped, "Don't look back!"

They ran on wildly pumping legs away from the cages, away from the six-foot high mass of quivering life that flopped into the clearing like gelatine dumped from a gargantuan bowl. They tried not to listen, they kept their eyes straight ahead, they ran without breaking their long, panic-driven strides.

The car was back in front of the house again, it's front bashed in. They jerked open the doors and slid in frantically. His shaking hand felt the key still in the ignition. He turned it and jabbed in the starter button.

"Les, it's coming this way!"

The gears ground together with a loud rasp and the car jerked forward. He didn't look behind, he just changed gears and kept pushing down on the accelerator until the car lurched into the lane again.

Les turned the car right and headed for the town he remembered passing through—it seemed like years before. He pushed the gas pedal to the floor and the car picked up speed. He couldn't see the road clearly without the headlights but he couldn't keep his foot up, it seemed to jam itself down on the accelerator. The car roared down the darkening road and Les drew in his first easy breath in four days as . . .

the being foamed and rocked across the ground, fury boiling in its tissues. The animal had failed, there was no food waiting, the food had gone. The being slithered in angry circles, searching, its visual cells picking at the ground, its sheathed and luminous formlessness scouring away the flaky dirt. Nothing. The being gurgled like a viscid tide for the house, for the clicking sound in . . .

Merv Ketter's arm jerked spasmodically and he sat up, eyes wide and staring. Pain drove jagged lines of consciousness into his brain—pain in his head, pain in his arm. The cone was like a burrowing spider there, clawing with razor legs, trying to cut its way out of his flesh. Merv struggled up to his knees, teeth gritted together, eyes clouding with the pain.

He had barely gained his feet when the crashing, splintering sound shook the house. He twitched violently, his lower jaw dropping. The digging, gouging fire in his arm increased and, suddenly he knew. With a whining gasp, he leaped into the hall and looked down the dark stairway pit.

the being undulated up the stairs, its seventy ingot eyes glowering, its shimmering deformity lurching up toward the animal. Maddened fury hissed and bubbled through its amorphous shape, it flopped and flung itself up the angular steps. The animal turned and fled toward

the back steps!—it was his only chance. He couldn't breathe, air seemed liquid in his lungs. His boot heels hammered down the hall and through the darkness of his bedroom. Behind, he heard the railings buckle and snap as the being reached the second floor, bent itself around into a U-shaped bladder, then threw its sodden form forward again.

Merv flung himself down the steep stairway, his palsied hand gripping at the railing, his heartbeat pounding at his chest like mallet blows. He cried out hoarsely as the pain in his arm flared again, almost making him lose consciousness.

As he reached the bottom step, he heard the doorway of his bedroom shattered violently and heard the gushing fury of the being as it

heaved and bucked into the backstair doorway and smashed it out to its own size. Below, it heard the pounding of the fleeing animal. Then adhesiveness lost hold and the being went grinding and rolling down the stairway, its seven hundred feelers pricking the casing and scraping at the splintering wood.

It hit the bottom step, crushed its huge misshapen bulk through the doorway and boiled across the kitchen floor.

In the living room Merv dashed for the mantel. Reaching up, he jerked down the Mauser rifle and whirled as the distended being cascaded its luminescent body through the doorway.

The room echoed and rang with sharp explosions as Merv emptied the rifle into the onrushing hulk. The bullets sprayed off its casing impotently and Merv jumped back with a scream of terror, the gun flung from his hands. His outflung arm knocked off the picture of his wife and he heard it shatter on the floor and, in his twisted mind, had the fleeting vision of it lying on the floor, Elsie's face smiling behind jagged glass.

Then his hand closed over something hard. And, suddenly, he knew exactly what to do.

As the glittering mass reared up and threw its liquidity toward him, Merv jumped to the side. The mantel splintered, the wall cracked open.

Then, as the being pulled itself up again and heaved over him, Merv jerked out the pin of the grenade and held it tightly to his chest.

Stupid beast! I'll kill you now for—

PAIN ! !

Tissues exploded, the casing split, the being ran across the floor like slag, a molten torrent of protoplasms.

Then silence in the room. *The being's minds snuffed out one by one as tenuous atmosphere starved each tissue of its life. The remains trembled slightly, agony flooded through the being's cells and glutinous joints. Thoughts trickled.*

Vital fluids trickling. Lamp beams giving warmth and life to pulsing matter. Organisms joining, cells dividing, the undulant contents of the food vat swelling, swelling, overpowering. Where are they! Where are the masters who gave me life that I might feed them and never lose my bulk or energy?

And then the being, which was born of tumorous hydroponics, died, having forgotten that it, itself, had eaten the masters as they slept, ingesting, with their bodies, all the knowledge of their minds.

On Saturday of the week of August 22nd, that year, there was a violent explosion in the desert and people twenty miles away picked up strange metals in their yards.

"A meteor," they said but that was because they had to say something.

Pattern for Survival ·····················

AND they stood beneath the crystal towers,
beneath the polished heights which, like scintillant mirrors,
caught rosy sunset on their faces until their city was one vivid,
coruscated blush.

Ras slipped an arm about the waist of his beloved.

"Happy?" he inquired, in a tender voice.

"Oh, yes," she breathed. "Here in our beautiful city where
there is peace and happiness for all, how could I be anything
but happy?"

Sunset cast its roseate benediction upon their soft embrace.

THE END

The clatter ceased. His hands curled in like blossoms and
his eyes fell shut. The prose was wine. It trickled on the taste
buds of his mind, a dizzying potion. I've done it again, he
recognized, by George in heaven, I've done it again.

Satisfaction towed him out to sea. He went down for the
third time beneath its happy drag. Surfacing then, reborn, he
estimated wordage, addressed envelope, slid in manuscript,
weighed total, affixed stamps and sealed. Another brief sub-
mergence in the waters of delight, then up withal and to the
mailbox.

It was almost twelve as Richard Allen Shaggley hobbled
down the quiet street in his shabby overcoat. He had to hurry
or he'd miss the pick-up and he mustn't do that. Ras And The
City of Crystal was too superlative to wait another day. He
wanted it to reach the editor immediately. It was a certain
sale.

Circuiting the giant, pipe-strewn hole (When, in the name
of heaven would they finish repairing that blasted sewer?),
he limped on hurriedly, envelope clutched in rigid fingers,
heart a turmoil of vibration.

Noon. He reached the mailbox and cast about anxious glances for the postman. No sign of him. A sigh of pleasure and relief escaped his chapped lips. Face aglow, Richard Allen Shaggley listened to the envelope thump gently on the bottom of the mailbox.

The happy author shuffled off, coughing.

Al's legs were bothering him again. He shambled up the quiet street, teeth gritted slightly, leather sack pulling down his weary shoulder. Getting old, he thought, haven't got the drive any more. Rheumatism in the legs. Bad; makes it hard to do the route.

At twelve fifteen, he reached the dark green mailbox and drew the keys from his pocket. Stooping, with a groan, he opened up the box and drew out its contents.

A smiling eased his pain-tensed face; he nodded once. Another yarn by Shaggley. Probably be snatched up right way. The man could really write.

Rising with a grunt, Al slid the envelope into his sack, relocked the mailbox, then trudged off, still smiling to himself. Makes a man proud, he thought, carrying his stories; even if my legs do hurt.

Al was a Shaggley fan.

When Rick arrived from lunch a little after three that afternoon, there was a note from his secretary on the desk.

New ms. from Shaggley just arrived, it read. *Beautiful job. Don't forget R.A. wants to see it when you're through. S.*

Delight cast illumination across the editor's hatchet face. By George in heaven, this was manna from what had threatened to be a fruitless afternoon. Lips drawn back in what, for him, was smiling, he dropped into his leather chair, restrained emphatic finger twitchings for the blue pencil (No need of it for a Shaggley yarn!) and plucked the envelope from the cracked glass surface of his desk. By George, a Shaggley story; what luck! R.A. would beam.

He sank into the cushion, instantly absorbed in the opening nuance of the tale. A tremor of transport palsied outer sense. Breathless, he plunged on into the story depths. What balance, what delineation! How the man could write. Distractedly, he brushed plaster dust off his pin-stripe sleeve.

As he read, the wind picked up again, fluttering his strawlike hair, buffeting like tepid wings against his brow. Unconsciously, he raised his hand and traced a delicate finger along the scar which trailed like livid thread across his cheek and lower temple.

The wind grew stronger. It moaned by pretzeled I-beams and scattered brown-edged papers on the soggy rug. Rick stirred restlessly and stabbed a glance at the gaping fissure in the wall (When, in the name of heaven, would they finish those repairs?), then returned, joy renewed, to Shaggley's manuscript.

Finishing at last, he fingered away a tear of bittersweetness and depressed an intercom key.

"Another check for Shaggley," he ordered, then tossed the snapped-off key across his shoulder.

At three-thirty, he brought the manuscript to R.A.'s office and left it there.

At four, the publisher laughed and cried over it, gnarled fingers rubbing at the scabrous bald patch on his head.

Old hunchbacked Dick Allen set type for Shaggley's story that very afternoon, vision blurred by happy tears beneath his eyeshade, liquid coughing unheard above the busy clatter of his machine.

The story hit the stand a little after six. The scar-faced dealer shifted on his tired legs as he read it over six times before, reluctantly, offering it for sale.

At half past six, the little bald-patched man came hobbling down the street. A hard day's work, a well-earned rest, he thought, stopping at the corner newsstand for some reading matter.

He gasped. By George in heaven, a new Shaggley story! What luck!

The only copy too. He left a quarter for the dealer who wasn't there at the moment.

He took the story home, shambling by skeletal ruins (Strange, those burned buildings hadn't been replaced yet), reading as he went.

He finished the story before arriving home. Over supper, he read it once again, shaking his lumpy head at the marvel of its impact, the unbreakable magic of its workmanship. It inspires, he thought.

But not tonight. Now was the time for putting things

away: the cover on the typewriter, the shabby overcoat, threadbare pin-stripe, eye-shade, mailman's cap and leather sack all in their proper places.

He was asleep by ten, dreaming about mushrooms. And, in the morning, wondering once again why those first observers had not described the cloud as more like a toadstool.

By six A.M. Shaggley, breakfasted, was at the typewriter.

This is the story, he wrote, of how Ras met the beautiful priestess of Shahglee and she fell in love with him.

Steel ••

THE two men came out of the station rolling a covered object. They rolled it along the platform until they reached the middle of the train, then grunted as they lifted it up the steps, the sweat running down their bodies. One of its wheels fell off and bounced down the metal steps and a man coming up behind them picked it up and handed it to the man who was wearing a rumpled brown suit.

"Thanks," said the man in the brown suit and he put the wheel in his side coat pocket.

Inside the car, the men pushed the covered object down the aisle. With one of its wheels off, it was lop-sided and the man in the brown suit—his name was Kelly—had to keep his shoulder braced against it to keep it from toppling over. He breathed heavily and licked away tiny balls of sweat that kept forming over his upper lip.

When they reached the middle of the car, the man in the wrinkled blue suit pushed forward one of the seat backs so there were four seats, two facing two. Then the two men pushed the covered object between the seats and Kelly reached through a slit in the covering and felt around until he found the right button.

The covered object sat down heavily on a seat by the window.

"Oh, God, listen to'm squeak," said Kelly.

The other man, Pole, shrugged and sat down with a sigh.

"What d'ya expect?" he asked.

Kelly was pulling off his suit coat. He dropped it down on the opposite seat and sat down beside the covered object.

"Well, we'll get 'im some o' that stuff soon's we're paid off," he said, worriedly.

"If we can find some," said Pole who was almost as thin as one. He sat slumped back against the hot seat watching Kelly mop at his sweaty cheeks.

"Why shouldn't we?" asked Kelly, pushing the damp handkerchief down under his shirt collar.

"Because they don't make it no more," Pole said with the false patience of a man who has had to say the same thing too many times.

"Well, that's crazy," said Kelly. He pulled off his hat and patted at the bald-spot in the center of his rust-colored hair. "There's still plenty B-twos in the business."

"Not many," said Pole, bracing one foot upon the covered object.

"*Don't*," said Kelly.

Pole let his foot drop heavily and a curse fell slowly from his lips. Kelly ran the handkerchief around the lining of his hat. He started to put the hat on again, then changed his mind and dropped it on top of his coat.

"Christ, it's hot," he said.

"It'll get hotter," said Pole.

Across the aisle a man put his suitcase up on the rack, took off his suit coat and sat down, puffing. Kelly looked at him, then turned back.

"Ya think it'll be hotter in Maynard, huh?" he asked.

Pole nodded. Kelly swallowed dryly.

"Wish we could have another o' them beers," he said.

Pole stared out the window at the heat waves rising from the concrete platform.

"I had three beers," said Kelly, "and I'm just as thirsty as I was when I started."

"Yeah," said Pole.

"Might as well've not had a beer since Philly," said Kelly.

Pole said, "Yeah."

Kelly sat there staring at Pole a moment. Pole had dark hair and white skin and his hands were the hands of a man who should be bigger than Pole was. But the hands were as clever as they were big. Pole's one o' the best, Kelly thought, one o' the best.

"Ya think he'll be all right?" he asked.

Pole grunted and smiled for an instant without being amused.

"If he don't get hit," he said.

"No, no, I mean it," said Kelly.

Pole's dark, lifeless eyes left the station and shifted over to Kelly.

"So do I," he said.

"Come on," Kelly said.

"Steel," said Pole, "ya know just as well as me. He's shot t'hell."

"That ain't true," said Kelly, shifting uncomfortably. "All he needs is a little work. A little overhaul 'n' he'll be good as new."

"Yeah, a little three-four grand overhaul," Pole said, "with parts they don't make no more." He looked out the window again.

"Oh . . . it ain't as bad as that," said Kelly. "Jesus, the way you talk you'd think he was ready for scrap."

"Ain't he?" Pole asked.

"No," said Kelly angrily, "he ain't."

Pole shrugged and his long white fingers rose and fell in his lap.

"Just cause he's a little old," said Kelly.

"Old." Pole grunted. "Ancient."

"Oh . . ." Kelly took a deep breath of the hot air in the car and blew it out through his broad nose. He looked at the covered object like a father who was angry with his son's faults but angrier with those who mentioned the faults of his son.

"Plenty o' fight left in him," he said.

Pole watched the people walking on the platform. He watched a porter pushing a wagon full of piled suitcases.

"Well . . . is he okay?" Kelly asked finally as if he hated to ask.

Pole looked over at him.

"I dunno, Steel," he said. "He needs work. Ya know that.

The trigger spring in his left arm's been rewired so many damn times it's almost shot. He's got no protection on that side. The left side of his face's all beat in, the eye lens is cracked. The leg cables is worn, they're pulled slack, the tension's gone to hell. Christ, even his gyro's off."

Pole looked out at the platform again with a disgusted hiss.

"Not to mention the oil paste he ain't got in 'im," he said.

"We'll get 'im some," Kelly said.

"Yeah, *after* the fight, *after* the fight!" Pole snapped, "What about *before* the fight? He'll be creakin' around that ring like a goddam—*steam shovel*. It'll be a miracle if he goes two rounds. They'll prob'ly ride us outta town on a pole."

Kelly swallowed. "I don't think it's that bad," he said.

"The *hell* it ain't," said Pole. "It's worse. Wait'll that crowd gets a load of 'Battling Maxo' from Philadelphia. Oh —*Christ*, they'll blow a nut. We'll be lucky if we get our five hundred bucks."

"Well, the contract's signed," said Kelly firmly. "They can't back out now. I got a copy right in the old pocket." He leaned over and patted at his coat.

"That contract's for Battling Maxo," said Pole. "Not for this—steam shovel here."

"Maxo's gonna do all right," said Kelly as if he was trying hard to believe it. "He's not as bad off as you say."

"Against a B-*seven*?" Pole asked.

"It's just a *starter* B-seven," said Kelly. "It ain't got the kinks out yet."

Pole turned away.

"Battling Maxo," he said. "One-round Maxo. The battling steam shovel."

"Aw, shut the hell up!" Kelly snapped suddenly, getting redder. "You're always knockin' 'im down. Well, he's been doin' OK for twelve years now and he'll keep on doin' OK. So he needs some oil paste. And he needs a little work. So *what*? With five hundred bucks we can get him all the paste he needs. And a new trigger spring for his arm and—and new leg cables! And everything. Chris-*sake*."

He fell back against the seat, chest shuddering with breath and rubbed at his cheeks with his wet handkerchief. He looked aside at Maxo. Abruptly, he reached over a hand and patted Maxo's covered knee clumsily and the steel clanked hollowly under his touch.

"You're doin' all right," said Kelly to his fighter.

The train was moving across a sun-baked prairie. All the windows were open but the wind that blew in was like blasts from an oven.

Kelly sat reading his paper, his shirt sticking wetly to his broad chest. Pole had taken his coat off too and was staring morosely out the window at the grass-tufted prairie that went as far as he could see. Maxo sat under his covering, his heavy steel frame rocking a little with the motion of the train.

Kelly put down his paper.

"Not even a word," he said.

"What d'ya expect?" Pole asked. "They don't cover Maynard."

"Maxo ain't just some clunk from Maynard," said Kelly. "He was big time. Ya'd think they'd"—he shrugged—"remember him."

"Why? For a coupla prelims in the Garden three years ago?" Pole asked.

"It wasn't no three years, buddy," said Kelly definitely.

"It was in 1977," said Pole, "and now it's 1980. That's three years where I come from."

"It was late '77," said Kelly. "Right before Christmas. Don't ya remember? Just before—Marge and me . . ."

Kelly didn't finish. He stared down at the paper as if Marge's picture were on it—the way she looked the day she left him.

"What's the difference?" Pole asked, "They don't remember *them* for Chrissake. With a coupla thousand o' the damn things floatin' around? How could they remember 'em? About the only ones who get space are the champeens and the new models."

Pole looked at Maxo. "I hear Mawling's puttin' out a B-nine this year," he said.

Kelly refocused his eyes. "Yeah?" he said uninterestedly.

"Hyper-triggers in both arms—and legs. All steeled aluminum. Triple gyro. Triple-twisted wiring. God, they'll be beautiful."

Kelly put down the paper.

"Think they'd remember him," he muttered. "It wasn't so long ago."

His face relaxed in a smile of recollection.

"Boy, will I ever forget that night," he said. "No one gives us a tumble. It was all Dimsy the Rock, Dimsy the Rock. Three t'one for Dimsy the Rock. Dimsy the Rock—fourth rankin' light heavy. On his way t'the top."

He chuckled deep in his chest. "And did we ever put him away," he said. "Oooh." He grunted with savage pleasure. "I can see that left cross now. *Bang!* Right in the chops. And old Dimsy the Rock hittin' the canvas like a—like a rock, yeah, *just* like a rock!"

He laughed happily. "Boy, what a night, what a night," he said. "Will I ever forget that night?"

Pole looked at Kelly with a somber face. Then he turned away and stared at the dusty sun-baked plain again.

"I wonder," he muttered.

Kelly saw the man across the aisle looking again at the covered Maxo. He caught the man's eye and smiled, then gestured with his head toward Maxo.

"That's my fighter," he said, loudly.

The man smiled politely, cupping a hand behind one ear.

"My fighter," said Kelly. "Battling Maxo. Ever hear of 'im?"

The man stared at Kelly a moment before shaking his head.

Kelly smiled. "Yeah, he was almost light heavyweight champ once," he told the man. The man nodded politely.

On an impulse, Kelly got up and stepped across the aisle. He reversed the seatback in front of the man and sat down facing him.

"Pretty damn hot," he said.

The man smiled. "Yes. Yes it is," he said.

"No new trains out here yet, huh?"

"No," said the man. "Not yet."

"Got all the new ones back in Philly," said Kelly. "That's where"—he gestured with his head—"my friend 'n' I come from. And Maxo."

Kelly stuck out his hand.

"The name's Kelly," he said. "Tim Kelly."

The man looked surprised. His grip was loose.

"Maxwell," he said.

When he drew back his hand he rubbed it unobtrusively on his pants leg.

"I used t'be called 'Steel' Kelly," said Kelly. "Used t'be in the business m'self. Before the war o' course. I was a light heavy."

"Oh?"

"Yeah. That's right. Called me 'Steel' cause I never got knocked down once. Not once. I was even number nine in the ranks once. Yeah."

"I see." The man waited patiently.

"My—fighter," said Kelly, gesturing toward Maxo with his head again. "He's a light heavy too. We're fightin' in Maynard t'night. You goin' that far?"

"Uh—no," said the man. "No, I'm—getting off at Hayes."

"Oh." Kelly nodded. "Too bad. Gonna be a good scrap." He let out a heavy breath. "Yeah, he was—fourth in the ranks once. He'll be back too. He—uh—knocked down Dimsy the Rock in late '77. Maybe ya read about that."

"I don't believe . . ."

"Oh. Uh-huh." Kelly nodded. "Well . . . it was in all the East Coast papers. You know. New York, Boston, Philly. Yeah it—got a hell of a spread. Biggest upset o' the year."

He scratched at his bald spot.

"He's a B-two y'know but—that means he's the second model Mawling put out," he explained, seeing the look on the man's face. "That was back in—let's see—'67, I think it was. Yeah, '67."

He made a smacking sound with his lips. "Yeah, that was a good model," he said. "The best. Maxo's still goin' strong." He shrugged depreciatingly. "I don't go for these new ones," he said. "You know. The ones made o' steeled aluminum with all the doo-dads."

The man stared at Kelly blankly.

"Too— . . . flashy—flimsy. Nothin' . . ." Kelly bunched his big fist in front of his chest and made a face. "Nothin' solid," he said. "No. Mawling don't make 'em like Maxo no more."

"I see," said the man.

Kelly smiled.

"Yeah," he said. "Used t'be in the game m'self. When there was enough men, o' course. Before the bans." He shook his head, then smiled quickly. "Well," he said, "we'll take this B-seven. Don't even know what his name is," he said, laughing.

His face sobered for an instant and he swallowed.

"We'll take 'im," he said.

Later on, when the man had gotten off the train, Kelly went back to his seat. He put his feet up on the opposite seat and, lying back his head, he covered his face with the newspaper.

"Get a little shut-eye," he said.

Pole grunted.

Kelly sat slouched back, staring at the newspaper next to his eyes. He felt Maxo bumping against his side a little. He listened to the squeaking of Maxo's joints. "Be all right," he muttered to himself.

"What?" Pole asked.

Kelly swallowed. "I didn't say anything," he said.

When they got off the train at six o'clock that evening they pushed Maxo around the station and onto the sidewalk. Across the street from them a man sitting in his taxi called them.

"We got no taxi money," said Pole.

"We can't just push 'im through the streets," Kelly said. "Besides, we don't even know where Kruger Stadium is."

"What are we supposed to eat with then?"

"We'll be loaded after the fight," said Kelly. "I'll buy you a steak three inches thick."

Sighing, Pole helped Kelly push the heavy Maxo across the street that was still so hot they could feel it through their shoes. Kelly started sweating right away and licking at his upper lip.

"God, how d'they live out here?" he asked.

When they were putting Maxo inside the cab the base wheel came out again and Pole, with a snarl, kicked it away.

"What're ya doin'?" Kelly asked.

"Oh . . . sh—" Pole got into the taxi and slumped back against the warm leather of the seat while Kelly hurried over the soft tar pavement and picked up the wheel.

"Chris-sake," Kelly muttered as he got in the cab. "What's the—?"

"Where to, chief?" the driver asked.

"Kruger Stadium," Kelly said.

"You're there." The cab driver pushed in the rotor button and the car glided away from the curb.

"What the hell's wrong with you?" Kelly asked Pole in a

low voice. "We wait more'n half a damn year t'get us a bout and you been nothin' but bellyaches from the start."

"Some bout," said Pole. "Maynard, Kansas—the prize-fightin' center o' the nation."

"It's a start, ain't it?" Kelly said. "It'll keep us in coffee 'n' cakes a while, won't it? It'll put Maxo back in shape. And if we take it, it could lead to——"

Pole glanced over disgustedly.

"I don't *get* you," Kelly said quietly. "He's our fighter. What're ya writin' 'im off for? Don't ya want 'im t'win?"

"I'm a class-A mechanic, Steel," Pole said in his falsely patient voice. "I'm not a day-dreamin' kid. We got a piece o' dead iron here, not a B-seven. It's simple mechanics, Steel, that's all. Maxo'll be lucky if he comes out o' that ring with his head still on."

Kelly turned away angrily.

"It's a *starter* B-seven," he muttered. "Full o' kinks. *Full* of 'em."

"Sure, sure," said Pole.

They sat silently a while looking out the window, Maxo between them, the broad steel shoulders bumping against theirs. Kelly stared at the building, his hands clenching and unclenching in his lap as if he was getting ready to go fifteen rounds.

"That a B-fighter ya got there?" the driver asked over his shoulder.

Kelly started and looked forward. He managed a smile.

"That's right," he said.

"Fightin' t'night?"

"Yeah. Battling Maxo. Maybe ya heard of 'im."

"Nope."

"He was almost light heavyweight champ once," said Kelly. "That right?"

"Yes sir. Ya heard o' Dimsy the Rock, ain't ya?"

"Don't think so."

"Well, Dimsy the——"

Kelly stopped and glanced over at Pole who was shifting irritably on the seat.

"Dimsy the Rock was number *three* in the light heavy ranks. Right on his way t'the top they all said. Well, my boy put 'im away in the fourth round. Left-crossed 'im—*bang!* Almost put Dimsy through the ropes. It was beautiful."

"That right?" asked the driver.

"Yes sir. You get a chance, stop by t'night at the stadium. You'll see a good fight."

"Have you seen this Maynard Flash?" Pole asked the driver suddenly.

"The Flash? You bet. Man, there's a fighter on his way. Won seven straight. He'll be up there soon ya can bet ya life. Matter o' fact he's fightin' t'night too. With some B-two heap from back East I hear."

The driver snickered. "Flash'll slaughter 'im," he said.

Kelly stared at the back of the driver's head, the skin tight across his cheek bones.

"Yeah?" he said, flatly.

"Man, he'll—"

The driver broke off suddenly and looked back. "Hey, you ain't—" he started, then turned front again. "Hey, I didn't know, mister," he said. "I was only ribbin'."

"Skip it," Pole said, "You're right."

Kelly's head snapped around and he glared at the sallow-face Pole.

"*Shut up*," he said in a low voice.

He fell back against the seat and stared out the window, his face hard.

"I'm gonna get 'im some oil paste," he said after they'd ridden a block.

"Swell," said Pole, "We'll eat the tools."

"Go to hell," said Kelly.

The cab pulled up in front of the brick-fronted stadium and they lifted Maxo out onto the sidewalk. While Pole tilted him, Kelly squatted down and slid the base wheel back into its slot. Then Kelly paid the driver the exact fare and they started pushing Maxo toward the alley.

"Look," said Kelly, nodding toward the poster board in front of the stadium. The third fight listed was

MAYNARD FLASH
(B-7, L.H.)
vs.
BATTLING MAXO
(B-2, L.H.)

"Big deal," said Pole.

Kelly's smile disappeared. He started to say something, then pressed his lips together. He shook his head irritably and big drops of his sweat fell to the sidewalk.

Maxo creaked as they pushed him down the alley and carried him up the steps to the door. The base wheel fell out again and bounced down the cement steps. Neither one of them said anything.

It was hotter inside. The air didn't move.

"Refreshing like a closet," Pole said.

"Get the wheel," Kelly said and started down the narrow hallway leaving Pole with Maxo. Pole leaned Maxo against the wall and turned for the door.

Kelly came to a half-glassed office door and knocked.

"Yeah," said a voice inside. Kelly went in, taking off his hat.

The fat bald man looked up from his desk. His skull glistened with sweat.

"I'm Battling Maxo's owner," said Kelly, smiling. He extended his big hand but the man ignored it.

"Was wonderin' if you'd make it," said the man whose name was Mr. Waddow. "Your fighter in decent shape?"

"The best," said Kelly cheerfully. "The best. My mechanic —he's class-A—just took 'im apart and put 'im together again before we left Philly."

The man looked unconvinced.

"He's in good shape," said Kelly.

"You're lucky t'get a bout with a B-two," said Mr. Waddow. "We ain't used nothin' less than B-fours for more than two years now. The fighter we was after got stuck in a car wreck though and got ruined."

Kelly nooded. "Well, ya got nothin' t'worry about," he said. "My fighter's in top shape. He's the one knocked down Dimsy the Rock in Madison Square year or so ago."

"I want a good fight," said the fat man.

"You'll get a good fight," Kelly said, feeling a tight pain in his stomach muscles. "Maxo's in good shape. You'll see. He's in top shape."

"I just want a good fight."

Kelly stared at the fat man a moment. Then he said, "You got a ready room we can use? The mechanic 'n' me'd like t'get something t'eat."

"Third door down the hall on the right side," said Mr. Waddow. "Your bout's at eight thirty."

Kelly nodded. "OK."

"Be there," said Mr. Waddow turning back to his work.

"Uh . . . what about—?" Kelly started.

"You get ya money after ya deliver a fight," Mr. Waddow cut him off.

Kelly's smile faltered.

"Okay," he said. "See ya then."

When Mr. Waddow didn't answer, he turned for the door.

"Don't slam the door," Mr. Waddow said. Kelly didn't.

"Come on," he said to Pole when he was in the hall again. They pushed Maxo down to the ready room and put him inside it.

"What about checkin' 'im over?" Kelly said.

"What about my gut?" snapped Pole. "I ain't eaten in six hours."

Kelly blew out a heavy breath. "All right, let's go then," he said.

They put Maxo in a corner of the room.

"We should be able t'lock him in," Kelly said.

"Why? Ya think somebody's gonna steal 'im?"

"He's valuable," said Kelly.

"Sure, he's a priceless antique," said Pole.

Kelly closed the door three times before the latch caught. He turned away from it, shaking his head worriedly. As they started down the hall he looked at his wrist and saw for the fiftieth time the white band where his pawned watch had been.

"What time is it?" he asked.

"Six twenty-five," said Pole.

"We'll have t'make it fast," Kelly said. "I want ya t'check 'im over good before the fight."

"What for?" asked Pole.

"Did ya hear me?" Kelly said angrily.

"Sure, sure," Pole said.

"He's gonna take that son-of-a-bitch B-seven," Kelly said, barely opening his lips.

"Sure he is," said Pole. "With his teeth."

"Hurry up," Kelly said, ignoring him. "We ain't got all night. Did ya get the wheel?"

Pole handed it to him.

"Some town," Kelly said disgustedly as they came back in the side door of the stadium.

"I told ya they wouldn't have any oil paste here," Pole

said. "Why should they? B-twos are dead. Maxo's probably the only one in a thousand miles."

Kelly walked quickly down the hall, opened the door of the ready room and went in. He crossed over to Maxo and pulled off the covering.

"Get to it," he said. "There ain't much time."

Blowing out a slow, tired breath, Pole took off his wrinkled blue coat and tossed it over the bench standing against the wall. He dragged a small table over to where Maxo was, then rolled up his sleeves. Kelly took off his hat and coat and watched while Pole worked loose the nut that held the tool cavity door shut. He stood with his big hands on his hips while Pole drew out the tools one by one and laid them down on the table.

"Rust," Pole muttered. He rubbed a finger around the inside of the cavity and held it up, copper colored rust flaking off the tip.

"Come on," Kelly said, irritably. He sat down on the bench and watched as Pole pried off the sectional plates on Maxo's chest. His eyes ran up over Maxo's leonine head. If I didn't see them coils, he thought once more, I'd swear he was real. Only the mechanics in a B-fighter could tell it wasn't real men in there. Sometimes people were actually fooled and sent in letters complaining that real men were being used. Even from ringside the flesh tones looked human. Mawling had a special patent on that.

Kelly's face relaxed as he smiled fondly at Maxo.

"Good boy," he murmured. Pole didn't hear. Kelly watched the sure-handed mechanic probe with his electric pick, examining connections and potency centers.

"Is he all right?" he asked, without thinking.

"Sure, he's great," Pole said. He plucked out a tiny steel-caged tube. "If this doesn't blow out," he said.

"Why should it?"

"It's sub-par," Pole said jadedly. "I told ya that after the last fight eight months ago."

Kelly swallowed. "We'll get 'im a new one after this bout," he said.

"Seventy-five bucks," muttered Pole as if he were watching the money fly away on green wings.

"It'll hold," Kelly said, more to himself than to Pole.

Pole shrugged. He put back the tube and pressed in the row of buttons on the main autonomic board. Maxo stirred.

"Take it easy on the left arm," said Kelly, "Save it."

"If it don't work here, it won't work out there," said Pole.

He jabbed at a button and Maxo's left arm began moving with little, circling motions. Pole pushed over the safety-block switch that would keep Maxo from counterpunching and stepped back. He threw a right at Maxo's chin and the robot's arm jumped up with a hitching motion to cover his face. Maxo's left eye flickered like a ruby catching the sun.

"If that eye cell goes . . ." Pole said.

"It won't," said Kelly tensely. He watched Pole throw another punch at the left side of Maxo's head. He saw the tiny ripple of the flexo-covered cheek, then the arm jerked up again. It squeaked.

"That's enough," he said. "It works. Try the rest of 'im."

"He's gonna get more than two punches throwed at his head," Pole said.

"His arm's all right," Kelly said. "Try something else I said."

Pole reached inside Maxo and activated the leg cable centers. Maxo began shifting around. He lifted his left leg and shook off the base wheel automatically. Then he was standing lightly on his black-shoed feet, feeling at the floor like a cured cripple testing for stance.

Pole reached forward and jabbed in the FULL button, then jumped back as Maxo's eye beams centered on him and the robot moved forward, broad shoulders rocking slowly, arms up defensively.

"Christ," Pole muttered, "they'll hear 'im squeakin' in the back row."

Kelly grimaced, teeth set. He watched Pole throw another right and Maxo's arm lurch up raggedly. His throat moved with a convulsive swallow and he seemed to have trouble breathing the close air in the little room.

Pole shifted around the floor quickly, side to side. Maxo followed lumberingly, changing direction with visibly jerking motions.

"Oh, he's beautiful," Pole said, stopping. "Just beautiful." Maxo came up, arms still raised, and Pole jabbed in under them, pushing the OFF button. Maxo stopped.

"Look, we'll have t'put 'im on defense, Steel," Pole said, "That's all there is to it. He'll get chopped t'pieces if we have 'im movin' in."

Kelly cleared his throat. "No," he said.

"Oh for—will ya use ya *head?*" snapped Pole. "He's a B-two f'Chris-sake. He's gonna get slaughtered anyway. Let's save the pieces."

"They want 'im on the offense," said Kelly. "It's in the contract."

Pole turned away with a hiss.

"What's the use?" he muttered.

"Test 'im some more."

"What for? He's as good as he'll ever be."

"Will ya do what I say!" Kelly shouted, all the tension exploding out of him.

Pole turned back and jabbed in a button. Maxo's left arm shot out. There was a snapping noise inside it and it fell against Maxo's side with a dead clank.

Kelly started up, his face stricken. "Jesus, what did ya *do!*" he cried. He ran over to where Pole was pushing the button again. Maxo's arm didn't move.

"I *told* ya not t'fool with that arm!" Kelly yelled. "What the hell's the *matter* with ya!" His voice cracked in the middle of the sentence.

Pole didn't answer. He picked up his pry and began working off the left shoulder plate.

"So help me God, if you broke that arm . . ." Kelly warned in a low, snaking voice.

"If *I* broke it!" Pole snapped. "Listen, you dumb mick! This heap has been runnin' on borrowed time for three years now! Don't talk t'me about breakages!"

Kelly clenched his teeth, his eyes small and deadly.

"Open it up," he said.

"Son-of-a—" Pole muttered as he got the plate off, "You find another goddam mechanic that coulda kep' this steam shovel together any better these last years. You just *find* one."

Kelly didn't answer. He stood rigidly, watching while Pole put down the curved plate and looked inside.

When Pole touched it, the trigger spring broke in half and part of it jumped across the room.

Kelly stared at the shoulder pit with horrified eyes.

"Oh, Christ," he said in a shaking voice. "Oh, *Christ.*"

Pole started to say something, then stopped. He looked at the ashen-faced Kelly without moving.

Kelly's eyes moved to Pole.

"Fix it," he said, hoarsely.

Pole swallowed. "Steel, I—"

"*Fix it!*"

"I can't! That spring's been fixin' t'break for—"

"You broke it! Now *fix* it!" Kelly clamped rigid fingers on Pole's arm. Pole jerked back.

"Let go of me!" he said.

"What's the matter with you!" Kelly cried. "Are you crazy? He's got t'be fixed. He's got t'be!"

"Steel, he needs a new spring."

"Well, get it!"

"They don't *have* 'em here, Steel," Pole said. "I told ya. And if they did have 'em, we ain't got the sixteen fifty t'get one."

"Oh—Oh, Jesus," said Kelly. His hand fell away and he stumbled to the other side of the room. He sank down on the bench and stared without blinking at the tall motionless Maxo.

He sat there a long time, just staring, while Pole stood watching him, the pry still in his hand. He saw Kelly's broad chest rise and fall with spasmodic movements. Kelly's face was a blank.

"If he don't watch 'em," muttered Kelly, finally.

"What?"

Kelly looked up, his mouth set in a straight, hard line. "If he don't watch, it'll work," he said.

"What're ya talkin' about?"

Kelly stood up and started unbuttoning his shirt.

"What're ya—"

Pole stopped dead, his mouth falling open. "Are you crazy?" he asked.

Kelly kept unbuttoning his shirt. He pulled it off and tossed it on the bench.

"Steel, you're out o' your mind!" Pole said. "You can't do that!"

Kelly didn't say anything.

"But you'll—Steel, you're *crazy!*"

"We deliver a fight or we don't get paid," Kelly said.

"But—Jesus, you'll get *killed!*"

Kelly pulled off his undershirt. His chest was beefy, there was red hair swirled around it. "Have to shave this off," he said.

"Steel, come on," Pole said. "You—"

His eyes widened as Kelly sat down on the bench and started unlacing his shoes.

"They'll never let ya," Pole said. "You can't make 'em think you're a—" He stopped and took a jerky step forward. "Steel, fuh Chrissake!"

Kelly looked up at Pole with dead eyes.

"You'll help me," he said.

"But they—"

"Nobody knows what Maxo looks like," Kelly said. "And only Waddow saw me. If he don't watch the bouts we'll be all right."

"But—"

"They won't know," Kelly said. "The B's bleed and bruise too."

"Steel, come on," Pole said shakily. He took a deep breath and calmed himself. He sat down hurriedly beside the broad-shouldered Irishman.

"Look," he said. "I got a sister back East—in Maryland. If I wire 'er, she'll send us the dough t'get back."

Kelly got up and unbuckled his belt.

"Steel, I know a guy in Philly with a B-five wants t'sell cheap," Pole said desperately. "We could scurry up the cash and—Steel, fuh Chrissake, you'll get killed! It's a B-seven! Don't ya understand? A B-seven! You'll be mangled!"

Kelly was working the dark trunks over Maxo's hips.

"I won't let ya do it, Steel," Pole said, "I'll go to—"

He broke off with a sucked-in gasp as Kelly whirled and moved over quickly to haul him to his feet. Kelly's grip was like the jaws of a trap and there was nothing left of him in his eyes.

"You'll help me," Kelly said in a low, trembling voice. "You'll help me or I'll beat ya brains out on the wall."

"You'll get killed," Pole murmured.

"Then I will," said Kelly.

Mr. Waddow came out of his office as Pole was walking the covered Kelly toward the ring.

"Come on, come on," Mr. Waddow said. "They're waitin' on ya."

Pole nodded jerkily and guided Kelly down the hall.

"Where's the owner?" Mr. Waddow called after them.

Pole swallowed quickly. "In the audience," he said.

Mr. Waddow grunted and, as they walked on, Pole heard the door to the office close. Breath emptied from him.

"I should've told 'im," he muttered.

"I'd o' killed ya," Kelly said, his voice muffled under the covering.

Crowd sounds leaked back into the hall now as they turned a corner. Under the canvas covering, Kelly felt a drop of sweat trickle down his temple.

"Listen," he said, "you'll have t'towel me off between rounds."

"Between what rounds?" Pole asked tensely. "You won't even last one."

"Shut up."

"You think you're just up against some tough fighter?" Pole asked. "You're up against a machine! Don't ya—"

"I said shut up."

"Oh . . . you dumb—" Pole swallowed. "If I towel ya off, they'll know," he said.

"They ain't seen a B-two in years," Kelly broke in. "If anyone asks, tell 'em it's an oil leak."

"Sure," said Pole disgustedly. He bit his lips. "Steel, ya'll never get away with it."

The last part of his sentence was drowned out as, suddenly, they were among the crowd, walking down the sloping aisle toward the ring. Kelly held his knees locked and walked a little stiffly. He drew in a long, deep breath and let it out slowly. He'd have to breathe in small gasps and exhalations through his nose while he was in the ring. The people couldn't see his chest moving or they'd know.

The heat burdened in around him like a hanging weight. It was like walking along the sloping floor of an ocean of heat and sound. He heard voices drifting past him as he moved.

"Ya'll take 'im home in a box!"

"Well, if it ain't *Rattlin'* Maxo!"

And the inevitable, "*Scrap iron!*"

Kelly swallowed dryly, feeling a tight drawing sensation in

his loins. Thirsty, he thought. The momentary vision of the bar across from the Kansas City train station crossed his mind. The dim-lit booth, the cool fan breeze on the back of his neck, the icy, sweat-beaded bottle chilling his palm. He swallowed again. He hadn't allowed himself one drink in the last hour. The less he drank the less he'd sweat, he knew.

"Watch it."

He felt Pole's hand slide in through the opening in the back of the covering, felt the mechanic's hand grab his arm and check him.

"Ring steps," Pole said out of a corner of his mouth.

Kelly edged his right foot forward until the shoe tip touched the riser of the bottom step. Then he lifted his foot to the step and started up.

At the top, Pole's fingers tightenend around his arm again.

"Ropes," Pole said, guardedly.

It was hard getting through the ropes with the covering on. Kelly almost fell and hoots and catcalls came at him like spears out of the din. Kelly felt the canvas give slightly under his feet and then Pole pushed the stool against the back of his legs and he sat down a little too jerkily.

"Hey, get that derrick out o' here!" shouted a man in the second row. Laughter and hoots. "Scrap iron!" yelled some people.

Then Pole drew off the covering and put it down on the ring apron.

Kelly sat there staring at the Maynard Flash.

The B-seven was motionless, its gloved hands hanging across its legs. There was imitation blonde hair, crew cut, growing out of its skull pores. Its face was that of an impassive Adonis. The simulation of muscle curve on its body and limbs was almost perfect. For a moment Kelly almost thought that years had been peeled away and he was in the business again, facing a young contender. He swallowed carefully. Pole crouched beside him, pretending to fiddle with an arm plate.

"Steel, don't," he muttered again.

Kelly didn't answer. He felt a desperate desire to suck in a lungful of air and bellow his chest. He drew in small patches of air through his nose and let them trickle out. He kept staring at the Maynard Flash, thinking of the array of instant-reaction centers inside that smooth arch of chest. The drawing sensation reached his stomach. It was like a cold hand pulling in at strands of muscle and ligament.

A red-faced man in a white suit climbed into the ring and reached up for the microphone which was swinging down to him.

"Ladies and gentlemen," he announced, "the opening bout of the evening. A ten-round light heavyweight bout. From Philadelphia, the B-two, *Battling Maxo*."

The crowd booed and hissed. They threw up paper airplanes and shouted "*Scrap iron!*"

"His opponent, our own B-seven, the *Maynard Flash!*"

Cheers and wild clapping. The Flash's mechanic touched a button under the left armpit and the B-seven jumped up and held his arms over his head in the victory gesture. The crowd laughed happily.

"*Jesus*," Pole muttered, "I never saw that. Must be a new gimmick."

Kelly blinked to relieve his eyes.

"Three more bouts to follow," said the red-faced man and then the microphone drew up and he left the ring. There was no referee. B-fighters never clinched—their machinery rejected it—and there was no knock-down count. A felled B-fighter stayed down. The new B-nine, it was claimed by the Mawling publicity staff, would be able to get up, which would make for livelier and longer bouts.

Pole pretended to check over Kelly.

"Steel, it's your last chance," he begged.

"*Get out*," said Kelly without moving his lips.

Pole looked at Kelly's immobile eyes a moment, then sucked in a ragged breath and straightened up.

"Stay away from him," he warned as he started through the ropes.

Across the ring, the Flash was standing in its corner, hitting its gloves together as if it were a real young fighter anxious to get the fight started. Kelly stood up and Pole drew the stool away. Kelly stood watching the B-seven, seeing how its eye centers were zeroing in on him. There was a cold sinking in his stomach.

The bell rang.

The B-seven moved out smoothly from its corner with a mechanical glide, its arms raised in the traditional way, gloved hands wavering in tiny circles in front of it. It moved quickly toward Kelly who edged out of his corner automatically, his mind feeling, abruptly, frozen. He felt his own hands rise as if someone else had lifted them and his legs were like dead wood under him. He kept his gaze on the bright unmoving eyes of the Maynard Flash.

They came together. The B-seven's left flicked out and Kelly blocked it, feeling the rock-hard fist of the Flash even through his glove. The first moved out again. Kelly drew back his head and felt a warm breeze across his mouth. His own left shot out and banged against the Flash's nose. It was like hitting a door knob. Pain flared in Kelly's arm and his jaw muscles went hard as he struggled to keep his face blank.

The B-seven feinted with a left and Kelly knocked it aside. He couldn't stop the right that blurred in after it and grazed his left temple. He jerked his head away and the B-seven threw a left that hit him over the ear. Kelly lurched back, throwing out a left that the B-seven brushed aside. Kelly caught his footing and hit the Flash's jaw solidly with a right uppercut. He felt a jolt of pain run up his arm. The Flash's head didn't budge. He shot out a left that hit Kelly on the right shoulder.

Kelly back-pedaled instinctively. Then he heard someone yell, "Get 'im a bicycle!" and he remembered what Mr. Waddow had said. He moved in again, his lips aching they were pressed together so tightly.

A left caught him under the heart and he felt the impact shudder through his frame. Pain stabbed at his heart. He threw a spasmodic left which banged against the B-seven's nose again. There was only pain. Kelly stepped back and staggered as a hard right caught him high on the chest. He started to move back. The B-seven hit him on the chest again. Kelly lost his balance and stepped back quickly to catch equilibrium. The crowd booed. The B-seven moved in without making a single mechanical sound.

Kelly regained his balance and stopped. He threw a hard right that missed. The momentum of his blow threw him off center and the Flash's left drove hard against his upper right arm. The arm went numb. Even as Kelly was sucking in a teeth-clenched gasp the B-seven shot in a hard right under his guard that slammed into Kelly's spongy stomach. Kelly felt the breath go out of him. His right slapped ineffectively across the Flash's right cheek. The Flash's eyes glinted.

As the B-seven moved in again, Kelly side-stepped and, for a moment, the radial eye centers lost him. Kelly moved out of range dizzily, pulling air in through his nostrils.

"Get that heap out o' there!" some man screamed.

"Scrap iron, scrap iron!"

Breath shook in Kelly's throat. He swallowed quickly and started foreward just as the Flash picked him up again. Taking a chance, he sucked in breath through his mouth hoping that his movements would keep the people from seeing. Then he was up to the B-seven. He stepped in close, hoping to out-time electrical impulse, and threw a hard right at the Flash's body.

The B-seven's left shot up and Kelly's blow was deflected by the iron wrist. Kelly's left was thrown off too and then the Flash's left shot in and drove the breath out of Kelly again. Kelly's left barely hit the Flash's rock-hard chest. He staggered back, the B-seven following. He kept jabbing but the B-seven kept deflecting the blows and counterjabbing with almost the same piston-like motion. Kelly's head kept snapping back. He fell back more and saw the right coming straight at him. He couldn't stop it.

The blow drove in like a steel battering-ram. Spears of pain shot behind Kelly's eyes and through his head. A black cloud seemed to flood across the ring. His muffled cry was drowned out by the screaming crowd as he toppled back, his nose and mouth trickling bright blood that looked as good as the dye they used in the B-fighters.

The rope checked his fall, pressing in rough and hard against his back. He swayed there, right arm hanging limp, left arm raised defensively. He blinked his eyes instinctively, trying to focus them. I'm a robot, he thought, a robot.

The Flash stepped in and drove a violent right into Kelly's chest, a left to his stomach. Kelly doubled over, gagging. A right slammed off his skull like a hammer blow, driving him back against the ropes again. The crowd screamed.

Kelly saw the blurred outline of the Maynard Flash. He felt another blow smash into his chest like a club. With a sob he threw a wild left that the B-seven brushed off. Another sharp blow landed on Kelly's shoulder. He lifted his right and managed to deflect the worst of a left thrown at his jaw. Another right concaved his stomach. He doubled over. A hammering right drove him back on the ropes. He felt hot salty blood in his mouth and the roar of the crowd seemed to swallow him. Stay up!—he screamed at himself. Stay up goddam you! The ring wavered before him like dark water.

With a desperate surge of energy, he threw a right as hard as he could at the tall beautiful figure in front of him. Something cracked in his wrist and hand and a wave of searing pain shot up his arm. His throat-locked cry went unheard. His arm fell, his left went down and the crowd shrieked and howled for the Flash to finish it.

There was only inches between them now. The B-seven rained in blows that didn't miss. Kelly lurched and staggered under the impact of them. His head snapped from side to side. Blood ran across his face in scarlet ribbons. His arm hung like a dead branch at his side. He kept getting slammed back against the ropes, bouncing forward and getting slammed back again. He couldn't see any more. He could only hear the screaming of the crowd and the endless swishing and thudding of the B-seven's gloves. Stay up, he thought. I have to stay up. He drew in his head and hunched his shoulders to protect himself.

He was like that seven seconds before the bell when a clubbing right on the side of his head sent him crashing to the canvas.

He lay there gasping for breath. Suddenly, he started to get up, then, equally as suddenly, realized that he couldn't. He fell forward again and lay on his stomach on the warm canvas, his head throbbing with pain. He could hear the booing and hissing of the dissatisfied crowd.

When Pole finally managed to get him up and slip the cover over his head the crowd was jeering so loudly that Kelly couldn't hear Pole's voice. He felt the mechanic's big hand inside the covering, guiding him, but he fell down climbing through the ropes and almost fell again on the steps. His legs were like rubber tubes. Stay up. His brain still murmured the words.

In the ready room he collapsed. Pole tried to get him up on the bench but he couldn't. Finally, he bunched up his blue coat under Kelly's head and, kneeling, he started patting with his handkerchief at the trickles of blood.

"You dumb bastard," he kept muttering in a thin, shaking voice. "You dumb bastard."

Kelly lifted his left hand and brushed away Pole's hand.

"Go—get the—money," he gasped hoarsely.

"What?"

"The money!" gasped Kelly through his teeth.

"But—"

"Now!" Kelly's voice was barely intelligible.

Pole straightened up and stood looking down at Kelly a moment. Then he turned and went out.

Kelly lay there drawing in breath and exhaling it with wheezing sounds. He couldn't move his right hand and he knew it was broken. He felt the blood trickling from his nose and mouth. His body throbbed with pain.

After a few moments he struggled up on his left elbow and turned his head, pain crackling along his neck muscles. When he saw that Maxo was all right he put his head down again. A smile twisted up one corner of his lips.

When Pole came back, Kelly lifted his head painfully. Pole came over and knelt down. He started patting at the blood again.

"Ya get it?" Kelly asked in a crusty whisper.

Pole blew out a slow breath.

"Well?"

Pole swallowed. "Half of it," he said.

Kelly stared up at him blankly, his mouth fallen open. His eyes didn't believe it.

"He said he wouldn't pay five C's for a one rounder."

"What d'ya mean?" Kelly's voice cracked. He tried to get up and put down his right hand. With a strangled cry he fell back, his face white. His head thrashed on the coat pillow, his eyes shut tightly.

"No," he moaned, "No. No. No. No. No."

Pole was looking at his hand and wrist. "Jesus God," he whispered.

Kelly's eyes opened and he stared up dizzily at the mechanic.

"He can't—he can't do that," he gasped.

Pole licked his dry lips.

"Steel, there—ain't a thing we can do. He's got a bunch o' toughs in the office with 'im. I can't . . ." He lowered his head. "And if—you was t'go there he'd know what ya done. And—he might even take back the two and a half."

Kelly lay on his back staring up at the naked bulb without blinking. His chest labored and shuddered with breath.

"No," he murmured. "No."

He lay there for a long time without talking. Pole got some water and cleaned off his face and gave him a drink. He opened up his small suitcase and patched up Kelly's face. He put Kelly's right arm in a sling.

Fifteen minutes later Kelly spoke.

"We'll go back by bus," he said.

"What?" Pole asked.

"We'll go by bus," Kelly said slowly. "That'll only cost, oh, fifty-six bucks." He swallowed and shifted on his back. "That'll leave almost two C's. We can get 'im a—a new trigger spring and a—eye lens and—" He blinked his eyes and held them shut a moment as the room started fading again.

"And oil paste," he said then. "Loads of it. He'll be—good as new again."

Kelly looked up at Pole. "Then we'll be all set up," he said. "Maxo'll be in good shape again. And we can get us some decent bouts." He swallowed and breathed laborously. "That's all he needs is a little work. New spring, a new eye lens. That'll shape 'im up. We'll show those bastards what a B-two can do. Old Maxo'll show 'em. *Right?*"

Pole looked down at the big Irishman and sighed.

"Sure, Steel," he said.

The Test ·····················

THE night before the test, Les helped his father study in the dining room. Jim and Tommy were asleep upstairs and, in the living room, Terry was sewing, her face expressionless as the needle moved with a swiftly rhythmic piercing and drawing.

Tom Parker sat very straight, his lean, vein-ribbed hands clasped together on the table top, his pale blue eyes looking intently at his son's lips as though it might help him to understand better.

He was 80 and this was his fourth test.

"All right," Les said, reading from the sample test Doctor Trask had gotten them. "Repeat the following sequences of numbers."

"Sequence of numbers," Tom murmured, trying to assimilate the words as they came. But words were not quickly assimilated any more; they seemed to lie upon the tissues of his brain like insects on a sluggish carnivore. He said the words in his mind again—*sequence of . . . sequence of numbers*—there he had it. He looked at his son and waited.

"Well?" he said, impatiently, after a moment's silence.

"Dad, I've already given you the first one," Les told him.

"Well . . ." His father grasped for the proper words. "Kindly give me the—the . . . do me the kindness of . . ."

Les exhaled wearily. "Eight-five-eleven-six," he said.

The old lips stirred, the old machinery of Tom's mind began turning slowly.

"Eight . . . f—ive . . ." The pale eyes blinked slowly. "Elevensix," Tom finished in a breath, then straightened himself proudly.

Yes, good, he thought—very good. They wouldn't fool him tomorrow; he'd beat their murderous law. His lips pressed together and his hands clasped tightly on the white table cloth.

"What?" he said then, refocusing his eyes as Les said something. "Speak up," he said, irritably. "Speak up."

"I gave you another sequence," Les said quietly. "Here, I'll read it again."

Tom leaned forward a little, ears straining.

"Nine-two-sixteen-seven-three," Les said.

Tom cleared his throat with effort. "Speak slower," he told his son. He hadn't quite gotten that. How did they expect anyone to retain such a ridiculously long string of numbers?

"What, *what?*" he asked angrily as Les read the numbers again.

"Dad, the examiner will be reading the questions faster than I'm reading them. You—"

"I'm quite aware of that," Tom interrupted stiffly, "Quite aware. Let me remind you . . . however, this is . . . not a test. It's study, it's for *study*. Foolish to go rushing through everything. *Foolish*. I have to learn this—this . . . this *test*," he finished, angry at his son and angry at the way desired words hid themselves from his mind.

Les shrugged and looked down at the test again. "Nine-two-sixteen-seven-three," he read slowly.

"Nine-two-six-seven—"

"Sixteen-seven, Dad."

"I said that."

"You said six, Dad."

"Don't you suppose I know what I said!"

Les closed his eyes a moment. "All right, Dad," he said.

"Well, are you going to read it again or not?" Tom asked him sharply.

Les read the numbers off again and, as he listened to his father stumble through the sequence, he glanced into the living room at Terry.

She was sitting there, features motionless, sewing. She'd turned off the radio and he knew she could hear the old man faltering with the numbers.

All right, Les heard himself saying in his mind as if he spoke to her. All right, I know he's old and useless. Do you want me to tell him that to his face and drive a knife into his back? You know and I know that he won't pass the test. Allow me, at least, this brief hypocrisy. Tomorrow the sentence will be passed. Don't make me pass it tonight and break the old man's heart.

"That's correct, I believe," Les heard the dignified voice of his father say and he refocused his eyes on the gaunt, seamed face.

"Yes, that's right," he said, hastily.

He felt like a traitor when a slight smile trembled at the corners of his father's mouth. I'm cheating him, he thought.

"Let's go on to something else," he heard his father say and he looked down quickly at the sheet. What would be easy for him? he thought, despising himself for thinking it.

"Well, come on, Leslie," his father said in a restrained voice. "We have no time to waste."

Tom looked at his son thumbing through the pages and his hands closed into fists. Tomorrow, his life was in the balance and his son just browsed through the test paper as if nothing important were going to happen tomorrow.

"Come on, come on," he said peevishly.

Les picked up a pencil that had string attached to it and

drew a half-inch circle on a piece of blank paper. He held out the pencil to his father.

"Suspend the pencil point over the circle for three minutes," he said, suddenly afraid he'd picked the wrong question. He'd seen his father's hands trembling at meal times or fumbling with the buttons and zippers of his clothes.

Swallowing nervously, Les picked up the stop watch, started it, and nodded to his father.

Tom took a quivering breath as he leaned over the paper and tried to hold the slightly swaying pencil above the circle. Les saw him lean on his elbow, something he wouldn't be allowed to do on the test; but he said nothing.

He sat there looking at his father. Whatever color there had been was leaving the old man's face and Les could see clearly the tiny red lines of broken vessels under the skin of his cheeks. He looked at the dry skin, creased and brownish, dappled with liver spots. Eighty years old, he thought—how does a man feel when he's 80 years old?

He looked in at Terry again. For a moment, her gaze shifted and they were looking at each other, neither of them smiling or making any sign. Then Terry looked back to her sewing.

"I believe that's three minutes," Tom said in a taut voice.

Les looked down at the stop watch. "A minute and a half, Dad," he said, wondering if he should have lied again.

"Well, keep your eyes on the watch then," his father said, perturbedly, the pencil penduluming completely out of the circle. "This is supposed to be a test, not a—a—a party."

Les kept his eyes on the wavering pencil point, feeling a sense of utter futility at the realization that this was only pretense, that nothing they did could save his father's life.

At least, he thought, the examinations weren't given by the sons and daughters who had voted the law into being. At least he wouldn't have to stamp the black INADEQUATE on his father's test and thus pronounce the sentence.

The pencil wavered over the circle edge again and was returned as Tom moved his arm slightly on the table, a motion that would automatically disqualify him on that question.

"That watch is slow!" Tom said in a sudden fury.

Les caught his breath and looked down at the watch. Two and a half minutes. "Three minutes," he said, pushing in the plunger.

Tom slapped down the pencil irritably. "There," he said.

"Fool test anyway." His voice grew morose. "Don't prove a thing. Not a thing."

"You want to do some money questions, Dad?"

"Are they the next questions in the test?" Tom asked, looking over suspiciously to check for himself.

"Yes," Les lied, knowing that his father's eyes were too weak to see even though Tom always refused to admit he needed glasses. "Oh, wait a second, there's one before that," he added, thinking it would be easier for his father. "They ask you to tell time."

"That's a foolish question," Tom muttered. "What do they—"

He reached across the table irritably and picked up the watch and glanced down at its face. "Ten fifteen," he said, scornfully.

Before Les could think to stop himself, he said. "But it's 11:15, Dad."

His father looked, for a moment, as though his face had been slapped. Then he picked up the watch again and stared down at it, lips twitching, and Les had the horrible premonition that Tom was going to insist it really was 10:15.

"Well, that's what I meant," Tom said abruptly. "Slipped out wrong. Course it's 11:15, any fool can see that. Eleven fifteen. Watch is no good. Numbers too close. Ought to throw it away. Now—"

Tom reached into his vest-pocket and pulled out his own gold watch. "Here's a *watch*," he said, proudly. "Been telling perfect time for . . . sixty years! That's a watch. Not like this."

He tossed Les's watch down contemptuously and it flipped over on its face and the crystal broke.

"Look at that," Tom said quickly, to cover the jolting of embarrassment. "Watch can't take anything."

He avoided Les's eyes by looking down at his own watch. His mouth tightened as he opened the back and looked at Mary's picture; Mary when she was in her thirties, golden-haired and lovely.

Thank God, she didn't have to take these tests, he thought —at least she was spared that. Tom had never thought he could believe that Mary's accidental death at 57 was fortunate, but that was before the tests.

He closed the watch and put it away.

"You just leave that watch with me, tonight," he said grumpily. "I'll see you get a decent . . . uh, *crystal* tomorrow."

"That's all right, Dad. It's just an old watch."

"That's *all* right," Tom said. "That's all right. You just leave it with me. I'll get you a decent . . . crystal. Get you one that won't break, one that won't break. You just leave it with me."

Tom did the money questions then, questions like *How many quarters in a five dollar bill?* and *If I took 36 cents from your dollar, how much change would you have left?*

They were written questions and Les sat there timing his father. It was quiet in the house, warm. Everything seemed very normal and ordinary with the two of them sitting there and Terry sewing in the living room.

That was the horror.

Life went on as usual. No one spoke of dying. The government sent out letters and the tests were given and those who failed were requested to appear at the government center for their injections. The law operated, the death rate was steady, the population problem was contained—all officially, impersonally, without a cry or a sensation.

But it was still loved people who were being killed.

"Never mind hanging over that watch," his father said. "I can do these questions without you . . . hanging over that watch."

"Dad, the examiners will be looking at their watches."

"The examiners are the examiners," Tom snapped. "You're not an examiner."

"Dad, I'm trying to help y—"

"Well, help me then, *help* me. Don't sit there hanging over that watch."

"This is your test, Dad, not mine," Les started, a flush of anger creeping up his cheeks. "If—"

"My test, yes, my test!" his father suddenly raged. "You all saw to that, didn't you? All saw to it that—that—"

Words failed again, angry thoughts piling up in his brain.

"You don't have to yell, Dad."

"I'm not yelling!"

"Dad, the boys are sleeping!" Terry suddenly broke in.

"I don't care if—!" Tom broke off suddenly and leaned back in the chair, the pencil falling unnoticed from his fingers and rolling across the table cloth. He sat shivering, his thin chest rising and falling in jerks, his hands twitching uncontrollably on his lap.

"Do you want to go on, Dad?" Les asked, restraining his nervous anger.

"I don't ask much," Tom mumbled to himself. "Don't ask much in life."

"Dad, shall we go on?"

His father stiffened. "*If you can spare the time,*" he said with slow, indignant pride. "*If you can spare the time.*"

Les looked at the test paper, his fingers gripping the stapled sheets rigidly. Psychological questions? No, he couldn't ask them. How did you ask your 80-year-old father his views on sex?—your flint-surfaced father to whom the most innocuous remark was "obscene."

"Well?" his father asked in a rising voice.

"There doesn't seem to be anymore," Les said. "We've been at it almost four hours now."

"What about all those pages you just skipped?"

"Most of those are for the . . . the physical, Dad."

He saw his father's lips press together and was afraid Tom was going to say something about that again. But all his father said was, "A fine friend. Fine friend."

"Dad, you—"

Les's voice broke off. There was no point in talking about it anymore. Tom knew perfectly well that Doctor Trask couldn't make out a bill of health for this test the way he'd done for the three tests previous.

Les knew how frightened and insulted the old man was because he'd have to take off his clothes and be exposed to doctors who would probe and tap and ask offensive questions. He knew how afraid Tom was of the fact that when he re-dressed, he'd be watched from a peephole and someone would mark on a chart how well he dressed himself. He knew how it frightened his father to know that, when he ate in the government cafeteria at the midpoint of the day-long examination, eyes would be watching him again to see if he dropped a fork or a spoon or knocked over a glass of water or dribbled gravy on his shirt.

"They'll ask you to sign your name and address," Les said, wanting his father to forget about the physical and knowing how proud Tom was of his handwriting.

Pretending that he grudged it, the old man picked up the pencil and wrote. I'll fool them, he thought as the pencil moved across the page with strong, sure motions.

Mr. Thomas Parker, he wrote, 2719 Brighton Street, Blairtown, New York.

"And the date," Les said.

The old man wrote, January 17, 2003, and something cold moved in the old man's vitals.

Tomorrow was the test.

They lay beside each other, neither of them sleeping. They had barely spoken while undressing and when Les had leaned over to kiss her goodnight she'd murmured something he didn't hear.

Now he turned over on his side with a heavy sigh and faced her. In the darkness, she opened her eyes and looked over at him.

"Asleep?" she asked softly.

"No."

He said no more. He waited for her to start.

But she didn't start and, after a few moments, he said, "Well, I guess this is . . . it." He finished weakly because he didn't like the words; they sounded ridiculously melodramatic.

Terry didn't say anything right away. Then, as if thinking aloud, she said, "Do you think there's any chance that—"

Les tightened at the words because he knew what she was going to say.

"No," he said. "He'll never pass."

He heard Terry swallowing. Don't say it, he thought, pleadingly. Don't tell me I've been saying the same thing for fifteen years. I know it. I said it because I thought it was true.

Suddenly, he wished he'd signed the Request For Removal years before. They needed desperately to be free of Tom; for the good of their children and themselves. But how did you put that need into words without feeling like a murderer? You couldn't say: I hope the old man fails, I hope they kill him. Yet anything else you said was only a hypocritical substitute for those words because that was exactly how you felt.

Medical terms, he thought—charts about declining crops and lowered standard of living and hunger ratio and degrading health level—they'd used all those as arguments to support passage of the law. Well, they were lies—obvious, groundless lies. The law had been passed because people wanted to be left alone, because they wanted to live their own lives.

"Les, what if he passes?" Terry said.

He felt his hands tightening on the mattress.

"Les?"

"I don't know, honey," he said.

Her voice was firm in the darkness. It was a voice at the end of patience. "You have to know," it said.

He moved his head restlessly on the pillow. "Honey, don't push it," he begged. "Please."

"Les, if he passes that test it means five more years. Five more years, Les. Have you thought what that means?"

"Honey, he can't pass that test."

"But, what if he does?"

"Terry, he missed three-quarters of the questions I asked him tonight. His hearing is almost gone, his eyes are bad, his heart is weak, he has arthritis." His fist beat down hopelessly on the bed. "He won't even pass the *physical*," he said, feeling himself tighten in self-hatred for assuring her that Tom was doomed.

If only he could forget the past and take his father for what he was now—a helpless, mid-jading old man who was ruining their lives. But it was hard to forget how he'd loved and respected his father, hard to forget the hikes in the country, the fishing trips, the long talks at night and all the many things his father and he had shared together.

That was why he'd never had the strength to sign the request. It was a simple form to fill out, much simpler than waiting for the five-year tests. But it had meant signing away the life of his father, requesting the government to dispose of him like some unwanted garbage. He could never do that.

And yet, now his father was 80 and, in spite of moral upbringing, in spite of life-taught Christian principles, he and Terry were horribly afraid that old Tom might pass the test and live another five years with them—another five years of fumbling around the house, undoing instructions they gave to the boys, breaking things, wanting to help but only getting in the way and making life an agony of held-in nerves.

"You'd better sleep," Terry said to him.

He tried to but he couldn't. He lay staring at the dark ceiling and trying to find an answer but finding no answer.

The alarm went off at 6. Les didn't have to get up until 8 but he wanted to see his father off. He got out of bed and dressed quietly so he wouldn't wake up Terry.

She woke up anyway and looked up at him from her pillow After a moment, she pushed up on one elbow and looked sleepily at him.

"I'll get up and make you some breakfast," she said.

"That's all right," Les said. "You stay in bed."

"Don't you want me to get up?"

"Don't bother, honey," he said. "I want you to rest."

She lay down again and turned away so Les wouldn't see her face. She didn't know why she began to cry soundlessly; whether it was because he didn't want her to see his father or because of the test. But she couldn't stop. All she could do was hold herself rigid until the bedroom door had closed.

Then her shoulders trembled and a sob broke the barrier she had built in herself.

The door to his father's room was open as Les passed. He looked in and saw Tom sitting on the bed, leaning down and fastening his dark shoes. He saw the gnarled fingers shaking as they moved over the straps.

"Everything all right, Dad?" Les asked.

His father looked up in surprise. "What are you doing up this hour?" he asked.

"Thought I'd have breakfast with you," Les told him.

For a moment they looked at each other in silence. Then his father leaned over the shoes again. "That's not necessary," he heard the old man's voice telling him.

"Well, I think I'll have some breakfast anyway," he said and turned away so his father wouldn't argue.

"Oh . . . Leslie."

Les turned.

"I trust you didn't forget to leave that watch out," his father said. "I intend to take it to the jeweler's today and have a decent . . . decent crystal put on it, one that won't break."

"Dad, it's just an old watch," Les said. "It's not worth a nickel."

His father nodded slowly, one palm wavering before him as if to ward off argument. "Never-the-less," he stated slowly, "I intend to—"

"All right, Dad, all right. I'll put it on the kitchen table."

His father broke off and looked at him blankly a moment.

Then, as if it were impulse and not delayed will, he bent over his shoes again.

Les stood for a moment looking down at his father's gray hair, his gaunt, trembling fingers. Then he turned away.

The watch was still on the dining room table. Les picked it up and took it in to the kitchen table. The old man must have been reminding himself about the watch all night, he thought. Otherwise he wouldn't have managed to remember it.

He put fresh water in the coffee globe and pushed the buttons for two servings of bacon and eggs. Then he poured two glasses of orange juice and sat down at the table.

About fifteen minutes later, his father came down wearing his dark blue suit, his shoes carefully polished, his nails manicured, his hair slicked down and combed and brushed. He looked very neat and very old as he walked over to the coffee globe and looked in.

"Sit down, Dad," Les said. "I'll get it for you."

"I'm not helpless," his father said. "Stay where you are."

Les managed to smile. "I put some bacon and eggs on for us," he said.

"Not hungry," his father replied.

"You'll need a good breakfast in you, Dad."

"Never did eat a big breakfast," his father said, stiffly, still facing the stove. "Don't believe in it. Not good for the stomach."

Les closed his eyes a moment and across his face moved an expression of hopeless despair. Why did I bother getting up? he asked himself defeatedly. All we do is argue.

No. He felt himself stiffening. No, he'd be cheerful if it killed him.

"Sleep all right, Dad?" he asked.

"Course I slept all right," his father answered. "Always sleep fine. Fine. Did you think I wouldn't because of a—"

He broke off suddenly and turned accusingly at Les. "Where's that watch?" he demanded.

Les exhaled wearily and held up the watch. His father moved jerkily across the linoleum, took it from him and looked at it a moment, his old lips pursed.

"Shoddy workmanship," he said. "Shoddy." He put it carefully in his side coat pocket. "Get you a decent crystal," he muttered. "One that won't break."

Les nodded. "That'll be swell, Dad."

The coffee was ready then and Tom poured them each a cup. Les got up and turned off the automatic griller. He didn't feel like having bacon and eggs either now.

He sat across the table from his stern-faced father and felt hot coffee trickling down his throat. It tasted terrible but he knew that nothing in the world would have tasted good to him that morning.

"What time do you have to be there, Dad?" he asked to break the silence.

"Nine o'clock," Tom said.

"You're sure you don't want me to drive you there?"

"Not at all, not at all," his father said as though he were talking patiently to an irritably insistent child. "The tube is good enough. Get me there in plenty of time."

"All right, Dad," Les said and sat there staring into his coffee. There must be something he could say, he thought, but he couldn't think of anything. Silence hung over them for long minutes while Tom drank his black coffee in slow, methodical sips.

Les licked his lips nervously, then hid the trembling of them behind his cup. Talking, he thought, talking and talking—of cars and tube conveyers and examination schedules—when all the time both of them knew that Tom might be sentenced to death that day.

He was sorry he'd gotten up. It would have been better to wake up and just find his father gone. He wished it could happen that way—permanently. He wished he could wake up some morning and find his father's room empty—the two suits gone, the dark shoes gone, the work clothes gone, the handkerchiefs, the socks, the garters, the braces, the shaving equipment—all those mute evidences of a life gone.

But it wouldn't be like that. After Tom failed the test, it would be several weeks before the letter of final appointment came and then another week or so before the appointment itself. It would be a hideously slow process of packing and disposing of and giving away of possessions, a process of meals and meals and meals together, of talking to each other, of a last dinner, of a long drive to the government center, of a ride up in a silent, humming elevator, of—

Dear God!

He found himself shivering helplessly and was afraid for a moment that he was going to cry.

Then he looked up with a shocked expression as his father stood.

"I'll be going now," Tom said.

Les's eyes fled to the wall clock. "But it's only a quarter to 7," he said tensely. "It doesn't take that long to—"

"Like to be in plenty of time," his father said firmly. "Never like to be late."

"But my God, Dad, it only takes an hour at the most to get to the city," he said, feeling a terrible sinking in his stomach.

His father shook his head and Les knew he hadn't heard. "It's early, Dad," he said, loudly, his voice shaking a little.

"Never-the-less," his father said.

"But you haven't eaten anything."

"Never did eat a big breakfast," Tom started. "Not good for the—"

Les didn't hear the rest of it—the words about lifetime habit and not good for the digestion and everything else his father said. He felt waves of merciless horror breaking over him and he wanted to jump and throw his arms around the old man and tell him not to worry about the test because it didn't matter, because they loved him and would take care of him.

But he couldn't. He sat rigid with sick fright, looking up at his father. He couldn't even speak when his father turned at the kitchen door and said in a voice that was calmly dispassionate because it took every bit of strength the old man had to make it so, "I'll see you tonight, Leslie."

The door swung shut and the breeze that ruffled across Les's cheeks chilled him to the heart.

Suddenly, he jumped up with a startled grunt and rushed across the linoleum. As he pushed through the doorway he saw his father almost to the front door.

"Dad!"

Tom stopped and looked back in surprise as Les walked across the dining room, hearing the steps counted in his mind —one, two, three, four, five.

He stopped before his father and forced a faltering smile to his lips.

"Good luck, Dad," he said. "I'll . . . see you tonight."

He had been about to say, "I'll be rooting for you"; but he couldn't.

His father nodded once, just once, a curt nod as of one gentleman acknowledging another.

"Thank you," his father said and turned away.

When the door shut, it seemed as if, suddenly, it had become an impenetrable wall through which his father could never pass again.

Les moved to the window and watched the old man walk slowly down the path and turn left onto the sidewalk. He watched his father start up the street, then straighten himself, throw back his lean shoulders and walk erect and briskly into the gray of morning.

At first Les thought it was raining. But then he saw that the shimmering moistness wasn't on the window at all.

He couldn't go to work. He phoned in sick and stayed home. Terry got the boys off to school and, after they'd eaten breakfast, Les helped her clear away the morning dishes and put them in the washer. Terry didn't say anything about his staying home. She acted as if it were normal for him to be home on a weekday.

He spent the morning and afternoon puttering in the garage shop, starting seven different projects and losing interest in them.

Around 5, he went into the kitchen and had a can of beer while Terry made supper. He didn't say anything to her. He kept pacing around the living room, staring out the window at the overcast sky, then pacing again.

"I wonder where he is," he finally said, back in the kitchen again.

"He'll be back," she said and he stiffened a moment, thinking he heard disgust in her voice. Then he relaxed, knowing it was only his imagination.

When he dressed after taking a shower, it was was five forty. The boys were home from playing and they all sat down to supper. Les noticed a place set for his father and wondered if Terry had set it there for his benefit.

He couldn't eat anything. He kept cutting the meat into smaller and smaller pieces and mashing butter into his baked potato without tasting any of it.

"What is it?" he asked as Jim spoke to him.

"Dad, if grandpa don't pass the test, he gets a month, don't he?"

Les felt his stomach muscles tightening as he stared at his older son. *Gets a month, don't he?*—the last of Jim's question muttered on in his brain.

"What are you talking about?" he asked.

"My Civics book says old people get a month to live after they don't pass their test. That's right, isn't it?"

"No, it *isn't*," Tommy broke in. "Harry Senker's grandma got her letter after only two weeks."

"How do you know?" Jim asked his nine-year-old brother. "Did you see it?"

"That's enough," Les said.

"Don't *have* t'see it!" Tommy argued, "Harry told me that—"

"That's *enough!*"

The two boys looked suddenly at their white-faced father.

"We won't talk about it," he said.

"But what—"

"*Jimmy*," Terry said, warningly.

Jimmy looked at his mother, then, after a moment, went back to his food and they all ate in silence.

The death of their grandfather means nothing to them, Les thought bitterly—nothing at all. He swallowed and tried to relax the tightness in his body. Well, why *should* it mean anything to them? he told himself; it's not their time to worry yet. Why force it on them now? They'll have it soon enough.

When the front door opened and shut at 6:10, Les stood up so quickly, he knocked over an empty glass.

"Les, *don't*," Terry said suddenly and he knew, immediately, that she was right. His father wouldn't like him to come rushing from the kitchen with questions.

He slumped down on the chair again and stared at his barely touched food, his heart throbbing. As he picked up his fork with tight fingers, he heard the old man cross the dining room rug and start up the stairs. He glanced at Terry and her throat moved.

He couldn't eat. He sat there breathing heavily, and picking at the food. Upstairs, he heard the door to his father's room close.

It was when Terry was putting the pie on the table that Les excused himself quickly and got up.

He was at the foot of the stairs when the kitchen door was pushed open. "Les," he heard her say, urgently.

He stood there silently as she came up to him.

"Isn't it better we leave him alone?" she asked.

"But, honey, I—"

"Les, if he'd passed the test, he would have come into the kitchen and told us."

"Honey, he wouldn't know if—"

"He'd know if he passed, you know that. He told us about it the last two times. If he'd passed, he'd have—"

Her voice broke off and she shuddered at the way he was looking at her. In the heavy silence, she heard a sudden splattering of rain on the windows.

They looked at each other a long moment. Then Les said, "I'm going up."

"Les," she murmured.

"I won't say anything to upset him," he said. "I'll . . ."

A moment longer they stared at each other. Then he turned away and trudged up the steps. Terry watched him go with a bleak, hopeless look on her face.

Les stood before the closed door a minute, bracing himself. I won't upset him, he told himself; I won't.

He knocked softly, wondering, in that second, if he were making a mistake. Maybe he should have left the old man alone, he thought unhappily.

In the bedroom, he heard a rustling movement on the bed, then the sound of his father's feet touching the floor.

"Who is it?" he heard Tom ask.

Les caught his breath. "It's me, Dad," he said.

"What do you want?"

"May I see you?"

Silence inside. "Well . . ." he heard his father say then and his voice stopped. Les heard him get up and heard the sound of his footsteps on the floor. Then there was the sound of paper rattling and a bureau drawer being carefully shut.

Finally the door opened.

Tom was wearing his old red bathrobe over his clothes and he'd taken off his shoes and put his slippers on.

"May I come in, Dad?" Les asked quietly.

His father hesitated a moment. Then he said, "Come in," but it wasn't an invitation. It was more as if he'd said, This is your house; I can't keep you from this room.

Les was going to tell his father that he didn't want to disturb him but he couldn't. He went in and stood in the middle of the throw rug, waiting.

"Sit down," his father said and Les sat down on the upright chair that Tom hung his clothes on at night. His father waited until Les was seated and then sank down on the bed with a grunt.

For a long time they looked at each other without speaking like total strangers each waiting for the other one to speak. How did the test go? Les heard the words repeated in his mind. How did the test go, how did the test go? He couldn't speak the words. How did the—

"I suppose you want to know what . . . happened," his father said then, controlling himself visibly.

"Yes," Les said "I . . ." He caught himself. "Yes," he repeated and waited.

Old Tom looked down at the floor for a moment. Then, suddenly, he raised his head and looked defiantly at his son.

"*I didn't go,*" he said.

Les felt as if all his strength had suddenly been sucked into the floor. He sat there, motionless, staring at his father.

"Had no intention of going," his father hurried on. "No intention of going through all that foolishness. Physical tests, m-mental tests, putting b-b-*blocks* in a board and . . . Lord knows what all! Had no intention of going."

He stopped and stared at his son with angry eyes as if he were daring Les to say he had done wrong.

But Les couldn't say anything.

A long time passed. Les swallowed and managed to summon the words. "What are you . . . going to do?"

"Never mind that, never mind," his father said, almost as if he were grateful for the question. "Don't you worry about your Dad. Your Dad knows how to take care of himself."

And suddenly Les heard the bureau drawer shutting again, the rustling of a paper bag. He almost looked around at the bureau to see if the bag were still there. His head twitched as he fought down the impulse.

"W-ell," he faltered, not realizing how stricken and lost his expression was.

"Just never mind now," his father said again, quietly, almost gently. "It's not your problem to worry about. Not your problem at all."

But it is! Les heard the words cried out in his mind. But he didn't speak them. Something in the old man stopped him; a sort of fierce strength, a taut dignity he knew he mustn't touch.

"I'd like to rest now," he heard Tom say then and he felt as if he'd been struck violently in the stomach. I'd like to rest now, to rest now—the words echoed down long tunnels of the mind as he stood. Rest now, rest now . . .

He found himself being ushered to the door where he turned and looked at his father. Goodbye. The word stuck in him.

Then his father smiled and said, "Good night, Leslie."

"Dad."

He felt the old man's hand in his own, stronger than his, more steady; calming him, reassuring him. He felt his father's left hand grip his shoulder.

"Good night, son," his father said and, in the moment they stood close together Les saw, over the old man's shoulder, the crumpled drugstore bag lying in the corner of the room as though it had been thrown there so as not to be seen.

Then he was standing in wordless terror in the hall, listening to the latch clicking shut and knowing that, although his father wasn't locking the door, he couldn't go into his father's room.

For a long time he stood staring at the closed door, shivering without control. Then he turned away.

Terry was waiting for him at the foot of the stairs, her face drained of color. She asked the question with her eyes as he came down to her.

"He . . . didn't go," was all he said.

She made a tiny, startled sound in her throat. "But—"

"He's been to the drugstore," Les said. "I . . . saw the bag in the corner of the room. He threw it away so I wouldn't see it but I . . . saw it."

For a moment, it seemed as if she were starting for the stairs but it was only a momentary straining of her body.

"He must have shown the druggist the letter about the test," Les said. "The . . . druggist must have given him . . . pills. Like they all do."

They stood silently in the dining room while rain drummed against the windows.

"What shall we do?" she asked, almost inaudibly.

"Nothing," he murmured. His throat moved convulsively and breath shuddered through him. "*Nothing.*"

Then he was walking numbly back to the kitchen and he could feel her arm tight around him as if she were trying to press her love to him because she could not speak of love.

All evening, they sat there in the kitchen. After she put the boys to bed, she came back and they sat in the kitchen drinking coffee and talking in quiet, lonely voices.

Near midnight, they left the kitchen and just before they went upstairs, Les stopped by the dining room table and found the watch with a shiny new crystal on it. He couldn't even touch it.

They went upstairs and walked past the door of Tom's bedroom. There was no sound inside. They got undressed and got in bed together and Terry set the clock the way she set it every night. In a few hours they both managed to fall asleep.

And all night there was silence in the old man's room. And the next day, silence.

Clothes Make the Man •••••••••••••••••

I WENT out on the terrace to get away from the gabbing cocktailers.

I sat down in a dark corner, stretched out my legs and sighed in complete boredom.

The terrace door opened again and a man reeled out of the noisome gaiety. He staggered to the railing and looked out over the city.

"Oh, my God," he said, running a palsied hand through his thin hair. He shook his head wearily and gazed at the light on top of the Empire State Building.

Then he turned with a groan and stumbled toward me. He tripped on my shoes and almost fell on his face.

"Uh-oh," he muttered, flopping into another chair. "You must excuse me, sir."

"Nothing," I said.

"May I beg your indulgence, sir?" he inquired.

I started to speak but he set out begging it immediately.

"Listen," he said, waving a fat finger. "Listen, I'm telling you a story that's impossible."

He bent forward in the dark and stared at me as best he could through martini-clouded eyes. Then he fell back on the chair breathing steam whistles. He belched once.

"Listen now," he said. "Make no mistake. There are stranger things in heaven and earth and so on. You think I'm drunk. You're absolutely right. But why? You could never tell.

"My brother," he said, despairingly, "is no longer a man."

"End of story," I suggested.

"It all began a couple of months ago. He's publicity head for the Jenkins ad agency. Topnotch man.

"That is," he sobbed, "I mean to say . . . he was."

He mused quietly, "Topnotch man."

Out of his breast pocket he dragged a handkerchief and blew a trumpet call which made me writhe.

"They used to come to him," he recalled, "all of them. There he'd sit in his office with his hat on his head, his shiny shoes on the desk. Charlie! they'd scream, give us an idea. He'd turn his hat once around (called it his thinking cap) and say, Boys! Cut it *this* way. And out of his lips would pour the damnedest ideas you ever heard. What a man!"

At this point he goggled at the moon and blew his nose again.

"So?"

"What a man," he repeated. "Best in the business. Give him his hat—that was a gag, of course. We thought."

I sighed and closed my eyes.

"He was a funny guy," said my narrator. "A funny guy."

"Ha," I said.

"He was a fashion plate. That's what he was. Suits had to be just right. Hats just right. Shoes, socks, everything custom made.

"Why, I remember once Charlie and his wife Miranda, the missus and me—we all drove out to the country. It was hot. I took off my suit coat.

"But would he? No sir! Man isn't a man without his coat, says he.

"We went to this nice place with a stream and a grassy plot for sitting. It was awful hot. Miranda and my wife took off their shoes and waded in the water. I even joined them. But him! Ha!"

"Ha!"

"Not him," he said. "There I was, no shoes and socks, pants and shirt sleeves rolled up, wading like a kid. And up there, watching amused, was Charlie, still dressed to kill. We called him. Come on Charlie, off with the shoes!

"Oh, no. A man isn't a man without his shoes, he said. I couldn't even walk without them. This burned Miranda up. Half the time, she says, I don't know whether I'm married to a man or a wardrobe.

"That's the way he was," he sighed, "that's the way."

"End of story," I said.

"No," he said, his voice tingling; with horror I suppose.

"Now comes the terrible part," he said. "You know what I said about his clothes. Terrible fussy. Even his underwear had to be fitted."

"Mmm," I said.

"One day," he went on, his voice sinking to an awed murmur, "someone at the office took his hat for a gag.

"Charlie seemed to pretend he couldn't think. Hardly said a word. Just fumbled. Kept saying, hat, hat and staring out the window. I took him home.

"Miranda and I put him on the bed and while I was talking to her in the living room, we heard an awful thump. We ran in the bedroom.

"Charlie was crumpled up on the floor. We helped him up. His legs buckled under. What's wrong we asked him. Shoes, shoes, he said. We sat him on the bed. He picked up his shoes. They fell out of his hands.

"Gloves, gloves, he said. We stared at him. Gloves! he shrieked. Miranda was scared. She got him a pair and dropped them on his lap. He drew them on slowly and painfully. Then he bent over and put his shoes on.

"He got up and walked around the room as if he were testing his feet.

"Hat, he said and went to the closet. He stuck a hat on his head. And then—would you believe it?—he said, What the hell's the idea of taking me home? I've got work to do and I've got to fire the bastard who stole my hat. Back to the office he goes.

"You believe that?" he asked.

"Why not?" I answered, wearily.

"Well, he said, "I guess you can figure the rest. Miranda tells me that day before I left: Is *that* why the bum is so quiet in bed? I have to stick a hat on him every night?

"I was embarrassed."

He paused and sighed.

"Things got bad after that," he went on. "Without a hat Charlie couldn't think. Without shoes he couldn't walk. Without gloves he couldn't move his fingers. Even in summer he wore gloves. Doctors gave up. A psychiatrist went on a vacation after Charlie visited him."

"Finish it up," I said. "I have to leave soon."

"There isn't much more," he said. "Things got worse and worse. Charlie had to hire a man to dress him. Miranda got sick of him and moved into the guest room. My brother was losing everything.

"Then came *that* morning . . ."

He shuddered.

"I went to see how he was. The door to his apartment was wide open. I went in fast. The place was like a tomb.

"I called for Charlie's valet. Not a sound. I went in the bedroom.

"There was Charlie lying on his bed still as a corpse, mumbling to himself. Without a word, I got a hat and stuck it on his head. Where's your man? I asked. Where's Miranda?

"He stared at me with trembling lips. Charlie, what is it? I asked.

"My suit, he said.

"What suit? I asked him. What are you talking about?

"My suit, he whimpered, *it went to work this morning.*

"I figured he was out of his mind.

"My grey pin-stripe, he said hysterically. The one I wore yesterday. My valet screamed and I woke up. He was looking at the closet. I looked. My God!

"Right in front of the mirror, my underwear was assembling itself. One of my white shirts fluttered over the undershirt, the pants pulled up into a figure, a coat was thrown over the shirt, a tie was knotted. Socks and shoes went under the trousers.

The coat arm reached up, took a hat off the closet shelf and stuck it in the air where the head would be if it had a head. Then the hat doffed itself once.

"Cut it this way, Charlie, a voice said and laughed like hell. The suit walked off. My valet ran off. Miranda's out.

"Charlie finished his story and I took his hat off so he could faint. I phoned for an ambulance."

The man shifted in his chair.

"That was last week," he said. "I've still got the shakes."

"That it?" I asked.

"About it," he said. "They tell me Charlie is getting weaker. Still in the hospital. Sits there on his bed with his grey hat sagging over his ears mumbling to himself. Can't talk, even with his hat on."

He mopped some perspiration off his face.

"That's not the worst part," he said, sobbing. "They tell me that Miranda is . . ."

He gulped.

"Is going steady with the suit. Telling all her friends the damn thing has more sex appeal than Charlie ever had."

"No," I said.

"Yes," he said. "She's in there now. Came in a little while ago."

He sank back in silent meditation.

I got up and stretched. We exchanged a glance and he fainted dead away.

I paid no attention. I went in and got Miranda and we left.

Blood Son ••••••••••••••••••••••••••••••

THE PEOPLE on the block decided definitely that Jules was crazy when they heard about his composition.

There had been suspicions for a long time.

He made people shiver with his blank stare. His coarse

gutteral tongue sounded unnatural in his frail body. The paleness of his skin upset many children. It seemed to hang loose around his flesh. He hated sunlight.

And his ideas were a little out of place for the people who lived on the block.

Jules wanted to be a vampire.

People declared it common knowledge that he was born on a night when winds uprooted trees. They said he was born with three teeth. They said he'd used them to fasten himself on his mother's breast drawing blood with the milk.

They said he used to cackle and bark in his crib after dark They said he walked at two months and sat staring at the moon whenever it shone.

Those were things that people said.

His parents were always worried about him. An only child, they noticed his flaws quickly.

They thought he was blind until the doctor told them it was just a vacuous stare. He told them that Jules, with his large head, might be a genius or an idiot. It turned out he was an idiot.

He never spoke a word until he was five. Then, one night coming up to supper, he sat down at the table and said "Death."

His parents were torn between delight and disgust. They finally settled for a place in between the two feelings. They decided that Jules couldn't have realized what the word meant.

But Jules did.

From that night on, he built up such a large vocabulary that everyone who knew him was astonished. He not only acquired every word spoken to him, words from signs, magazines, books; he made up his own words.

Like—nightouch. Or—killove. They were really several words that melted into each other. They said things Jules felt but couldn't explain with other words.

He used to sit on the porch while the other children played hopscotch, stickball and other games. He sat there and stared at the sidewalk and made up words.

Until he was twelve Jules kept pretty much out of trouble.

Of course there was the time they found him undressing Olive Jones in an alley. And another time he was discovered dissecting a kitten on his bed.

But there were many years in between. Those scandals were forgotten.

In general he went through childhood merely disgusting people.

He went to school but never studied. He spent about two or three terms in each grade. The teachers all knew him by his first name. In some subjects like reading and writing he was almost brilliant.

In others he was hopeless.

One Saturday when he was twelve, Jules went to the movies. He saw "Dracula."

When the show was over he walked, a throbbing nerve mass, through the little girl and boy ranks.

He went home and locked himself in the bathroom for two hours.

His parents pounded on the door and threatened but he wouldn't come out.

Finally he unlocked the door and sat down at the supper table. He had a bandage on his thumb and a satisfied look on his face.

The morning after he went to the library. It was Sunday. He sat on the steps all day waiting for it to open. Finally he went home.

The next morning he came back instead of going to school.

He found *Dracula* on the shelves. He couldn't borrow it because he wasn't a member and to be a member he had to bring in one of his parents.

So he stuck the book down his pants and left the library and never brought it back.

He went to the park and sat down and read the book through. It was late evening before he finished.

He started at the beginning again, reading as he ran from street light to street light, all the way home.

He didn't hear a word of the scolding he got for missing lunch and supper. He ate, went in his room and read the book to the finish. They asked him where he got the book. He said he found it.

As the days passed Jules read the story over and over. He never went to school.

Late at night, when he had fallen into an exhausted slumber, his mother used to take the book into the living room and show it to her husband.

One night they noticed that Jules had underlined certain sentences with dark shaky pencil lines.

Like: "The lips were crimson with fresh blood and the stream had trickled over her chin and stained the purity of her lawn death robe."

Or: "When the blood began to spurt out, he took my hands in one of his, holding them tight and, with the other seized my neck and pressed my mouth to the wound . . ."

When his mother saw this, she threw the book down the garbage chute.

In the next morning when Jules found the book missing he screamed and twisted his mother's arm until she told him where the book was.

Then he ran down to the cellar and dug in the piles of garbage until he found the book.

Coffee grounds and egg yolk on his hands and wrists, he went to the park and read it again.

For a month he read the book avidly. Then he knew it so well he threw it away and just thought about it.

Absence notes were coming from school. His mother yelled. Jules decided to go back for a while.

He wanted to write a composition.

One day he wrote it in class. When everyone was finished writing, the teacher asked if anyone wanted to read their composition to the class.

Jules raised his hand.

The teacher was surprised. But she felt charity. She wanted to encourage him. She drew in her tiny jab of a chin and smiled.

"All right," she said, "Pay attention children. Jules is going to read us his composition."

Jules stood up. He was excited. The paper shook in his hands.

"My Ambition by . . ."

"Come to the front of the class, Jules, dear."

Jules went to the front of the class. The teacher smiled lovingly. Jules started again.

"My Ambition by Jules Dracula."

The smile sagged.

"When I grow up I want to be a vampire."

The teacher's smiling lips jerked down and out. Her eyes popped wide.

"I want to live forever and get even with everybody and make all the girls vampires. I want to smell of death."

"Jules!"

"I want to have a foul breath that stinks of dead earth and crypts and sweet coffins."

The teacher shuddered. Her hands twitched on her green blotter. She couldn't believe her ears. She looked at the children. They were gaping. Some of them were giggling. But not the girls.

"I want to be all cold and have rotten flesh with stolen blood in the veins."

"That will . . . hrrumph!"

The teacher cleared her throat mightily.

"That will be all Jules," she said.

Jules talked louder and desperately.

"I want to sink my terrible white teeth in my victims' necks. I want them to . . . "

"Jules! Go to your seat this instant!"

"I want them to slide like razors in the flesh and into the veins," read Jules ferociously.

The teacher jolted to her feet. Children were shivering. None of them were giggling.

"Then I want to draw my teeth out and let the blood flow easy in my mouth and run hot in my throat and . . . "

The teacher grabbed his arm. Jules tore away and ran to a corner. Barricaded behind a stool he yelled:

"And drip off my tongue and run out my lips down my victims' throats! I want to drink girls' blood!"

The teacher lunged for him. She dragged him out of the corner. He clawed at her and screamed all the way to the door and the principal's office.

"That is my ambition! That is my ambition! *That is my ambition!*"

It was grim.

Jules was locked in his room. The teacher and the principal sat with Jules' parents. They were talking in sepulchral voices.

They were recounting the scene.

All along the block parents were discussing it. Most of them didn't believe it at first. They thought their children made it up.

Then they thought what horrible children they'd raised if the children could make up such things.

So they believed it.

After that everyone watched Jules like a hawk. People avoided his touch and look. Parents pulled their children off the street when he approached. Everyone whispered tales of him.

There were more absence notes.

Jules told his mother he wasn't going to school anymore. Nothing would change his mind. He never went again.

When a truant officer came to the apartment Jules would run over the roofs until he was far away from there.

A year wasted by.

Jules wandered the streets searching for something; he didn't know what. He looked in alleys. He looked in garbage cans. He looked in lots. He looked on the east side and the west side and in the middle.

He couldn't find what he wanted.

He rarely slept. He never spoke. He stared down all the time. He forgot his special words.

Then.

One day in the park, Jules strolled through the zoo.

An electric shock passed through him when he saw the vampire bat.

His eyes grew wide and his discolored teeth shone dully in a wide smile.

From that day on, Jules went daily to the zoo and looked at the bat. He spoke to it and called it the Count. He felt in his heart it was really a man who had changed.

A rebirth of culture struck him.

He stole another book from the library. It told all about wild life.

He found the page on the vampire bat. He tore it out and threw the book away.

He learned the selection by heart.

He knew how the bat made its wound. How it lapped up the blood like a kitten drinking cream. How it walked on folded wing stalks and hind legs like a black furry spider. Why it took no nourishment but blood.

Month after month Jules stared at the bat and talked to it. It became the one comfort in his life. The one symbol of dreams come true.

*   *   *

One day Jules noticed that the bottom of the wire covering the cage had come loose.

He looked around, his black eyes shifting. He didn't see anyone looking. It was a cloudy day. Not many people were there.

Jules tugged at the wire.

It moved a little.

Then he saw a man come out of the monkey house. So he pulled back his hand and strolled away whistling a song he had just made up.

Late at night, when he was supposed to be asleep he would walk barefoot past his parents' room. He would hear his father and mother snoring. He would hurry out, put on his shoes and run to the zoo.

Everytime the watchman was not around, Jules would tug at the wiring.

He kept on pulling it loose.

When he was finished and had to run home, he pushed the wire in again. Then no one could tell.

All day Jules would stand in front of the cage and look at the Count and chuckle and tell him he'd soon be free again.

He told the Count all the things he knew. He told the Count he was going to practice climbing down walls head first.

He told the Count not to worry. He'd soon be out. Then, together, they could go all around and drink girls' blood.

One night Jules pulled the wire out and crawled under it into the cage.

It was very dark.

He crept on his knees to the little wooden house. He listened to see if he could hear the Count squeaking.

He stuck his arm in the black doorway. He kept whispering.

He jumped when he felt a needle jab in his finger.

With a look of great pleasure on his thin face, Jules drew the fluttering hairy bat to him.

He climbed down from the cage with it and ran out of the zoo; out of the park. He ran down the silent streets.

It was getting late in the morning. Light touched the dark skies with grey. He couldn't go home. He had to have a place.

He went down an alley and climbed over a fence. He held tight to the bat. It lapped at the dribble of blood from his finger.

He went across a yard and into a little deserted shack.

It was dark inside and damp. It was full of rubble and tin cans and soggy cardboard and excrement.

Jules made sure there was no way the bat could escape.

Then he pulled the door tight and put a stick through the metal loop.

He felt his heart beating hard and his limbs trembling. He let go of the bat. It flew to a dark corner and hung on the wood.

Jules feverishly tore off his shirt. His lips shook. He smiled a crazy smile.

He reached down into his pants pocket and took out a little pen knife he had stolen from his mother.

He opened it and ran a finger over the blade. It sliced through the flesh.

With shaking fingers he jabbed at his throat. He hacked. The blood ran through his fingers.

"Count! Count!" he cried in frenzied joy. "Drink my red blood! Drink me! Drink me!"

He stumbled over the tin cans and slipped and felt for the bat. It sprang from the wood and soared across the shack and fastened itself on the other side.

Tears ran down Jules' cheeks.

He gritted his teeth. The blood ran across his shoulders and across his thin hairless chest.

His body shook in fever. He staggered back toward the other side. He tripped and felt his side torn open on the sharp edge of a tin can.

His hands went out. They clutched the bat. He placed it against his throat. He sank on his back on the cool wet earth. He sighed.

He started to moan and clutch at his chest. His stomach heaved. The black bat on his neck silently lapped his blood.

Jules felt his life seeping away.

He thought of all the years past. The waiting. His parents. School. Dracula. Dreams. For this. This sudden glory.

Jules' eyes flickered open.

The inside of the reeking shack swam about him.

It was hard to breathe. He opened his mouth to gasp in the air. He sucked it in. It was foul. It made him cough. His skinny body lurched on the cold ground.

Mists crept away in his brain.

One by one like drawn veils.

Suddenly his mind was filled with terrible clarity.

He felt the aching pain in his side.

He knew he was lying half naked on garbage and letting a flying bat drink his blood.

With a strangled cry, he reached up and tore away the furry throbbing bat. He flung it away from him. It came back, fanning his face with its vibrating wings.

Jules staggered to his feet.

He felt for the door. He could hardly see. He tried to stop his throat from bleeding so.

He managed to get the door open.

Then, lurching into the dark yard, he fell on his face in the long grass blades.

He tried to call out for help.

But no sounds save a bubbling mockery of words came from his lips.

He heard the fluttering wings.

Then, suddenly they were gone.

Strong fingers lifted him gently. Through dying eyes Jules saw the tall dark man whose eyes shone like rubies.

"My son," the man said.

Trespass ✦✦✦✦✦✦✦✦✦✦✦✦✦✦✦✦✦✦✦✦✦✦✦✦✦✦✦✦✦✦✦

IN THE hall he put down his suitcase. "How have you been?" he asked.

"Fine," she said, with a smile.

She helped him off with his coat and hat and put them in the hall closet.

"This Indiana January sure feels cold after six months in South America."

"I bet it does," she said.

They walked into the living-room, arms around each other.

"What have you been doing with yourself?" he asked.

"Oh . . . not too much," she said. "Thinking about you."

He smiled and hugged her.

"That's a lot," he said.

Her smile flickered a moment, then returned. She held his hand tightly. And, suddenly, although he didn't realize it at first, she was wordless. He'd gone over this moment in his mind so often that the sharpness of its anti-climax later struck him. She smiled and looked into his eyes while he spoke but the smile kept fading and her eyes kept evading his at the very moments he wanted their attention most.

Later in the kitchen she sat across from him as he drank the third cup of her hot, rich coffee.

"I won't sleep tonight," he said, grinning, "but I don't want to."

Her smile was only obliging. The coffee burned his throat and he noticed she wasn't drinking any of the first cup she'd poured for herself.

"No coffee for you?" he asked.

"No, I . . . I don't drink it anymore."

"On a diet or something?"

He saw her throat move.

"Sort of," she said.

"That's silly," he said. "Your figure is perfect."

She seemed about to say something. Then she hesitated. He put down his cup.

"Ann, is . . ."

"Something wrong?" she finished.

He nodded.

She lowered her eyes. She bit her lower lip and clasped her hands before her on the table. Then her eyes closed and he got the feeling that she was shutting herself away from something hopelessly terrible.

"Honey, what is it?"

"I guess . . . the best way is to just . . . just up and tell you."

"Well, of course, sweetheart," he said anxiously. "What is it? Did something happen while I was gone?"

"Yes. And no."

"I don't understand."

She was looking at him suddenly. The look was haunted and it made him shudder.

"I'm going to have a baby," she said.

He was about to cry out—but that's wonderful. He was about to jump up and embrace her and dance her around the room.

Then it hit him, driving the color from his face.

"What?" he said.

She didn't answer because she knew he'd heard.

"How . . . long have you known this?" he asked, watching her eyes hold motionless on his face.

She drew in a shaking breath and he knew her answer would be the wrong one. It was.

"Three weeks," she said.

He sat there looking blankly at her and stirring the coffee without realizing. Then he noticed and, slowly, he drew out the spoon and put it down beside the cup.

He tried to say the word but he couldn't. It trembled in his vocal chords. He tensed himself.

"Who?" he asked her, his voice toneless and weak.

Her eyes were black on him, her face ashen. Her lips trembled when she told him.

She said, "No one."

"What?"

"David," she said carefully, "I . . ."

Then her shoulders slumped.

"No one, David. No one."

It took a moment for the reaction to hit him. She saw it on his face before he turned it away from her. Then she stood up and looked down at him, her voice shaking.

"David, I swear to God I never had anything to do with any man while you were gone!"

He sank back numbly against the chair back. God, O God, what could he say? A man comes back from six months in the jungle and his wife tells him she's pregnant and asks him to believe that . . .

His teeth set on edge. He felt as if he were involved in the beginning of some hideously smutty joke. He swallowed and looked down at his trembling hands. Ann, Ann! He wanted to pick up his cup and hurl it against the wall.

"David, you've got to bel—"

He stumbled up and out of the room. She was behind him quickly, clutching for his hand.

"David, you've got to believe me. I'll go insane if you don't.

It's the only strength that's kept me going—the hope that you'd believe me. If you don't . . ."

Her words broke off and they stared bleakly at each other. He felt her hand holding his. Cold.

"Ann, what do you want me to believe? That my child was conceived five months after I left you?"

"David, if I were guilty would I . . . be so open in telling you? You know how I feel about our marriage. About you."

Her voice lowered.

"If I'd done what you think I've done, I wouldn't tell you," she said, "I'd kill myself."

He kept looking helplessly at her, as if the answer lay in her anxious face. Finally he spoke.

"We'll . . . go to Doctor Kleinman," he said. "We'll . . ."

Her hand dropped away from his.

"You don't believe me, do you?"

His voice was tortured.

"You know what you're asking of me, don't you?" he said. "Don't you, Ann? I'm a scientist. I can't accept the incredible . . . just like that. Don't you think I want to believe you? But . . ."

She stood before him a long time. Then she turned away a little and her voice was well controlled.

"All right," she said quietly, "do what you think is best."

Then she walked out of the room. He watched her go. Then he turned and walked slowly to the mantel. He stood looking at the kewpie doll sitting there with its legs hanging down over the edge. *Coney Island* read the words on her dress. They'd won it on their honeymoon trip eight years before.

His eyes fell shut suddenly.

Homecoming.

The word was a dead word now.

"Now that the welcomes are done for," said Doctor Kleinman, "what are you doing here? Catch a bug in the jungle?"

Collier sat slumped in the chair. For a few seconds he glanced out the window. Then he turned back to Kleinman and told him quickly.

When he'd finished they looked at each other for a silent moment.

"It's not possible, is it?" Collier said then.

Kleinman pressed his lips together. A grim smile flickered briefly on his face.

"What can I say?" he said. "No, it's impossible? No, not as far as observation goes? I do not know, David. We assume that the sperms survive in the cervix canal no more than three to five days, maybe a little longer. But, even if they do . . ."

"They can't fertilize??" Collier finished.

Kleinman didn't nod or answer but Collier knew the answer. Knew it in simple words that were pronouncing doom on his life.

"There's no hope then," he said quietly.

Kleinman pressed his lips together again and ran a reflective finger along the edge of his letter opener.

"Unless," he said, "it is to speak to Ann and make her understand you will not desert her. It is probably fear which makes her speak as she does."

" . . . will not desert her," Collier echoed in an inaudible whisper and shook his head.

"I suggest nothing, mind you," Kleinman went on. "Only that it is possible Ann is too hysterically frightened to tell you the truth."

Collier rose, drained of vitality.

"All right," he said indecisively, "I'll speak to her again. Maybe we can . . . work it out."

But when he told her what Kleinman had said she just sat in the chair and looked at him without expression on her face.

"And that's it," she said. "You've decided."

He swallowed.

"I don't think you know what you're asking of me," he said.

"Yes, I know what I'm asking," she answered. "Just that you believe in me."

He started to speak in rising anger, then checked himself.

"Ann," he said, "just *tell* me. I'll do my best to understand."

Now she was losing temper too. He watched her hands tighten, then tremble on her lap.

"I hate to spoil your noble scene," she said. "But I'm not pregnant by another man. Do you understand me—believe me?"

She wasn't hysterical now or frightened or on the defensive. He stood there looking down at her, feeling numb and confused. She never had lied to him before and yet . . . what was he to think?

She went back to her reading then and he kept standing and watching her. These are the facts, his mind insisted. He turned away from her. Did he really know Ann? Was it possible she was something entirely strange to him now? Those six months?

What had happened during those six months?

He stood making up the living-room couch with sheets and the old comforter they had used when they were first married. As he looked down at the thick quilting and the gaudy patterns now faded from innumerable washings, a grim smile touched his lips.

Homecoming.

He straightened up with a tired sigh and walked over to where the record player scratched gently. He lifted the arm up and put on the next record. He looked at the inside cover of the album as Tschaikowsky's *Swan Lake* started.

To my very own darling. Ann.

They hadn't spoken all afternoon or evening. After supper she'd gotten a book from the case and gone upstairs. He'd sat in the living room trying to read *The Fort Tribune*, trying even harder to relax. Yet how could he? Could a man relax in his home with his wife who carried a child that wasn't his? The newspaper had finally slipped from his lax fingers and fallen to the floor.

Now he sat staring endlessly at the rug, trying to figure it out.

Was it possible the doctors were wrong? Could the life cell exist and maintain its fertilizing capacity for, not days, but months? Maybe, he thought, he'd rather believe that than believe Ann could commit adultery. Theirs had always been an ideal relationship, as close an approximation of The Perfect Marriage as one could allow possible. Now this.

He ran a shaking hand through his hair. Breath shuddered through him and there was a tightness in his chest he could not relieve. A man comes home from six months in the . . .

Put it out of your mind!—he ordered himself, then forced himself to pick up the paper and read every word in it including comics and the astrology column. *You will receive a big surprise today*, the syndicated seer told him.

He flung down the paper and looked at the mantel clock. After ten. He'd been sitting there over an hour while Ann sat up in bed reading. He wondered what book was taking the place of affection and understanding.

He rose wearily. The record player was scratching again.

After brushing his teeth he went out into the hall and started for the stairs. At the bedroom door he hesitated, glanced in. The light was out. He stopped and listened to her breathing and knew she wasn't asleep.

He almost started in as a rushing sense of need for her covered him. But then he remembered that she was going to have a baby and it couldn't possibly be his baby. The thought made him stiffen. It turned him around, thin-lipped, and took him down the stairs and he slapped down the wall switch to plunge the living room into darkness.

He felt for the couch and sank down on it. He sat for a while in the dark smoking a cigarette. Then he pressed the stub into an ashtray and lay back. The room was cold. He climbed under the sheets and comforter and lay there shivering. Homecoming. The word oppressed him again.

He must have slept a little while, he thought, staring up at the black ceiling. He held up his watch and looked at the luminous hands. Three twenty. He grunted and rolled onto his side. Then he raised up and shook the pillow to puff it up.

He lay there thinking of her. Six months away and here, on the first night home, he was on the living room couch while she lay upstairs in bed. He wondered if she were frightened. She still had a little fear of the darkness left over from her childhood. She used to hug against him and press her cheek against his shoulder and go to sleep with a happy sigh.

He tortured himself thinking about it. More than anything else he wanted to rush up the stairs and crawl in beside her, feel her warm body against him. Why don't you? asked his sleepy mind. Because she's carrying someone else's child, came the obedient answer. Because she's sinned.

He twisted his head impatiently on the pillow. Sinned. The word sounded ridiculous. He rolled onto his back again and reached for a cigarette. He lay there smoking slowly, watching the glowing tip move in the blackness.

It was no use. He sat up swiftly and fumbled for the ashtray. He had to have it out with her, that was all. If he reasoned with her, she'd tell him what had happened. Then they'd have something to go on. It was better that way.

Rationalization, said his mind. He ignored it as he trudged up the icy steps and hesitated outside the bedroom.

He went in slowly, trying to remember how the furniture was placed. He found the small nightlamp on the bureau and turned the knob. The tiny glow pushed away darkness from itself.

He shivered under his heavy robe. The room was freezing, all the windows open wide. But, as he turned, he saw Ann lying there clad only in a thin nightgown. He moved quickly to the bed and pulled the bedclothes up over her, trying not to look at her body. Not now, he thought, not at a time like this. It would distort everything.

He stood over the bed and watched her sleep. Her hair was spread darkly over the pillow. He looked at her white skin, her soft red lips. She's a beautiful woman, he almost spoke the words aloud.

He turned his head away. All right, the word was ridiculous but it was true. What else would you call the betrayal of marriage? Was there a better word than sinned?

His lips tightened. He was remembering how she'd always wanted a baby. Well, she had one now.

He noticed the book next to her on the bed and picked it up. *Basic Physics.* What on earth was she reading that for? She'd never shown the remotest interest in the sciences except for perhaps a little sociology, a smattering of anthropology. He looked down curiously at her.

He wanted to wake her up but he couldn't. He knew he'd be struck dumb as soon as her eyes opened. I've been thinking, I want to discuss this sensibly, his mind prompted. It sounded like a soap opera line.

That was the crux of it, the fact that he was incapable of discussing it with her sensibly or not. He couldn't leave her, neither could he thrash it out as he'd planned. He felt a tightening of anger at his vacillation. Well, he defended angrily, how can a man adjust to such a circumstance? A man comes home from six months in . . .

He moved back from the bed and sank down on the small chair that stood beside the bureau. He sat there shivering a little and watching her face. It was such a childlike face, so innocent.

As he watched she stirred in her sleep, writhing uncomfortably under the blankets. A whimper moved her lips, then suddenly, her right hand reached up and heaved the blankets aside so that they slid off the edge of the bed. Her feet kicked them away completely. Then a great sigh trembled her body and she rolled onto her side and slept, despite the shivering that began almost immediately.

Again he stood, dismayed at her actions. She'd never been a restless sleeper. Was it a habit she'd acquired while he was gone? It's guilt—his mind said, disconcertingly. He twitched at the infuriating idea and, walking over to the bed, he tossed the blankets over her roughly.

When he straightened up he saw that her eyes were on him. He started to smile, then wrenched it from his lips.

"You're going to get pneumonia if you keep throwing off the bedclothes," he said irritably.

She blinked. "What?" she said.

"I said . . ." he started, then stopped. There was too much anger piling up in him. He fought it off.

"You're kicking off the blankets," he said, in a flat voice.

"Oh," she said, "I . . . I've been doing it for about a week now."

He looked at her. What now?—the thought came.

"Would you get me a drink of water?" she asked.

He nodded, glad for the excuse to take his eyes from her. He padded into the hall and bathroom and ran the water until it got cold, then filled up the glass.

"Thank you," she said softly as he handed it to her.

"Welcome."

She drank all of it in one swallow then looked up guiltily.

"Would you . . . mind getting me another one?"

He looked at her for a moment, then took the glass and brought her another drink. She drank it just as quickly.

"What have you been eating?" he asked, feeling a strange tightness at finally talking to her but about such an irrelevant topic.

"Salt . . . I guess," she said.

"You must have had an awful lot."

"I have, David."

"That's not good.'

"I know." She looked at him imploringly.

"What do you want—another glass?" he asked.

She lowered her eyes. He shrugged. He didn't think it was right but he didn't care to argue about it. He went to the bathroom and got her the third drink. When he got back her eyes were closed. He said, "Here is your water," but she was asleep. He put down the glass.

As he watched her he almost felt an uncontrollable desire to lie beside her, hold her close and kiss her lips and face. He thought of all the nights he'd lain awake in the sweltering tent thinking about Ann. Rolling his head on the pillow almost in agony because she was so far away. He had the same feeling now. And yet, although he stood beside her, he couldn't touch her.

Turning abruptly, he snapped off the nightlamp and left the bedroom. He went downstairs and threw himself down on the couch and dared his brain not to fall asleep. His brain conceded and he fell into a blank, uneasy slumber.

When she came into the kitchen the next morning she was coughing and sneezing.

"What did you do, throw off the blankets again?" he said.

"Again?" she asked.

"Don't you remember me coming up there?"

She looked at him blankly.

"No," she said.

They looked at each other for a moment. Then he went to the cupboard and took out two cups.

"Can you drink coffee?" he asked.

She hesitated a moment. Then she said, "Yes."

He put the cups down on the table, then sat down and waited. When the coffee started spurting up into the glass dome of the pot, Ann stood and picked up a potholder. Collier watched her pour the black, steaming fluid into the cups. Her hand shook a little as she poured his cup and he shrank back to avoid getting splashed.

He waited until she was sitting down, then asked grumpily, "What are you reading *Basic Physics* for?"

Again the blank, uncertain look.

"I don't know," she said. "It just . . . caught my interest for some reason."

He spooned sugar into his coffee and stirred, hearing her pour cream into hers.

"I . . . thought you . . ." He took a breath. "I thought you had to drink skimmed milk. Or something," he said.

"I felt like a cup of coffee."

"I see."

He sat there looking morosely at the table, drinking the burning coffee in slow sips. He forced himself to sink into a dull, edgeless cloud. He almost forgot she was there. The room disappeared, all its sights and sounds falling away.

Then her cup banged down. He started.

"If you're not going to talk to me, we might as well end it right now!" she said angrily. "If you think I'm going to stick around until you feel like talking to me, you're wrong!"

"What would you like me to do!" he flared back. "If you found out I'd fathered some other woman's child, how would you feel?"

She closed her eyes and a look of strained patience held her face tautly.

"Listen, David," she said, "for the last time, *I have not committed adultery.* I know it spoils your role of the injured spouse but I can't help that. You can make me swear on a hundred Bibles and I'll still tell you the same thing. You can put truth serum in me and I'll tell you the same thing. You can strap me to a lie detector and my story will still be the same. David, I'm . . . !"

She couldn't finish. A spasm of coughing began shaking her body. Her face darkened and tears ran down her cheeks as she gripped the side of the table with whitened fingers, gasping for breath.

For a moment he forgot everything except that she was in pain. He jumped up and ran to the sink for water. Then he patted her back gently while she drank. She thanked him in a choking voice. He patted her back once more, almost longingly.

"You'd better stay in bed today," he said, "that's a bad cough you have. And I'd . . . you'd better pin down the blankets so you don't . . ."

"David, what are you going to do?" she asked unhappily.

"Do?"

She didn't explain.

"I'm . . . not sure, Ann," he said. "I want with all my heart to believe you. But . . ."

"But you can't. Well, that's that."

"Oh, *stop* jumping to conclusions! Can't you give me some time to work it out? For God's sake, I've only been home one day."

For a brief moment he thought he saw something of the old warmth in her eyes. Maybe she could see, behind his anger, how much he wanted to stay. She picked up her coffee.

"Work it out then," she said. "*I* know what the truth is. If you don't believe me . . . then work it out your own clever way."

"Thank you," he said.

When he left the house she was back in bed, bundled up warmly, coughing and reading avidly, *An Introduction To Chemistry*.

"Dave!"

Professor Mead's studious face broke into a grin. He put down the tweezers he'd been moving the microscope slide with and shoved out his right hand. Johnny Mead, former All-American quarterback, was twenty-seven, tall and broad, sporting a perpetual crewcut. He held Collier's hand in a firm grip.

"How's it been, boy?" he asked. "Had enough of those Matto Grosso vermin?"

"More than enough," Collier said, smiling.

"You're looking good, Dave," Mead said. "Nice and tan. You must make quite a sight around this campus of leprous-skinned faculty."

They moved across the wide laboratory toward Mead's office, passing students bent over their microscopes and working the testing instruments. Collier got a momentary feeling of return, then lost it in the irony that he should get the feeling here and not at home.

Mead closed the door and waved Collier to a chair.

"Well, tell me all about it, Dave," he said. "Your daring exploits in the tropics."

Collier cleared his throat.

"Well, if you don't mind, Johnny," he said, "there's something else I want to talk to you about now."

"Fire away, boy."

Collier hesitated.

"Understand now," he said, "I'm telling you this under

strictest confidence and only because I consider you my best friend."

Mead leaned forward in his chair, the look of youthful exuberance fading as he saw that Collier was worried.

Collier told him.

"No, Dave," Johnny said when he was finished.

"Listen, Johnny," Collier went on, "I know it sounds crazy. But she's insisted so forcibly that she's innocent that . . . well, frankly, I'm at a loss. Either she's had such an emotional breakdown that her mind has rejected the memory of . . . of . . ."

His hands stirred helplessly in his lap.

"Or?" Johnny said.

Collier took a deep breath.

"Or else she's telling the truth," he said.

"But . . ."

"I know, I know," Collier said. "I've been to our doctor. Kleinman, you know him."

Johnny nodded.

"Well, I've been to him and he said the same thing you don't have to say. That it's impossible for a woman to become pregnant five months after intercourse. I know that but . . ."

"What?"

"Isn't there some other way."

Johnny looked at him without speaking. Collier's head dropped forward and his eyes closed. After a moment he made a sound of bitter amusement.

"Isn't there some other way," he mocked himself. "What a stupid question."

"She insists she's had no . . ."

Collier nodded wearily.

"Yes," he said. "She . . . Yes."

"I don't know," Johnny said, running the tip of a forefinger over his lower lip. "Maybe she's hysterical. Maybe . . . David, maybe she isn't pregnant at all."

"What!"

Collier's head snapped up, his eyes looking eagerly into Johnny's.

"Don't jump the gun, Dave. I don't want that on my conscience. But, well . . . hasn't Ann always wanted a baby? I think she has—wanted it bad. Well . . . it may be just a crazy theory but I think it's possible that the emotional . . . *drain* of being separated from you for six months could cause a false pregnancy."

A wild hope began to surge in Collier, irrational he knew but one he clutched at, desperately.

"I think you should talk to her again," Johnny said. "Try to get more information from her. Maybe even do what she suggests and try hypnosis, truth serum, anything. But . . . boy, don't give up! I *know* Ann. And I trust her."

As he half ran down the street he kept thinking how little credit was due him for finding the trust he needed. But, at least, thank God, he had it for now. It filled him with hope, it made him want to cry out—it has to be true, it *has* to be!

Then, as he turned into the path of the house, he stopped so quickly that he almost fell forward and his breath drew in with a gasp.

Ann was standing on the porch in her nightgown, an icy January wind whipping the fragile silk around the full contours of her body. She stood on the frost-covered boards in her bare feet, one hand on the railing.

"Oh, my God," muttered Collier in a strangled voice as he raced up the path to grab her.

Her flesh was bluish and like ice when he caught her and when he looked into her wide, staring eyes, a bolt of panic drove through him.

He half led, half dragged her into the warm living room and set her down in the easy chair before the fireplace. Her teeth were chattering and breath passed her lips in wheezing gasps. His hands shook as he ran around frantically getting blankets, plugging in the heating pad and placing it under her icy feet, breaking up wood with frenzied motions and starting a fire, making hot coffee.

Finally, when he'd done everything he could, he knelt before her and held her frigid hands in his. And, as he listened to the shivering of her body reflected in her breath, a sense of utter anguish wrenched at his insides.

"Ann, Ann, what's the *matter* with you?" he almost sobbed. "Are you out of your mind?"

She tried to answer but could not. She huddled beneath the blankets, her eyes pleading with him.

"You don't have to talk, sweetheart," he said. "It's all right."

"I . . . I . . . I . . . h-had to go out," she said.

And that was all. He stayed there before her, his eyes never leaving her face. And, even though she was shaking and gripped by painful seizures of coughing, she seemed to realize his faith in her because she smiled at him and, in her eyes, he saw that she was happy.

By supper time she had a raging fever. He put her in bed and gave her nothing to eat but all the water she wanted. Her temperature fluctuated, her flushed burning skin becoming cold and clammy in almost seconds.

Collier called Kleinman about six and the doctor arrived fifteen minutes later. He went directly to the bedroom and checked Ann. His face became grave and he motioned Collier into the hall.

"We must get her to the hospital," he said quietly.

Then he went downstairs and phoned for an ambulance. Collier went back in to the bedside and stood there holding her limp hand, looking down at her closed eyes, her feverish skin. Hospital, he thought, oh my God, the hospital.

Then a strange thing happened.

Kleinman returned and beckoned once more for Collier to come out in the hall. They stood there talking until the downstairs bell rang. Then Collier went down to let them in and the two orderlies and the interne followed him up the stairs carrying their stretcher.

They found Kleinman standing by the bed staring down at Ann in speechless amazement.

Collier ran to him.

"What is it!" he cried.

Kleinman lifted his head slowly.

"She is cured," he said in awed tones.

"What?"

The interne moved quickly to the bed. Kleinman spoke to him and to Collier.

"The fever is gone," he said. "Her temperature, her respiration, her pulse beat—all are normal. She has been completely cured of pneumonia in . . ."

He checked his pocket watch.

"In seventeen minutes," he said.

Collier sat in Kleinman's waiting room staring sightlessly at the magazine in his lap. Inside, Ann was being x-rayed.

There was no doubt anymore, Ann was pregnant. X-rays at six weeks had shown the fetus inside her. Once more their relationship suffered from doubt. He was still concerned for her health but, once more, was unable to speak to her and tell her that he believed in her. And, though he'd never actually told her of his renewed doubt, Ann had felt it. She avoided him at home, sleeping half the time, the other half reading omniverously. He still couldn't understand that. She'd gone through all his books on the physical sciences, then his texts on sociology, anthropology, philosophy, semantics, history and now she was reading geography books. There seemed no sense to it.

And, all during this period, while the form in her body changed from a small lump to a pear shape, to a globe, then an ovoid—she'd been eating an excess of salt. Doctor Kleinman kept warning her about it. Collier had tried to stop her but she wouldn't stop. Eating salt seemed a compulsion.

As a result she drank too much water. Now her weight had come to the point where the over-size fetus was pressing against her diaphragm causing breathing difficulty.

Just yesterday Ann's face had gone blue and Collier had rushed her to Kleinman's office. The doctor had done something to ease the condition. Collier didn't know what. Then Ann had been x-rayed and Kleinman told Collier to bring her back the next day.

The door opened and Kleinman led Ann out of his office. "Sit, my dear," he told her. "I want to talk to David."

Ann walked past Collier without looking at him and sat down on the leather couch. As he stood, he noticed her reaching for a magazine. *The Scientific American.* He sighed and shook his head as he walked into Kleinman's office.

As he moved for the chair, he thought, for what seemed the hundredth time, of the night she'd cried and told him she had to stay because there was no place else to go. Because she had no money of her own and her family was dead. She'd told him that if it wasn't for the fact that she was innocent she'd probably kill herself for the way he was treating her. He had stood beside the bed, silent and tense, while she cried, unable to argue, to console, even to reply. He'd just stood there until he could bear it no longer and then walked out of the room.

"What?" he said.

"I say look at these," Kleinman said grimly.

Kleinman's behavior had changed too in the past months, declining from confidence to a sort of confused anger.

Collier looked down at the two x-ray plates, glanced at the dates on them. One was from the day before, the other was the plate Kleinman had just taken.

"I don't . . ." Collier stared.

Kleinman told him. "Look at the size of the child."

Collier compared the plates more carefully. At first he didn't see. Then his startled eyes flicked up suddenly.

"Is it possible?" he said, feeling a crushing sense of the unreal on him.

"It has happened," was all Kleinman said.

"But . . . how?"

Kleinman shook his head and Collier saw the doctor's left hand on the desk grip into a fist as if he were angered by this new enigma.

"I have never seen the like of it," Kleinman said. "Complete bone structure by the seventh week. Facial form by the eighth week. Organs complete and functioning by the end of the second month. The mother's insane desire for salt. And now this . . ."

He picked up the plates and looked at them almost in belligerence.

"How can a child decrease its size?" he said.

Collier felt a pang of fear at the mystified tone in Kleinman's voice.

"It is clear, it is clear," Kleinman shook his head irritably. "The child had grown to excess proportions because of the mother drinking too much water. To such proportions that it was pressing dangerously against her diaphragm. And now, in one day, the pressure is gone, the size of the child markedly decreased."

Kleinman's hands snapped into hard fists.

"It is almost," he said nervously, "as if the child knows what is going on."

"No more salt!"

His voice rose in pitch as he jerked the salt shaker from her hand and stamped over to the cupboard. Then he took her glass of water and emptied most of it into the sink. He sat down again.

She sat with her eyes shut, her body trembling. He watched as tears ran slowly from her eyes and down her cheeks. Her teeth bit into her lower lip. Then her eyes opened; they were big, frightened eyes. She caught a sob in the middle and hastily brushed her tears aside. She sat there quietly.

"Sorry," she murmured and, for some reason, Collier got the impression that she wasn't talking to him.

She finished the remaining water in a gulp.

"You're drinking too much water again," he said. "You know what Doctor Kleinman said."

"I . . . try," she said, "But I can't help it. I feel such a need for salt and it makes me so thirsty."

"You'll have to quit drinking so much water," he said coldly. "You'll endanger the child."

She looked startled as her body twitched suddenly. Her hands slipped from the table to press against her swollen stomach. Her look implored him to help her.

"What is it?" he asked hurriedly.

"I don't know," she said. "The baby kicked."

He leaned back, muscles unknotted.

"That's to be expected," he said.

They sat quietly a while. Ann toyed with her food. Once he saw her reach out automatically for the salt, then raise her eyes in slight alarm when her fingers didn't find the shaker.

"David," she said after a few minutes.

He swallowed his food.

"What?"

"Why have you stayed with me?"

He couldn't answer.

"Is it because you believe me?"

"I don't know, Ann. I don't know."

The look of slight hope on her face left and she lowered her head.

"I thought," she said, "Maybe . . . because you were staying . . ."

The crying again. She sat there not even bothering to brush aside the tears that moved slowly down her cheeks and over her lips.

"Oh, Ann," he said, half irritably, half in sorrow.

He got up to go to her. As he did her body twitched again, this time more violently, and her face went blank. Again she cut off her sobs and rubbed at her cheeks with almost angry fingers.

"I can't *help* it," she said slowly and loudly.

Not to him. Collier was sure it was not to him.

"What are you talking about?" he said nervously.

He stood there looking down at his wife. She looked so helpless, so afraid. He wanted to pull her against himself and comfort her. He wanted to . . .

Still sitting, she leaned against his chest while he stroked her soft brown hair.

"Poor little girl," he said. "My poor little girl."

"Oh David, *David*, if only you'd believe me. I'd do anything to make you believe me, anything. I can't stand to have you so cold to me. Not when I know I haven't done anything wrong."

He stood there silently and his mind spoke to him. There is a chance, it said, a chance.

She seemed to guess what he was thinking. Because she looked up at him and there was absolute trust in her eyes.

"Anything, David, *anything*."

"Can you hear me, Ann?" he said.

"Yes," she said.

They were in Professor Mead's office. Ann lay on the couch, her eyes closed. Mead took the needle from Collier's fingers and put it on the desk. He sat on the corner of the desk and watched in grim silence.

"Who am I, Ann?"

"David."

"How do you feel, Ann?"

"Heavy. I feel heavy."

"Why?"

"The baby is so heavy."

Collier licked his lips. Why was he putting it off, asking these extraneous questions? He knew he wanted to ask. Was he too afraid? What if, despite her insistence on this, she gave the wrong answer?

He gripped his hands together tightly and his throat seemed to become a column of rock.

"Dave, not too long," Johnny cautioned.

Collier drew in a rasping breath.

"Is it . . ." he started, then swallowed with difficulty, "Is it . . . my child, Ann?"

She hesitated. She frowned. Her eyes flickered open for a second, then shut. Her entire body writhed. She seemed to be fighting the question. Then the color drained from her face.

"No," she said through clenched teeth.

Collier felt himself stiffening as if all his muscles and tendons were dough expanding and pushing out his flesh.

"Who's the father?" he asked, not realizing how loud and unnatural his voice was.

At that, Ann's body shuddered violently. There was a clicking sound in her throat and her head rolled limply on the pillow. At her sides, the white fists opened slowly.

Mead jumped over and put his fingers to her wrist. His face was taut as he felt for the pulsebeat. Satisfied, he lifted her right eyelid and peered at the eye.

"She's really out," he said, "I told you it wasn't a good idea to give serum to such a heavily pregnant woman. You should have done it months ago. Kleinman won't like this."

Collier sat there not hearing a word, his face a mask of hopeless distress.

"Is she all right?" he asked.

But the words hardly came out. He felt something shake in his chest. He didn't realize what it was until it was too late. Then he ran shaking hands over his cheeks and stared at the wet fingers with incredulous eyes. His mouth opened, closed. He tried to cut off the sobs but he could not.

He felt Johnny's arm around his shoulders.

"It's all right, boy," Johnny said.

Collier jammed his eyes shut, wishing that his whole body could be swallowed up in the swimming darkness before his gaze. His chest heaved with trembling breaths and he couldn't swallow the lump in his throat. His head kept shaking slowly. My life is ended, he thought, I loved and trusted her and she has betrayed me.

"Dave?" he heard Johnny say.

Collier grunted.

"I don't want to make things worse. But . . . well, there's still a hope, I think."

"Huh?"

"Ann didn't answer your question. She didn't say the father was . . . another man," he finished weakly.

Collier pushed angrily to his feet.

"Oh shut up, will you?" he said.

Later they carried her to the car and Collier drove her home.

Slowly he took off his coat and hat and let them drop on the hall chest. Then he shuffled into the living room and sank down on his chair. He lifted his feet to the ottoman with a weary grunt. He sat there, slumped over, staring at the wall.

Where was she?—he wondered. Upstairs reading probably, just as he'd left her this morning. She had a pile of library books by the bed. Rousseau, Locke, Hegel, Marx, Descartes, Darwin, Bergson, Freud, Whitehead, Jeans, Eddington, Einstein, Emerson, Dewey, Confucius, Plato, Aristotle, Spinoza, Kant, Schopenhauer, James—an endless assortment of books.

And the way she read them. As if she were sitting there and rapidly turning the pages without even looking at what was written on them. Yet he knew she was getting it all. Once in a while she'd let a phrase drop, a concept, an idea. She was getting every word.

But why?

Once he had gotten the wild idea that Ann had read something about acquired characteristics and was trying to pass along this knowledge to her unborn child. But he had quickly put aside that idea. Ann was intelligent enough to know that such a thing was patently impossible.

He sat there shaking his head slowly, a habit he'd acquired in the past few months. Why was he still with her? He kept asking himself the question. Somehow the months had slipped by and still he was living in this house. A hundred times he'd started to leave and changed his mind. Finally he'd given up and moved into the back bedroom. They lived now like landlord and tenant.

His nerves were starting to go. He found himself obsessed with an overwhelming impatience. If he was walking from one place to another he would suddenly feel a great rush of anger that he had not already completed the trip. He resented all transport, he wanted things done immediately. He snapped at his pupils whether they rated it or not. His classes were being so poorly conducted that he'd been called before Doctor

Peden, the head of the Geology Department. Peden hadn't been too hard on him because he knew about Ann but Collier knew he couldn't go on like this.

His eyes moved over the room. The rug was thick with dust. He'd tried going over it with the vacuum whenever he thought of it, but it piled up too fast to keep pace with. The whole house was going to pot. He had to take care of his laundry. The machine in the basement hadn't been used for months. He didn't know how to operate it and Ann never touched it now. He took the clothes to the laundromat downtown.

When he'd commented once on the slovenliness of the house, Ann had looked hurt and started to cry. She cried all the time now and always the same way. First, as if she were going to continue for an hour straight. Then, suddenly, with lurching abruptness, she would stop crying and wipe away the tears. He got the impression sometimes that it had something to do with the child, that she stopped for fear the crying would affect the baby. Or else it was the other way around, he thought, that the baby didn't like . . .

He closed his eyes as if to shut out the thought. His right hand tapped nervously and impatiently on the arm of the chair. He got up restlessly and walked around the room running a forefinger over flat surfaces, wiping the dust off on his handkerchief.

He stood staring malignantly at the heap of dishes in the sink, the unkempt condition of the curtains, the smeared linoleum. He felt like rushing upstairs and letting her know that, pregnancy or no pregnancy, she was going to snap out of this doldrum and act like a wife again or he was leaving.

He started through the dining room, then halfway to the stairs he hesitated, halted completely. He went back to the stove slowly and put the flame on underneath the coffee pot. The coffee would be stale but he'd rather drink it that way than make more.

What was the use? She'd try to talk to him and tell him she understood but then, as if she were under a spell, she'd start to cry. And, after a few moments, she'd get that startled look and stop crying. As a matter of fact she was even beginning to control her tears from the outset. As if she knew that the crying was not going to work so she may as well not start at all.

It was eerie.

The word brought him up short. That was it—eerie. The

pneumonia. The decrease in fetal size. The reading. The desire for salt. The crying and the stopping of it.

He found himself staring at the white wall over the stove. He found himself shuddering.

Ann didn't tell us the father was another man.

When he came in she was in the kitchen drinking coffee. Without a word he took the cup from her and poured the remainder of it into the sink.

"You're not supposed to drink coffee," he said.

He looked into the coffee pot. He'd left it almost full that morning   .

"Did you drink *all* of it?" he asked angrily.

She lowered her head.

"For God's sake, don't cry." he rasped.

"I . . . I won't," she said.

"Why do you drink coffee when you know you're not supposed to?"

"I just couldn't stand it anymore."

"*Oh-h,*" he said, clenching his teeth. He started out of the room.

"David, I can't help it," she called after him, "I can't drink water. I have to drink *something*. David, can't—can't you! . . ."

He went upstairs and took a shower. He couldn't concentrate on anything. He put down the soap and then forgot where. He stopped shaving before he was done and wiped off the lather. Then, later, while he was combing his hair, he noticed half his face still bearded and, with a muffled curse, he lathered again and finished.

The night was like all the others except for one thing. When he went into the bedroom for clean pajamas he saw that she was having difficulty focusing her eyes. And, while he lay in the back bedroom correcting test papers, he heard her giggling. Later he tossed around for several hours before he slept and all that time she kept giggling at something. He wanted to slam the door shut and drown out the sound but he couldn't. He had to leave the door open in case she needed him during the night.

At last he slept. For how long he didn't know. It seemed only a moment before he lay there blinking up at the dark ceiling.

"Now am I alien and forgotten, O lost of traveled night."
First he thought he was dreaming.
"Murk and strangeness, here am I in ever night, hot, hot."
He sat up suddenly then, his heart jolting.
It was Ann's voice.
He threw his legs over the side of the bed and found his
slippers. He pushed up quickly and padded to the door, shiver-
ing as the cold air chilled the rayon thinness of his pajamas. He
moved into the hall and heard her speaking again.
"Dream of goodbyes, forsaken, plunged in swelling liquors,
cry I for light, release me from torment and trial."
All spoken in a singsong rhythm, in a voice that was Ann's
and not Ann's, more high-pitched, more tense.
She was lying there on her back, her hands pressed to her
stomach. It was moving. He watched the flesh ripple under
the thinness of her nightgown. She should have been chilled
without any blankets but she seemed warm. The bedside lamp
was still on, the book—Science and Sanity, Korzybski—
fallen from her fingers and lying half open on the mattress.
It was her face. Sweat drops dotted it like hundreds of tiny
crystals. Her lips were drawn back from her teeth.
Her eyes wide open.
"Kin of the night, sickened of this pit, O send me not to
make the way!"
He felt a horrible fascination in standing there listening to
her. But she was in pain. It was obvious from her whitened
skin, the way her hands, like claws, raked the sheet at her sides
into mounds of wadded, sweat-streaked cotton.
"I cry, I cry," she said. "Rhyuio Gklemmo Fglwo!"
He slapped her face and her body lurched on the bed.
"He again, the hurting one!"
Her lips spread wide in a scream. He slapped her again and
focus came to her eyes. She lay there staring up at him in com-
plete horror. Her hands jumped to her cheeks, pressing against
them. She seemed to recoil into the bed. Her pupils shrank to
pinpoints in the milk-white of her eyes.
"No," she said, "No!"
"Ann, it's me, David! You're all right!"
She looked uncomprehendingly at him for a long moment,
her breasts heaving with tortured breaths.
Then, suddenly, she was relaxed and recognized him. Her

lower jaw went slack and a moan of relief filled her throat.

He sat down beside her and took her in his arms. She clung to him, crying, her face into his chest.

"All right, baby, let it out, let it out."

Again. The choking off of sobs, the suddenly dried eyes, the pulling away from him, the blank look.

"What is it?" he asked.

No answer. She stared at him.

"Baby, what *is* it? Why can't you cry?"

Something crossed her face, then slipped away.

"Baby, you should cry."

"I don't want to cry."

"Why not?"

"He won't let me," she blurted out.

Suddenly, they were both silent, staring at each other and, he knew, in an instant, that they were very close to the answer.

"*He?*" he asked.

"No," she said suddenly, "I don't mean it. I don't mean that. I don't mean *he*, I mean something else."

For a long time they sat there looking at each other. Then speaking no more, he made her lie down and covered her up. He got a blanket and stayed the rest of the night in the chair by the bureau. When he woke up in the morning, cramped and cold, he saw that she'd thrown off the blankets again.

Kleinman told him that Ann had adjusted to cold. There seemed to be something added to her system which was sending out heat to her when she needed it.

"And all this salt she takes." Kleinman threw up his hands. "It is beyond sense. You would think the child thrives on a saline diet. Yet she no longer gains excess weight. She does not drink water to combat the thirst. What does she do to ease the thirst?"

"Nothing," Collier said. "She is always thirsty."

"And the reading, it goes on?"

"Yes," said Collier.

"And the talking in her sleep?"

"Yes."

Kleinman shook his head.

"Never in my life," he said, "have I seen a pregnancy like this."

She finished up the last of the huge pile she'd been constantly augmenting. She took all the books back to the library.

A new development began.

She was seven months pregnant. It was May and Collier noticed that the oil was filthy, the tires were unnaturally worn and there was a dent in the left rear fender.

"Have you been using the car?" he asked her one Saturday morning. It was in the living room, the phonograph was playing Brahms.

"Why?" she asked. He told her and she said irritably, "If you already know, why do you ask me?"

"Have you?"

"Yes. I've been using the car. Is that permissible?"

"You needn't be sarcastic."

"Oh no," she said angrily. "I needn't get sarcastic. I've been pregnant seven months and not once have you believed that some other man isn't the father. No matter how many times I've told you that I'm innocent, you still won't say—I believe you. And *I'm* sarcastic. Oh, honest, David, you're a panic, a real panic."

She stamped over to the phonograph and turned it off.

"I'm *listening* to it," he said.

"That's too bad. I don't like it."

"Since when?"

"Oh, leave me alone."

He caught her by the wrist as she turned away.

"Listen," he said, "maybe you think the whole thing has been a vacation for me. I come home from six months research and find you pregnant. Not by me! I don't care what you say, I'm *not* the father and I nor anyone else knows any way but one for a woman to get pregnant. Still I haven't left. I've watched you turn into a book-reading machine. I've had to clean the house when I could, cook most of the meals, take care of our clothes—as well as teach every day at the college. I've had to look over you as I would a child, keeping you from kicking off the blankets, keeping you from eating too much salt, from drinking too much water, too much coffee, from smoking too much . . ."

"I've stopped smoking myself," she said, pulling away.

"Why?" he threw at her suddenly. She looked blank.

"Go ahead," he said, "say it. Because *he* doesn't like it."

"I stopped smoking myself," she repeated. "I can't stand them."

"And now you don't like music."

"It . . . hurts my stomach," she said, vaguely.

"Nonsense," he said.

Before he could stop her, she'd gone out the front door into the blazing sunlight. He went to the door and watched her get into the car clumsily. He started to call to her but she'd started the motor and couldn't hear him. He watched the car disappear up the block doing fifty in second gear.

"How long has she been gone now?" Johnny asked.

Collier glanced nervously at his watch.

"I don't know exactly," he said. "Since around nine-thirty, I guess. We'd argued, as I said . . ."

He broke off nervously and checked his watch again. It was past midnight.

"How long has she been driving like this?" Johnny asked.

"I don't know, Johnny. I told you I just found out."

"Doesn't her size . . . ?" started Johnny.

"No, the baby isn't big anymore." Collier spoke the astounding now in a matter-of-fact voice. He ran a shaky hand through his hair.

"You think we should call the police?" he asked.

"Wait a little."

"What if she's had an accident?" Collier said. "She's not the best driver in the world. Why in God's name did I let her go? Seven months pregnant and I let her go driving. Oh, I ought to be . . ."

He felt himself getting ready to crack. All this tension in his house, this strange and endlessly distressing pregnancy—it was getting to him. A man couldn't hold onto tension for seven months and not feel it. He could not keep his hands from shaking anymore. He'd developed a habit of persistent blinking to use up some of the nervous energy.

He paced across the rug to the fireplace and stood there tapping his nails nervously on the shelf.

"I think we should call the police," he said.

"Take it easy," Johnny warned.

"What would you advise?" Collier snapped.

"Sit down. Right there. That's it. Now, relax. She's all right, believe me. I'm not worried about Ann. She's probably had a flat or an engine failure somewhere in the middle of nowhere. How many times have I heard you go on about needing a new battery? It probably died, that's all."

"Well . . . wouldn't the police be able to find her a lot quicker?"

"All right, boy, if it'll make you happier, I'll call them."

Collier nodded, then started up as a car passed in the street. He rushed to the window and drew back the blinds. Then he bit his lips and turned back. He went back to the fireplace while Johnny moved for the hall phone. He listened to Johnny dialing, then twitched as the receiver was put down hurriedly.

"Here she is," Johnny said.

They led her into the front room, dizzy and confused. She didn't answer Collier's frantic questions. She headed straight for the kitchen as if she didn't notice them.

"Coffee," she said in a guttural voice.

At first Collier tried to stop her, then he felt Johnny's hand on his arm.

"Let her go," Johnny said. "It's time we got to the bottom of this."

She stood in front of the stove and turned the flame up high under the coffee pot. She ladled in careless spoonfuls, then slammed on the lid, and stood looking down at it studiedly.

Collier started to say something but, once more, Johnny restrained him. Collier stood restively in the kitchen doorway, watching his wife.

When the brown liquid started popping up into the dome, Ann grabbed the pot off the stove without using a potholder. Collier drew in his breath and gritted his teeth.

She poured out the steaming liquid and it sloshed up the sides of the used cup on the table. Then she slammed down the pot and reached hungrily for the cup.

She finished the whole pot in ten minutes.

She drank without cream or sugar, as if she didn't care what it tasted like. As if she didn't taste it at all.

Only when she'd finished did her face relax. She slumped back in the chair and sat there a long time. They watched her in silence.

Then she looked up at them and giggled.

She pushed up and fell against the table. Collier heard Johnny draw in sudden breath.

"My God," he said, "she's *drunk!*"

She was a heavy unwieldly form to get up the stairs, especially since she gave them no assistance. She kept humming to herself—a strange, discordant melody that seemed to move in indefinable tone steps, repeated and repeated like the sound of low wind. There was a beatific smile on her face.

"A lot of good that did," Collier muttered.

"Be patient, be patient," Johnny whispered back.

"Easy enough for you to. . . ."

"Shhh," Johnny quieted him but Ann didn't hear a word they said.

She stopped humming as soon as they put her down on the bed and had fallen into a deep sleep before they straightened up. Collier drew a thin blanket over her and put a pillow under her head. She didn't stir as he lifted her head.

Then the two men stood in silence beside the bed. Collier looked down at the wife he no longer understood. His mind swam with painful discordances and, through them all, burned the horrible strain of doubt that had never left him. Who was the father of her child? Even though he couldn't leave her, even though he felt a great loving pity for her—they could never be close again until he knew.

"I wonder where she goes?" Johnny asked. "When she drives, I mean."

"I don't know." Sullenly.

"She must have gone pretty far to wear down the tires so much. I wonder if. . . ."

That was when she started again.

"*Send me not,*" she said.

Johnny gripped Collier's arm.

"Is that it?" he asked.

"I don't know yet."

"*Black, black, drive me out, horror in these shores, heavy, heavy.*"

Collier shuddered.

"That's it," he said.

Johnny knelt hurriedly beside the bed and listened carefully.

"*Breathe me, implore my fathers, seek me out in washing pain, send me not to make the way.*"

Johnny stared at Ann's taut features. She looked as if she were in pain again. And yet it was not her face, Collier suddenly realized. The expression wasn't hers.

Ann threw off the blanket and thrashed on the bed, sweat breaking out on her face.

"*To walk on shores of orange sea, cool, to tread the crimson fields, cool, the raft of silent waters, cool, to ride upon the desertland, cool, return me fathers of my fathers, Rhyuio Gklemmo Fglwo.*"

Then she was silent except for tiny groans. At her sides, her hands clutched the sheets and her breaths were labored and uneven.

Johnny straightened up and looked at Collier. Neither of them spoke a word.

They sat with Kleinman.

"What you suggest is fantastic," the doctor said.

"Listen," Johnny said. "Let's run it down. One—the excess saline requirements, not the requirements of a normal pregnancy. Two—the cold, the way Ann's body adjusted to it, the way she was cured of pneumonia in minutes."

Collier sat staring numbly at his friend.

"All right," Johnny said, "first the salt. In the beginning it made Ann drink too much water. She gained weight and then her weight endangered the child. What happened? She no longer was allowed to drink water."

"Allowed?" Collier asked.

"Let me finish," Johnny said. "About the cold; it was as if the child needed cold and forced Ann to stay cold—until it realized that by acquiring itself some comfort it was endangering the very vessel it lived in. So it cured the vessel of pneumonia. It adjusted the vessel to cold."

"You talk as if. . . ." Kleinman started.

"The effects of cigarettes," Johnny said. "Excuse me, doctor. Ann could have smoked in moderation without endangering herself or the child. Yet she stopped altogether. It might have been an ethical point, true. Again, it might be that the child reacted violently to nicotine, and, in a sense, forbade her to. . . ."

Kleinman interrupted irritably.

"You talk as if the child were directing its mother rather than being helpless, subject to its mother's actions."

"Helpless?" was all Johnny said.

Kleinman didn't go on. He pressed his lips together in annoyed surrender and tapped nervously on his desk. Johnny waited a moment and then, seeing that Kleinman wasn't going to continue, he went on.

"Three—the aversion to music which she once loved. Why? Because it was music? I don't think so. *Because of the vibrations.* Vibrations which a normal child wouldn't even notice being so insulated from sound not only by the layers of its mother's epidermis but by the very structure of its own hearing apparatus. Apparently, this . . . child . . . has much keener hearing.

"The coffee," he said. "It made her drunk. Oh—it made *it* drunk."

"Now wait," Collier started, then broke off.

"And now," Johnny said, "as to her reading. It fits in too. All those books—more or less the basic works in every field of knowledge, a seemingly calculated study of mankind and his every thought."

"What are you driving at?" Collier spoke nervously.

"Think, Dave! All these things. The reading, the trips in the car. As if she were trying to get as much information as she could about life in our civilization. As if the child were. . . ."

"You are not implying that the child was. . . ." Kleinman began.

"Child?" Johnny said grimly. "I think we can stop referring to it as a child. Perhaps the body is childlike. But the mind—never."

They were deadly silent. Collier felt his heart pulsing strangely in his chest.

"Listen," Johnny said. "Last night Ann—or the . . . it—was drunk. Why? Maybe because of what it's learned, what it's seen. I hope so. Maybe it was sick and wanted to forget."

He leaned forward.

"Those visions Ann had; I think they tell the story—as crazy as it is. The deserts, the marshes, the crimson fields. Add the cold. Only one thing wasn't mentioned and I think that's probably because they don't exist."

"What?" Collier asked, reality scaling away from him.

"The canals," Johnny said. "Ann has a Martian in her womb."

For a long time they looked at him in incredulous silence. Then both started talking at once, protesting with nervous horror in their voices. Johnny waited until the first spasm of their words had passed.

"Is there a better answer?" he asked.

"But . . . how?" Kleinman asked heatedly. "How could such a pregnancy be effected?"

"I don't know," Johnny said. "But why? I think I know." Collier was afraid to ask.

"All through the years," Johnny said, "There's been no end of talk and writing about the Martians, about flying saucers. Books, stories, movies, articles—always with the same theme."

"I don't. . . ." Collier began.

"I think the invasion has finally come," Johnny said. "At least a tryout. I think this is their first attempt, an insidious, cruel attempt—invasion by flesh. To place an adult life cell from their own planet into the body of an Earth woman. Then, when this fully matured Martian mind is coupled to the form of an Earth child—the process of conquest begins. This is their experiment, I think, their test. If it works . . ."

He didn't finish.

"But . . . oh, that's insane," Collier said, trying to push away the fear that was crowding him in.

"So is her reading," said Johnny. "So are her trips in the car. So is her coffee drinking and her dislike of music and her pneumonia healing and her standing out in the cold and the reduction of body size and the visions and that crazy toneless song she sang. What do you want, Dave . . . a blueprint?"

Kleinman stood up and went to his filing cabinets. He pulled out a drawer and came back to the desk with a folder in his hand.

"I have had this is my files for three weeks now," he said. "I have not told you. I did not know how. But this information, this theory," he quickly amended, "compels me to . . ."

He pushed the x-ray slide across the desk to them.

They looked at it and Collier gasped. Johnny's voice was awed.

"A double heart," he said.

Then his left hand bunched into a fist.

"That clinches it!" he said. "Mars has two fifths the gravity of Earth. They'd need a double heart to drive their blood or whatever it is they have in their veins."

"But . . . it does not need this here," Kleinman said.

"Then there's some hope," Johnny said. "There are rough spots in this invasion. The Martian cell would, of genetic necessity, cause certain Martian characteristics in the child—the double heart, the acute hearing, the need for salt, I don't know why, the need for cold. In time—and if this experiment works —they may iron out these difficulties and be able to create a child with only the Martian mind and every physical characteristic Earthlike. I don't know but I suspect the Martian is also telepathic. Otherwise how would it have known it was in danger when Ann had pneumonia?"

The scene flitted suddenly across Collier's mind—him standing beside the bed, the thought—*the hospital, oh God, the hospital*. And, under Ann's flesh, a tiny alien brain, well versed by then in the terms of Earth, plucking at his thought. Hospital, investigation, discovery . . . He shuddered convulsively.

". . . we to do?" he caught the tail end of Kleinman's question. "Kill the . . . the *Martian* after it is born?"

"I don't know," Johnny said. "But if this . . . ," he shrugged, "this *child* is born alive and born normal—I don't think killing would help. I'm sure they must be watching. If the birth is normal—they might assume their experiment is a success whether we killed the child or not."

"A Caesarean?" Kleinman said.

"Maybe," Johnny said. "But . . . would they be sure they've failed if we had to use artificial means to destroy . . . their first invader? No, I don't think it's good enough. They'd try again, this time somewhere where no one could check on it—in an African village, in some unavailable town, in . . ."

"We can't leave that . . . that *thing* in her!" Collier said in horror.

"How do we know we can remove it?" Johnny said grimly, "and not kill Ann?"

"What?" Collier asked, feeling as if he were some brainless straight man for horror.

Johnny exhaled raggedly.

"I think we have to wait," he said. "I don't think we have any choice."

Then, seeing the look on Collier's face, he hurriedly added.

"It's not hopeless, boy. There are things in our favor. The double heart which might drive the blood too fast. The difficulties of combining alien cells. The fact that it's July and the heat might destroy the Martian. The fact that we can cut off all its salt supply. It can all help. But, most of all, because the Martian isn't happy. It drank to forget and—what were its words? O, send me not to make the way."

He looked grimly at them.

"Let's hope it dies of despair," he said.

"Or?" Collier asked hollowly.

"Or else this . . . miscegenation from space succeeds."

Collier dashed up the stairs, his heart pounding with a strange ambivalent beat. Knowing at last she was innocent was horribly balanced by knowledge of the danger she was in.

At the top of the stairs he stopped. The house was silent and hot in the late afternoon.

They were right, he suddenly realized, right in advising him not to tell her. It hadn't actually struck him until then, he'd thought it wrong not to let her know. He'd thought she wouldn't mind as long as she knew what it was, as long as she had his faith again.

But now he wondered. It was a terrifying thing, the import of it made him tremble. Might not the knowledge of this horror drive her into hysterics; she'd been bordering on breakdown for the past three months.

His mouth tightened and he walked into the room.

She lay on her back, her hands resting limply on her swollen stomach, her lifeless eyes staring up at the ceiling. He sat down, on the edge of the bed. She didn't look at him.

"Ann."

No answer. He felt himself shiver. I can't blame you, he thought, I've been harsh and thoughtless.

"Sweetheart," he said.

Her eyes moved slowly over and their gaze on him was cold and alien. It was the creature in her, he thought, she didn't realize how it controlled her. She must never realize. He knew that then, clearly.

He leaned over and pressed his cheek against hers.

"Darling," he said.

A dull, tired voice hardly audible. "What?"

"Can you hear me?" he said.

She didn't reply.

"Ann, about the baby."

There was a slight sign of life in her eyes.

"What about the baby?"

He swallowed.

"I . . . I know that . . . that it isn't the baby of . . . another man."

For a moment she stared at him. Then she muttered, "Bravo," and turned her head away.

He sat there, hands gripped into tight fists, thinking—well, that's that, I've killed her love completely.

But then her head turned back. There was something in her eyes, a tremulous question.

"What?" she said.

"I believe you," he said. "I know you've told me the truth. I'm apologizing with all my heart . . . if you'll let me."

For a long moment nothing seemed to register. Then she took her hands from her stomach and pressed them against her cheeks. Her wide brown eyes began to glisten as they looked at him.

"You're not . . . fooling me?" she asked him.

For a moment he hung suspended, then he threw himself against her.

"Oh, Ann, Ann," he said, "I'm sorry. I'm so sorry, Ann."

Her arms slid around his neck and held him. He felt her breasts shake with inner sobs. Her right hand caressed his hair.

"David, David . . ." She said it like that, over and over.

For a long time they remained there, silent and at peace. Then she asked:

"What made you change your mind?"

His throat moved.

"I just did," he said.

"But why?"

"No reason, honey. I mean, of course, there was a reason. I just realized that. . . ."

"You've doubted me for seven months, David. Why did you change your mind now?"

He felt a burst of rage at himself. Was there nothing he could tell her that would satisfy her?

"I think I've misjudged you," he said.

"Why?"

He sat up and looked at her without the answer. The look

of soft happiness was leaving her face. Her expression was taut and unyielding.

"Why, David?"

"I told you, sweet. . . ."

"You didn't tell me."

"Yes, I did. I said I think I've misjudged you."

"That's no reason."

"Ann, don't let's argue now. Does it matter if . . ."

"Yes, it matters a lot!" she said, her voice breaking, as her breath caught.

"And what about your biological assurances?" she said. "No woman can have a baby without being impregnated by a man. You always made that very clear. What about that? Have you given up your faith in biology and transferred it to me?"

"No, darling," he said. "I simply know things I didn't know before."

"What things?"

"I can't tell you."

"More secrets! Is this Kleinman's advice, just a trick to make my last month cozy? Don't lie to me, I know when you're lying to me."

"Ann, don't get so excited."

"I'm not excited!"

"You're shouting. Now stop it."

"I will not stop it! You toy with my feelings for more than half a year and now you want me to be calmly rational! Well, I won't be! I'm sick of you and your pompous attitude! I'm tired of . . . *Uhhh!*"

She lurched on the bed, her head snapping as she jerked her head from the pillow, all the color drained from her face in an instant. Her eyes on him were the eyes of a wounded child, dazed and shocked.

"*My insides!*" she gasped.

"Ann!"

She was half sitting now, her body shaking, a wild, despairing groan starting up in her throat. He grabbed her shoulders and tried to steady her. The Martian!—the thought clutched at his mind—it doesn't like her angry!

"It's all right baby, all r . . ."

"He's hurting me!" she cried. "He's hurting me, David! Oh God!"

"He can't hurt you," he heard himself say.

"No, no, no, I can't stand it," she said between clenched teeth. "*I can't stand it.*"

Then, as abruptly as the attack had come, her face relaxed utterly. Not so much with actual relaxation as with a complete absence of all feeling. She looked dizzily at David.

"I'm numb," she said quietly, "I . . . can't . . . feel . . . a . . ."

Slowly she sank back on the pillow and lay there a second with her eyes open. Then she smiled drowsily at Collier.

"Good night, David," she said.

And closed her eyes.

Kleinman stood beside the bed.

"She is in perfect coma," he said, quietly. "More accurately I should say under hypnotic trance. Her body functions normally but her brain has been . . . frozen."

Johnny looked at him.

"Suspended animation?"

"No, her body functions. She is just asleep. I cannot wake her."

They went downstairs to the living room.

"In a sense," Kleinman said, "she is better off. There will be no upsets now. Her body will function painlessly, effortlessly."

"The Martian must have done it," Johnny said, "to safeguard its . . . home."

Collier shuddered.

"I'm sorry, Dave," Johnny said.

They sat silent a moment.

"It must realize we know about it," Johnny said.

"Why?" asked Collier.

"It wouldn't be tipping off its hand completely if it thought there was still a chance of secrecy."

"Maybe it could not stand the pain," said Kleinman.

Johnny nodded. "Yes, maybe."

Collier sat there, his heart beating strainedly. Suddenly he clenched his fists and drove them down on his legs.

"Meanwhile, what are we supposed to do!" he said. "Are we helpless before this . . . this trespasser?"

"We can't take risks with Ann," was all Johnny said and Kleinman nodded once.

Collier sank back in the chair. He sat staring at the kewpie doll on the mantel. *Coney Island* read the doll's dress and on the belt—*Happy Days.*

"Rhyuio Gklemmo Fglwo!"

Ann writhed in unconscious labor on the hospital bed. Collier stood rigidly beside her, his eyes fastened to her sweat-streaked face. He wanted to run for Kleinman but he knew he shouldn't. She'd been like this twenty hours now—twenty hours of twisting, teeth-clenching agony. When it had started he'd cut his classes completely to stay with her.

He reached down trembling fingers to hold her damp hand. Her fingers clamped on his until the grip almost hurt. And, as he watched in numbed horror, he saw the face of the Earth-formed Martian passing across his wife's features—the slitted eyes, the thin, drawn-back lips, the white skin pulled rigidly over facial bones.

"*Pain! Pain! Spare me, fathers of my fathers, send me not to . . . !*"

There was a clicking in her throat, then silence. Her face suddenly relaxed and she lay there shivering weakly. He began to pat her face with a towel.

"In the yard, David," she muttered, still unconscious.

He bent over suddenly, his heart jolting.

"In the yard, David," she said. "I heard a sound and I went out. The stars were bright and there was a crescent moon. While I stood there I saw a white light come over the yard. I started to run back to the house but something hit me. Like a needle going into my back and my stomach. I cried out but then it was black and I couldn't remember. Anything. I tried to tell you David, but I couldn't remember, I couldn't remember, I couldn't . . ."

A hospital. In the corridor the father paces, his eyes feverish and haunted. The hall is hot and silent in the early August morning. He walks back and forth restlessly and his hands are white fists at his sides.

A door opens. The father whirls as a doctor comes out. The doctor draws down the cloth which has covered his mouth and nose. He looks at the man.

"*Your wife is well,*" *says the doctor.*

The father grabs the doctor's arm.

"*And the baby?*" *he asks.*

"*The baby is dead.*"

"Thank God," the father says.
Still wondering if in Africa, in Asia . . .

When Day is Dun ·•·•·•·•·•·•·•·•·•·•·•·•·•

> *Now bray goodnight to Earth*
> *For day is dun and man's estate*
> *Is cast into the vault of time*
> *Tuck in the graveclothes of forever*
> *Snuff the candle of attempt*
> *And let fall across our eyes*
> *That secret shroud of fusion*
> *With dark mystery.*

HE sat upon a rock and wrote his text on wood, using as pen a charcoaled finger. It is just, he mused, that the concluding theme should be set down with this digit in limbo, this beggarly palpus which once pointed at earth and sky to arrogate—I am your master, earth, your master, sky—and now lies grilled and temperate among the rubbish of our being.

I sit at Earth's wake and shed no tear.

Now he raised funereal eyes to float across the plain a glacial contemplation. Between his fingers rolled the sooty stylus and breath showed nasal evidence of his disgust. Now here am I, he brooded, perched upon a tepid boulder and inspecting that momentous joke which man has finally played upon himself.

He smote his brow and "Ah!" he cried, spiritually swept overboard. His great despairing head flopped forward on his chest and quavering moans beset his form. Birthright disemboweled, he sorrowed, golden chance arust, man has found the way—but to extinction.

Then he straightened up to make his back a ramrod of defiance. I shall not be a cur bowwowing, he avowed, this mortuary moment shall not have the best of me. Yea, though death bestride me and pluck with spectral fingers at my sores I shall not cry for less; I am inviolate.

The tatters quivered royally upon his shoulders. He bent to
write again:

> Now let me relish death
> As Earth gloats o'er her own demise
> With eyes of shimmering slag.

One leaden edge of tongue peeped out through barricades of
lip. Now he was hot.

> Birds crow a serenade to man
> Incinerated he
> Prostrate sautéed skeleton
> For all the gods to see
> Birds peck a saucy tune with bristly nibs
> Upon the xylophone of man's forgotten ribs.

"Capital! Capital!" he cried, stamping one unbooted foot
upon the ashy soil. In the excitement of the phrase, he dropped
his pen and stooped to pluck it up. Here, deposed antennae,
he grimaced the thought, and then he wrote again.

Odd it was, he scrolled, that man throughout his ill-tuned
history never ceased to plot man's own destruction.

> Chorus: More than fantastic
> This alien two
> Lived together
> And never knew.

He paused. How to continue, he wondered, how go on
with this concluding ledger of man's account. It demanded
bite, a trenchant instantaneity and yet deceptive calm like
forty fathom sea when gales are shrieking overhead. As there,
so here, he thought, I must suggest the titanic with polished
and well-mannered couplets. As for instance:

> Tell me here
> What difference there
> To burn in bias
> Or burn in fires.

I have no audience nor hope of one yet I go on composing
till what needs be said is said. And then I go—my own way.
He reached into his pocket for the twenty-seventh time and

drawing out the pistol, rolled its chamber with reflective finger. One bullet there he knew, his key to final rest. He gazed into the barrel's dark eye and did not quail. Yes, when it ends, he thought, when I have savored to the dregs this dark wine of most utter ruination, I shall press this to my head and blow away the last of man's complaints.

But now, he thought, back to my work. I have not done with mankind yet. A few words still remain, several discourteous racks of poesy. Shall I dispose so soon of what men always wanted most—the last word?

He flourished stylus, wrote:

> Be this the final entry
> In mankind's book of psalms
> He knit his shroud with atoms
> And dug his grave with bombs.

No. No, that did not catch the temper. He scratched it out. Let me see, he tapped a nail upon eroded teeth. What can I say? Ah!

> Man the better
> Man the higher
> Man the pumps
> The world's on fire.

But is this all quite fair, he mused amid chuckling, that I, as sole survivor, make such light of this unnatural tragedy which is the fall of man. Should I not instead sing out of mountainous regrets and summon tidal panegyrics which would wash away all bitterness with one great, cleansing surge. Should I not?

Man, man, he brooded, what have you done with your so excellent a world? Was it so small that you should scorn it, so drafty you should heat it to an incandescence, so unsightly you should rearrange its mountains and its seas?

"Ah," he said, "Oh . . . ah!"

His hands fell limp. A tear, two tears ran down his beak-shape nose to quiver on the tip, then fall upon the ground. And hiss.

What portent this, his mind groaned on, that I should be the last man's embittered tribe. The very last! Portent this, vast moment this—to be alone in all the world!

It is too much, he cried aloud within his head. I reel at the significance. He fingered the gun. How can I bear to hold this crushing weight upon my shoulders? Are my words appropriate, my sentiments all fit for this immensity of meaning?

He blinked, released the pistol. He was insulted by the question. What, I not up to it; what, my words inappropriate? He straightened up and bristled at the ash-envapored sky.

It is fitting, he declared, that these last measures be composed by a man alone. For shall a pack of masons clamor round the stone, entangling arms in clumsy eagerness to chisel out man's epitaph? And shall a host of scriveners haggle endlessly on man's obituary, muttering and wrangling like a coachless football team in huddle?

No this is best—one man to suffer beautiful agonies, one voice to speak the final words, then dot the i's and cross the t's and so farewell to man's domain—ending, if not sustaining, in gentle poetry.

And I that man, I that voice! Blessed with this final opportunity, my words alone without a million others to dilute them, my phrases only to ring out through all eternity, uncontradicted.

He sighed, he wrote again.

> It took this to make me individual
> The killing of all men
> Yea . . .

His head jerked up, alarmed, as, from far across the rubbled plain there came a sound.

"Eh?" he muttered. "What be that?"

He blinked, re-focused blood-streaked eyes, shook his head, squinted. And then his lower jaw slipped down and down until his mouth became a yawning cave.

A man was hobbling across the plain, waving a crooked arm at him. He watched the ashes rise in clouds of powder around the limping man and, in his mind, a great numbness struck.

A fellow creature! A comrade, another voice to hear, another . . .

The man stumbled up.

"Friend!" cried the man from out his startled face.

And abruptly, hearing this human voice usurp the mountainous, brooding silence, something suddenly snapped within the poet's brain.

"I shall not be robbed!" he cried. And he shot the man neatly between the eyes. Then he stepped across the peaceful body and went over to another rock of fused sidewalk.

He sat, shook back his sleeve. And, just before he bent to work again, he spun the empty chambers in his hand.

Ah, well, he sighed, for this moment, to have this glorious, shining doom alone—it was worth it.

Sonnet To a Parboiled Planet, he began . . .

The Curious Child ·························

LATE afternoon. An ordinary day, no different from a hundred other days. Sunlight was bronzing Jersey-facing windows, traffic herds were bleating in the streets, multitude heels clicked busily on the streets. Midtown offices were lethargic with waning labors. Five o'clock approaching on another day. In a few minutes the rush for subways, buses, taxis—in a few minutes, the great exodus.

Robert Graham sat at his desk finishing up a few last details, his pencil marking slowly across the sheets of paper. Finishing, he glanced up at the clock. Almost time to quit. He got up with a grunt and stretched slowly, exchanging a smile with the girl across the way. Then he went to the washroom and cleaned up, buttoned his collar and adjusted his tie, combed his dark hair into place. Everyone was getting ready to leave as clock hands stood seconds short of spelling five o'clock.

Back in the office, Robert Graham made a final check on his work. Then it was five and, dropping the papers into the basket labeled OUT, he moved for the coat rack. With wearied motions he slipped on his jacket and dropped the hat on his head. Another day ended. Now for the drive home, dinner, an evening at home—maybe television or a bridge game with the Olivers.

Robert Graham moved slowly down the hall toward people clustered around the elevator doors. He had to wait for two loads to go down before he got a place. Then he backed himself into the hot, crowded cubicle, the doors slid shut and he felt the floor droop beneath him.

As he descended he tried to remember what Lucille had asked him to pick up on the way home from work. Cinnamon? Pepper? Chives? He shook his head slowly. Lucille had told him to make a list but he'd refused. Lucille always told him to make a list and he always refused and always forgot later what it was he was supposed to get. Memory was an irksome thing.

The elevator doors slid open and he moved casually through the crowded lobby and out into the street.

Where it began.

My God, he thought, now where did I park the car? For a moment he felt vague amusement at the prospect of crumbling memory. Then he frowned and tried to remember.

There were several places he might have parked it that morning. There was one place right across from the building but a delivery truck had gotten there before he did. He hadn't had the time to wait and see if the truck were only going to be parked there a few moments so he'd driven on and turned right at the corner.

In the next block a woman in a yellow Pontiac had backed into an opening seconds before he could reach it. A few cars down there had been another spot but, stopping to let two women cross the street, he'd missed that one too.

But these thoughts weren't helping any. He still didn't remember where he was parked. He stopped walking and stood indecisively on the sidewalk, irritated by this ridiculous forgetfulness. He knew very well he was parked within a block or two of the building. Let's see, was it in that parking lot near the restaurant he ate lunch in—35 cents an hour—75 cents maximum—was it there?

No, not there. He felt sure of that.

A woman sagging under the weight of bundles collided with him. Robert Graham begged her pardon and moved against the building to get out of the way of traffic. He stood there peevishly trying to remember where he'd parked his car.

Well, this is absurd, he thought angrily. But anger didn't help; he still couldn't remember. His fingers twitched irritably. Come on, will you?—he asked himself. How many places were there he could have parked? Not many.

It was probably in front of the flower shop, he decided then. He often parked there.

He stepped away from the building impatiently and walked quickly to the corner where he turned right onto 22nd Street. He felt a trifle uneasy about not remembering where the car was parked. It was a small lapse, yes, but disconcerting when it came without any warning. He walked faster, feeling an unaccountable tenseness rising in his body.

The car wasn't in front of the flower shop.

He stood there looking blankly at the place where he usually parked. In his mind he visualized the green Ford standing at the curb, the whitewall tires, the—

The vision broke, it flowed apart and, abruptly, he found himself visualizing a blue Chevrolet standing there. He blinked once, his mind tripping over itself in confusion. His car was a green Ford, 1954 model. He didn't own that blue Chevrolet any more . . .

. . . did he?

Robert Graham felt his heart throbbing strangely, unnaturally, like a drum in a hollow room. What in God's name was wrong? First he forgot where he'd parked the car and now he didn't even seem sure what his car looked like. 1954 Ford, 1949 Chevrolet . . .

Suddenly, running through his mind were pictures of all the cars he'd ever owned from the air-cooled Franklin in 1932 to the '54 Ford. None of it made sense. It was as if the years were twisting over themselves, joining together past and present. 1947—the Plymouth, 1938—the Pontiac, 1945—Chevrolet, 1935 . . .

He stiffened with nervous impatience. This is ridiculous! He heard the words spilling across his aroused mind. I'm 37 years old, this is 1954 and I own a green Ford. He felt offended at this jumbled hodge-podge of memories, this mixture of the contemporary with the forgotten. Yes, it was very ridiculous when a man couldn't even remember where he'd parked his car. It was like a stupid dream. Yet it was more than that and, suddenly, he realized it.

It was frightening too.

A small thing really; just a parked car. But the car was part of his existence and that part had lost definition and that was frightening.

Enough, he told himself, let's get this thing straight. Where the hell am I parked? It was near there because he'd gotten to work on time and yet he hadn't reached downtown until a quarter of nine. *Chevrolet, Plymouth, Pontiac, Chevrolet, Dodge . . .* he ignored the car names streaming away in his mind. Where am I parked? Is it—

The thought broke off suddenly. Robert Graham stood rigid, an island in the tide of moving people, a look of stricken wonder on his face.

Since when did he own a car?

Muscle cords tensed, he stared at the curb with frightened eyes. What is it—oh, my God, *what is it?* Something fleeing from his mind, a knowledge severed and fading away, drifting . . .

Robert Graham relaxed and looked around him. Good Lord, what am I standing here for, he thought, I have to get home.

And he started for the subway.

Now what was it Lucille wanted? Cinnamon? Coffee? Paprika? God damn, why couldn't he remember? Well, never mind, he'd remember on the way home. He hurried around the corner, stopping to pick up the evening paper at the newsstand.

It was when he reached the entrance steps to the subway that he stopped again. He stood there while people pushed by him and clattered down into the dim passage.

Local to 14th Street—his mind was reciting—Brighton Express to—

But he lived in Manhattan.

Wait a minute now, wait—his mind hastened to prevent the return of that tight, restless feeling. 568 West 87th Street, that was where he lived. What was this nonsense about the Brighton Express? He started down the steps. That was where he used to live, in Brooklyn, 222 East 7th Street. But he didn't live there any . . .

He stopped again at the bottom of the steps, backing against the white-tiled wall with a confused look on his face. He lived in Brooklyn didn't he?—the little house near Prospect Park? He felt the muscles of his face tightening and felt breath rising shakily from his lungs. What is going on?—the question came feebly in his mind—what's the matter with me?

His head snapped around suddenly. What am I doing *here* when I own a car?—he thought confusedly.

A car? His cheek twitched. He didn't own a car. He—

Robert Graham started moving slowly, nervously down the passage. Manhattan, he was telling himself, I live in upper Manhattan, 568 West 87th Street, apartment 3-C. No, I don't, I live in Brooklyn at—5698 Manhill Avenue, Queens.

Queens! For God's sake he and Lucille hadn't lived in Queens for fifteen years!

57 Pine Drive, Allendale, New Jersey. Robert Graham stiffened, feeling a hot tightness in his stomach. His eyes moved dumbly around the murky passage, looking at the people who moved by him quickly, heading for the turnstiles. He stared at the sign next to him that showed a pink rhinoceros balancing on his horn a loaf of Feldman's Pumpernickel— *Fresher Than Tomorrow!* And his dazed mind struggled to catch hold of something rooted and immovable.

But addresses flowed across his mind in a bubbling current of numbers, streets, cities, states—Manhattan, Brooklyn, Queens, Staten Island, New Jersey—*No, for God's sake, he'd left Jersey when he was seventeen!*—5698 Manhill Avenue, 1902 Bedford Avenue, 57 Pine Drive, 3360 East 75th Street— *The Sheepshead Orphan Home.*

Robert Graham shuddered. It had been months since he'd thought of the orphan home where he'd spent seven years. He swallowed convulsively and realized that sweat was trickling down his temples, realized that he was still standing tensely in the subway passage, the newspaper clutched in his shaking hand while people rushed and jostled past his motionless form.

He closed his eyes and shuddered uncontrollably. All right, all right, he thought quickly, maybe I've been working too hard. The mind was a tricky mechanism after all—it could break down when you least expected it.

With trembling fingers he removed the wallet from his back trouser pocket. If I can't remember, he steadied himself, then I'll find the address on an identification card, that's all. I'll get home quickly, calmly and then I'll call Doctor Wolfe and—

Robert Graham stared at the driver's license in his wallet.

An almost inaudible whimper sounded in his throat. But I don't have a car, he heard his mind claiming, I don't—

His fingers twitched and the wallet fell to the concrete floor. Quickly, nervously, he bent over and picked it up. I'm sick, he thought, I'm *sick*, I have to get home right away. His eyes moved over the driver's license. *222 E. 7th Street, Brooklyn 18, N. Y.* He hurried down the passage, slipping the wallet into his coat pocket.

Something stopped him before the turnstiles—a twitch of memory, a stab of recollection—something about a failure to send change of address to the motor vehicle bureau; something about well-known furniture in an uptown Manhattan apartment, Lucille making supper and—

"Pardon it, mister, will you let me pass, please?" A young woman's irritated voice. Robert Graham backed quickly from the turnstile and moved against the tile wall again, a trickle of ice water down his back.

I don't know where I live.

He admitted it, confessed it to himself. I know all the places I've lived in all my life but I can't remember which one I live in *now.* It was insane but there it was. He remembered the apartment on 87th Street, and the little house in Brooklyn and the apartment in Queens and the bungalow on Staten Island and—

He felt dizzy standing there—dizzy and afraid. He wanted to grab someone and ask them to take him home, he wanted to tell them he was forgetting everything and they had to help him.

He took out the wallet again and opened it with shaking fingers. Social security number 128-16-5629—*Robert Graham.* That didn't help. A man knew his own name. But what about where he lived?

His library card—*Queens Public Library.* But he didn't live in Queens any more! He should have thrown that card away—it was long expired. Damn! His chest lurched and shuddered in with a gasp. What was happening to him? Nothing made sense. You left work on an ordinary Thursday afternoon and you—

Oh, no.

He forced together his shaking lips Thursday, it was Thursday. *Wasn't it?* His jaw sagged and he pulled it up tight as though he were suddenly afraid that his body were starting to come apart too. He stood shivering and sick-eyed in the dim passage looking at people push through the turnstiles, hearing the endless snap of the heavy wooden spokes as they turned.

What day is it? He had to face the question. It was Monday. He and Lucille had gone to the park yesterday and rowed around the lake. No, that wasn't right because he remembered settling that Barton-Dozier contract yesterday.

There was a clicking in his throat. He started away from the cool wall, then sank back, the wallet still clutched in his fingers. Thursday, he told himself with the stiffness of rigid will—it's Thursday, Thursday, *Thursday!* I left the offices of . . . of—

Oh, my God in heaven, who did he work for!

Again he started forward as if he were about to break into a terrified run. But he stopped with a trembling of legs and didn't know whether to go forward or backward or stay as he was.

Automatically, without even being conscious of it, he took a nickel from his trouser pocket and tried to put it into the turnstile slot.

Someone was crowding behind him. "What's the matter, bud?" Robert Graham heard the man say.

"This—this nickel," he said, "It doesn't go in."

The man stared at him a moment. Then his cheeks puffed out in repressed laughter. "Jeez," he said, "A nickel yet. Where you been?"

Robert Graham stared at the man, something cold and frightening pushing up from his stomach. Then, abruptly, he brushed past the man with a breathless grunt.

He stopped by the wall and looked back, his chest rising and falling jerkily with strained breaths. I don't know what I'm doing—he thought with a sense of absolute dread in him —I don't know where I'm going or where I live or who I work for. I don't even know what day it is! He felt sweat breaking out on his face and as he reached for his handkerchief he saw—

The newspaper! He held it up quickly and unfolded it.

Wednesday. A shuddering breath of relief emptied his lungs. There . . . there—at least there was something; something solid to hold onto. Wednesday. It was Wednesday. His throat moved convulsively. Thank God I know *that* much anyway.

He wiped away sweat. All right, he braced himself, something's happened to my mind. I have to get home and get proper care. Look in the wallet, there's got to be something with my address on it—a book club card, my draft card, my medical insurance card, my—

The paper fluttered down to the floor as Robert Graham's hands slapped frantically at his pockets. His fingers fled about his clothes and whimpering sounds filled his throat. No—oh, God, *no!*

"*I dropped it.*"

He said it aloud in a tight voice, suddenly refusing to let panic overwhelm him. I dropped it. Probably over by the turnstile. I was holding too many things in my hands—the paper, the nickel, the wallet. I dropped it. I'll go and find it now.

He walked slowly and rigidly down the passage, eyes moving over the floor that was dotted with blackened gum blobs and littered with candy wrappers, crushed soft-drink cups, newspaper scraps and torn open, flattened cigarette butts.

There was no wallet on the floor and there was no wallet near the turnstile.

He pressed one trembling hand to his cheek. No, no, this wasn't real, he assured himself, it was a dream, a crazy, distorted dream. He wandered about dazedly through the milling ranks of commuters, looking at the floor, searching for his wallet.

Maybe somebody picked it up—he suddenly thought.

"Pardon me," he said to the man in the change booth.

The man looked up with hurried annoyance and the people behind Robert Graham pressed their lips together with irritation.

"Well, what *is* it?" the man asked

"Did someone leave a wallet here?" Robert Graham asked him, "I—"

"No—no wallet."

Robert Graham stared blankly at him

"Mister, there's a lot of people waiting for change." the man said impatiently.

Robert Graham turned away and stumbled across the passage, breath faltering through his nostrils. He felt as if he were going to cry and he bit his lower lip. No, no, it wasn't true. He looked around with shocked, uncomprehending eyes. Everything seemed to be drifting away, existence clouding, his life obscured in a mist of riven memory.

"No!"

People stared at the taut-faced man who spoke the word so loudly as he stood in their hurrying midst.

No, this was absurd! This was the world, this was life, everyday life in 1954! He wasn't insane, he was as rational as the next man and he was going to get home fast.

Pretending he wasn't palsied with breaking nerves, he walked quickly back the passage toward the row of telephone booths against one side. All right, I can't remember where I live. I'll get the address from the directory. I'll look through every one. There can't be that many Robert—

Robert—

He stopped abruptly, paralyzed with fear. People hurried by him, rushing to their homes—people who knew where their homes were. People who knew their own last names.

"This is—"

Ridiculous? His hoarse, breathless voice couldn't finish the sentence. It wasn't ridiculous. It was terrifying, it was a sudden, complete horror in his life. His mind was going, it was going! He had to get home to, to, to—

Oh, my God!

Three women shied away from the trembling man who stood in the middle of the passage whimpering. They looked back at him curiously as they hurried by.

He shoved through the crowd frenziedly. "I have to get help," he kept muttering, "I have to get—"

There seemed to be a strange cloud moving down the passage with the approaching people. They didn't seem to see it, even though they were unable to walk right through it.

But he saw it. And a gagging cry started in his throat as he turned and staggered back down the passage on weakening legs. I don't know who I am—the words kept stabbing at him as he tried to escape—I don't know who I am! He turned and looked back over his shoulder. The cloud was drawing closer rapidly, it was only a few feet from him. He whirled.

The man screamed.

Then night flooded over him—night broken by spurts of light that were like fish in a dark lake, half seen as flashes of shimmering movement. He thought he saw a strange face. He thought he heard someone say,

"Come along now."

Then he collapsed. Then blackness swirled into his brain and he forgot everything.

He lay staring as the man talked to him, a strange hairless man in a glistening tunic.

"We've been looking for you a long time," the man said. "You see when you were a child of two living with your father, who was a scientist, you went into a time screen, out of curiosity, and accidentally set it into motion.

"We knew you'd gone back to 1919 but we didn't know where you'd gone. It was a hard search. But now you're back.

"We're sorry it was such a frightening experience but there was nothing we could do. You see, the closer we got to you the more your past and present was jumbled in your mind until, as we reached you, you lost hold of everything."

The man smiled thinly as Robert looked out dazedly at the strange, glittering city.

"You belong here," said the man, "Welcome."

The Funeral ••••••••••••••••••••••••••••••••

MORTON Silkline was in his office musing over floral arrangements for the Beaumont obsequies when the chiming strains of "I am Crossing o'er the Bar to Join the Choir Invisible" announced an entrant into Clooney's Cut-Rate Catafalque

Blinking meditation from his liver-colored eyes, Silkline knit his fingers to a placid clasp, then settled back against the sable leather of his chair, a smile of funereal welcome on his

lips. Out in the stillness of the hallway, footsteps sounded on
the muffling carpet, moving with a leisured pace and, just
before the tall man entered, the desk clock buzzed a curt ac-
knowledgment to 7:30.

Rising as if caught in the midst of a tête-à-tête with death's
bright angel, Morton Silkline circled the glossy desk on whispering feet and extended one flaccid-fingered hand.

"Ah, good evening, sir," he dulceted, his smile a precise
compendium of sympathy and welcome, his voice a calculated
drip of obeisance.

The man's handshake was cool and bone-cracking but Silkline managed to repress reaction to a momentary flicker of
agony in his cinnamon eyes.

"Won't you be seated?" he murmured, fluttering his bruised
hand toward The Grieved One's chair.

"Thank you," said the man, his voice a baritoned politeness
as he seated himself, unbuttoning the front of his velvet-
collared overcoat and placing his dark homburg on the glass
top of the desk.

"My name is Morton Silkline," Silkline offered as he re-
circled to his chair, settling on the cushion like a diffident
butterfly.

"Asper," said the man.

"May I say that I am proud to meet you, Mister Asper?"
Silkline purred.

"Thank you," said the man.

"Well, now," Silkline said, getting down to the business of
bereavement, "what can Clooney's do to ease your sorrow?"

The man crossed his dark-trousered legs. "I should like," he
said, "to make arrangements for a funeral service."

Silkline nodded once with an I-am-here-to-succor smile.

"Of course," he said, "you've come to the right place, sir."
His gaze elevated a few inches beyond the pale. "When loved
ones lie upon that lonely couch of everlasting sleep," he re-
cited, "let Clooney draw the coverlet."

His gaze returned and he smiled with a modest subservience.
"Mrs. Clooney," he said, "made that up. We like to pass it
along to those who come to us for comfort."

"Very nice," the man said. "Extremely poetic. But to details: I'd like to engage your largest parlor."

"I see," Silkline answered, restraining himself, only with

effort, from the rubbing together of hands. "That would be our Eternal Rest Room."

The man nodded affably. "Fine. And I would also like to buy your most expensive casket."

Silkline could barely restrain a boyish grin. His cardiac muscle flexing vigorously, he forced back folds of sorrowful solicitude across his face.

"I'm sure," he said, "that can be effected."

"With gold trimmings?" the man said.

"Why . . . yes," said Director Silkline, clicking audibly as he swallowed. "I'm certain that Clooney's can satisfy your every need in this time of grievous loss. Naturally—" His voice slipped a jot from the condoling to the fiduciary "—it will entail a bit more expenditure than might, otherwise, be—"

"The cost is of no importance," said the man, waving it away. "I want only the best of everything."

"It will be so, sir, it *will* be so," declared a fervent Morton Silkline.

"Capital," said the man.

"Now," Silkline went on, briskly, "will you be wishing our Mr. Mossmound to deliver his sermon *On Crossing The Great Divide* or have you a denominational ceremony in mind?"

"I think not," said the man, shaking his head, thoughtfully. "A friend of mine will speak at the services."

"Ah," said Silkline, nodding, "I see."

Reaching forward, he plucked the gold pen from its onyx holder, then with two fingers of his left hand, drew out an application form from the ivory box on his desk top. He looked up with the accredited expression for the Asking of Painful Questions.

"And," he said, "what is the name of the deceased, may I ask?"

"Asper," said the man.

Silkline glanced up, smiling politely. "A relative?" he inquired.

"Me," said the man.

Silkline's laugh was a faint coughing

"I beg your pardon?" he said. "I thought you said—"

"*Me*," the man repeated.

"But, I don't—"

"You see," the man explained, "I never had a proper going off. It was catch-as-catch-can, you might say; all improvised. Nothing—how shall I put it?—tasty." The man shrugged his wide shoulders. "I always regretted that," he said. "I always intended to make up for it."

Morton Silkline had returned the pen to its holder with a decisive jabbing of the hand and was on his feet, pulsing with a harsh distemper.

"Indeed, sir," he commented. "Indeed."

The man looked surprised at the vexation of Morton Silkline.

"I—" he began.

"I am as fully prepared as the next fellow for a trifling badinage," Silkline interrupted, "but not during work hours. I think you fail to realize, sir, just where you are. This is Clooney's, a much respected ossuary; not a place for trivial joking or—"

He shrank back and stared, open-mouthed, at the black-garbed man who was suddenly on his feet, eyes glittering with a light most unseemly.

"This," the man said, balefully, "is not a joke."

"Is not—" Silkline could manage no more.

"I came here," said the man, "with a most serious purpose in mind." His eyes glowed now like cherry-bright coals. "And I expect this purpose to be gratified," he said. "Do you understand?"

"I—"

"On Tuesday next," the man continued, "at 8:30 P.M., my friends and I will arrive here for the service. You will have everything prepared by then. Full payment will be made directly following the exequies. Are there any questions?"

"I—"

"I need hardly remind you," said the man, picking up his homberg, "that this affair is of the utmost importance to me." He paused potently before allowing his voice to sink to a forbidding basso profundo. "I expect all to go well."

Bowing a modicum from the waist, the man turned and moved in two regal strides across the office, pausing a moment at the door.

"Uh . . . one additional item," he said. "That mirror in the foyer . . . remove it. And, I might add, any others that my friends and I might chance upon during our stay in your parlors."

The man raised one gray-gloved hand. "And now good-night."

When Morton Silkline reached the hall, his customer was just flapping out a small window. Quite suddenly, Morton Silkline found the floor.

They arrived at 8:30, conversing as they entered the foyer of Clooney's to be met by a tremble-legged Morton Silkline about whose eyes hung the raccoon circles of sleepless nights.

"Good evening," greeted the tall man, noting, with a pleased nod, the absence of the wall mirror.

"Good—" was the total of Silkline's wordage.

His vocal cords went slack and his eyes, embossed with daze, moved from figure to figure in the tall man's coterie—the gnarl-faced hunchback whom Silkline heard addressed as Ygor; the peak-hatted crone upon whose cceremented shoulder a black cat crouched; the hulking hairy-handed man who clicked yellow teeth together and regarded Silkline with markedly more than casual eyes; the waxen-featured little man who licked his lips and smiled at Silkline as though he possessed some inner satisfaction; the half-dozen men and women in evening dress, all cherry-eyed and -lipped and—Silkline cringed—superbly toothed.

Silkline hung against the wall, mouth a circular entrance way, hands twitching feebly at his sides as the chatting assemblage passed him by, headed for the Eternal Rest Room.

"Join us," the tall man said.

Silkline stirred fitfully from the wall and stumble-wove an erratic path down the hallway, eyes still saucer-round with stupor.

"I trust," the man said pleasantly, "everything is well prepared."

"Oh," Silkline squeaked. "Oh—oh, yes."

"Sterling," said the man.

When the two of them entered the room, the others were grouped in an admiring semicircle about the casket.

"Is good," the hunchback was muttering to himself. "Is good box."

"Aye, be that a casket or be that a casket, Delphinia?" cackled the ancient crone and Delphinia replied, "Mrrrrow."

While the others nodded, smiling felicitous smiles and murmuring, "Ah. Ah."

Then one of the evening-dressed women said, "Let Ludwig see," and the semicircle split open so the tall man could pass.

He ran his long fingers over the gold work on the sides and top of the casket, nodding appreciatively. "Splendid," he murmured, voice husky with emotion. "Quite splendid. Just what I always wanted."

"You picked a beauty, lad," said a tall white-haired gentleman.

"Well, try it on fer size!" the chuckling crone declared.

Smiling boyishly, Ludwig climbed into the casket and wriggled into place. "A perfect fit," he said, contentedly.

"Master look good," mumbled Ygor, nodding crookedly. "Look good in box."

Then the hairy-handed man demanded they begin because he had an appointment at 9:15, and everyone hurried to their chairs.

"Come, duck," said the crone, waving a scrawny hand at the ossified Silkline. "Sit by my side. I likes the pretty boys, I do, eh, Delphinia?" Delphinia said, "Mrrrrrow."

"Please, Jenny," Ludwig Asper asked her, opening his eyes a moment. "Be serious. You know what this means to me."

The crone shrugged. "Aye. Aye," she muttered, then pulled off her peaked hat and fluffed at dank curls as the zombie-stiff Silkline quivered into place beside her, aided by the guiding hand of the little waxen-faced man.

"Hello, pretty boy," the crone whispered, leaning over and jabbing a spear-point elbow into Silkline's ribs.

Then the tall white-haired gentleman from the Carpathian zone rose and the service began.

"Good friends," said the gentleman, "we have gathered ourselves within these bud-wreathed walls to pay homage to our comrade, Ludwig Asper, whom the pious and unyielding fates have chosen to pluck from existence and place within that bleak sarcophagus of all eternity."

"*Ci-gît*," someone murmured; "*Chant du cygne*," another. Ygor wept and the waxen-featured little man, sitting on the other side of Morton Silkline, leaned over to murmur, "*Tasty*," but Silkline wasn't sure it was in reference to the funeral address.

"And thus," the gentleman from Carpathia went on, "we

collect our bitter selves about this, our comrade's bier; about this litter of sorrow, this cairn, this cromlech, this unhappy tumulus—"

"*Clearer, clearer,*" demanded Jenny, stamping one pointy-toed and petulant shoe. "Mrrrrow," said Delphinia and the crone winked one blood-laced eye at Silkline who shrank away only to brush against the little man who gazed at him with berry eyes and murmured once again, "*Tasty.*"

The white-haired gentleman paused long enough to gaze down his royal nose at the crone. Then he continued, "—this mastaba, this sorrowing tope, this ghat, this dread dokhma—"

"What did he say?" asked Ygor, pausing in mid-sob. "What, what?"

"This ain't no declamation tourney, lad," the crone declared. "Keep it crisp, I say."

Ludwig raised his head again, a look of pained embarrassment on his face, "Jenny," he said. "*Please.*"

"Aaaah . . . *toad's teeth!*" snapped the crone jadedly, and Delphinia moaned.

"*Requiescas in pace,* dear brother," the Count went on, testily. "The memory of you shall not perish with your untimely sepulture. You are, dear friend, not so much out of the game as playing on another field."

At which the hairy-handed man rose and hulked from the room with the guttural announcement, "Go," and Silkline felt himself rendered an icicle as he heard a sudden padding of clawed feet on the hallway rug and a baying which echoed back along the walls.

"Ullgate says he has a dinner appointment," the little man asided with a bright-eyed smile. Silkline's chair creaked with shuddering.

The white-haired gentleman stood tall and silent, his red eyes shut, his mouth tight-lipped with aristocratic pique.

"Count," pleaded Ludwig. "Please."

"Am I to endure these vlugar calumnies?" asked the Count. "These—"

"Well, *la-de-da,*" crooned Jenny to her cat.

"Silence, woman!" roared the Count, his head disappearing momentarily in a white, trailing vapor, then reappearing as he gained control.

Ludwig sat up, face a twist of aggravation. "Jenny," he declared, "I think you'd better leave."

"You think to throw old Jenny of Boston out?" the crone challenged. "Well, you got a think that's coming then!"

And, as a shriveling Silkline watched, the crone slapped on her pointed hat and sprouted minor lightning at the fingertips. A snail-backed Delphinia bristled ebony hairs as the Count stepped forward, hand outstretched, to clamp onto the crone's shoulder, then stiffened in mid-stride as sizzling fire ringed him.

"Haa!" crowed Jenny while a horror-stricken Silkline gagged, "My rug!"

"Jen-ny!" Ludwig cried, clambering out. The crone gestured and all the flowers in the room began exploding like popcorn.

"No-o," moaned Silkline as the curtains flared and split. Chairs were overthrown. The Count bicarbonated to a hissing stream of white which flew at Jenny—who flung up her arms and vanished, cat and all, in an orange spume as the air grew thick with squeaks and rib-winged flapping.

Just before the bulbous-eyed Morton Silkline toppled forward, the waxen-faced man leaned over, smiling toothfully, squeezed the Director's numbed arm and murmured, "Tasty."

Then Silkline was at one with the rug.

Morton Silkline slumped in his sable-leathered chair, still twitching slightly even though a week had passed since the nerve-splitting event. On his desk lay the note that Ludwig Asper had left pinned to his unconscious chest.

Sir, it read. *Accept, in addition to this bag of gold (which I trust will cover all costs) my regrets that full decorum was not effected by the guests at my funeral. For, save for that, the entire preparation was most satisfactory to me.*

Silkline put down the note and grazed a loving touch across the hill of glinting coins on his desk. Through judicious inquiry, he had gleaned the information that a connection in Mexico (namely, a cosmetician nephew in Carillo's Cut-Rate Catacomb) could safely dispose of the gold at mutual profit. All things considered, the affair had not been really as bad as all—

Morton Silkline looked up as something entered his office.

He would have chosen to leap back screaming and vanish in the flowered pattern of the wallpaper but he was too petrified. Once more gape-mouthed, he stared at the huge, tentacled, ocher-dripping shapelessness that weaved and swayed before him.

"A friend," it said politely, "recommended you to me."

Silkline sat bug-eyed for a lengthy moment but then his twitching hand accidentally touched the gold again. And he found strength.

"You've come," he said, breathing through his mouth, "to the right place—uh . . . sir. *Pomps*—" He swallowed mightily and braced himself "—*for all circumstances.*"

He reached for his pen, blowing away the yellow-green smoke which was beginning to obscure the office.

"Name of the deceased?" he asked, businesslike.

The Last Day ••••••••••••••••••••••••••••

HE woke up and the first thing he thought was —*the last night is gone.*

He had slept through half of it.

He lay there on the floor and looked up at the ceiling. The walls still glowed reddish from the outside light. There was no sound in the livingroom but that of snoring.

He looked around.

There were bodies sprawled out all over the room. They were on the couch, slumped on chairs, curled up on the floor. Some were covered with rugs. Two of them were naked.

He raised up on one elbow and winced at the shooting pains in his head. He closed his eyes and held them tightly shut for a moment. Then he opened them again. He ran his tongue over the inside of his dry mouth. There was still a stale taste of liquor and food in his mouth.

He rested on his elbow as he looked around the room again, his mind slowly registering the scene.

Nancy and Bill lying in each other's arms, both naked.

Norman curled up in an arm chair, his thin face taut as he slept. Mort and Mel lying on the floor, covered with dirty throw rugs. Both snoring. Others on the floor.

Outside the red glow.

He looked at the window and his throat moved. He blinked. He looked down over his long body. He swallowed again.

I'm alive, he thought, and it's all true.

He rubbed his eyes. He took a deep breath of the dead air in the apartment.

He knocked over a glass as he struggled to his feet. The liquor and soda sloshed over the rug and soaked into the dark blue weave.

He looked around at the other glasses, broken, kicked over, hurled against the wall. He looked at the bottles all over, all empty.

He stood staring around the room. He looked at the record player overturned, the albums all strewn around, jagged pieces of records in crazy patterns on the rug.

He remembered.

It was Mort who had started it the night before. He had suddenly rushed to the playing record machine and shouted drunkenly,

"What the hell is music anymore! Just a lot of noise!"

And he had driven the point of his shoe against the front of the record player and knocked it against the wall. He had lurched over and down on his knees. He had struggled up with the player in his beefy arms and heaved the entire thing over on its back and kicked it again.

"The hell with music!" he had yelled, "I hate the crap anyway!"

Then he'd started to drag records out of their albums and their envelopes and snap them over his kneecap.

"Come on!" he'd yelled to everybody, "Come on!"

And it had caught on. The way all crazy ideas had caught on in those last few days.

Mel had jumped up from making love to a girl. He had flung records out the windows, scaling them far across the street. And Charlie had put aside his gun for a moment to stand at the windows too and try to hit people in the street with thrown records.

Richard had watched the dark saucers bounce and shatter on the sidewalks below. He'd even thrown one himself. Then he'd just turned away and let the others rage. He'd taken Mel's girl into the bedroom and had relations with her.

He thought about that as he stood waveringly in the reddish light of the room.

He closed his eyes a moment.

Then he looked at Nancy and remembered taking her too sometime in the jumble of wild hours that had been yesterday and last night.

She looked vile now, he thought. She'd always been an animal. Before, though, she'd had to veil it. Now, in the final twilight of everything she could revel in the only thing she'd ever really cared about.

He wondered if there were any people left in the world with real dignity. The kind that was still there when it no longer was necessary to impress people with it.

He stepped over the body of a sleeping girl. She had on only a slip. He looked down at her tangled hair, at her red lips smeared, the tight unhappy frown printed on her face.

He glanced into the bedroom as he passed it. There were three girls and two men in the bed.

He found the body in the bathroom.

It was thrown carelessly in the tub and the shower curtain torn down to cover it. Only the legs showed, dangling ridiculously over the front rim of the tub.

He drew back the curtain and looked at the blood-soaked shirt, at the white, still face.

Charlie.

He shook his head, then turned away and washed his face and hands at the sink. It didn't matter. Nothing mattered. As a matter of fact, Charlie was one of the lucky ones now. A member of the legion who had put their heads into ovens, or cut their wrists or taken pills or done away with themselves in the accepted fashions of suicide.

As he looked at his tired face in the mirror he thought of cutting his wrists. But he knew he couldn't. Because it took more than just despair to incite self-destruction.

He took a drink of water. Lucky, he thought, there's still water running. He didn't suppose there was a soul left to run the water system. Or the electric system or the gas system or the telephone system or any system for that matter.

What fool would work on the last day of the world?

*   *   *   *

Spencer was in the kitchen when Richard went in.

He was sitting in his shorts at the table looking at his hands. On the stove some eggs were frying. The gas was working then too, Richard thought.

"Hello," he said to Spencer.

Spencer grunted without looking up. He stared at his hands. Richard let it go. He turned the gas down a little. He took bread out of the cupboard and put it in the electric toaster. But the toaster didn't work. He shrugged and forgot about it.

"What time is it?"

Spencer was looking at him with the question.

Richard looked at his watch.

"It stopped," he said.

They looked at each other.

"Oh," Spencer said. Then he asked, "What day is it?"

Richard thought. "Sunday, I think," he said.

"I wonder if people are at church," Spencer said.

"Who cares?"

Richard opened the refrigerator.

"There aren't any more eggs," Spencer said.

Richard shut the door.

"No more eggs," he said dully, "No more chickens. No more anything."

He leaned against the wall with a shuddering breath and looked out the window at the red sky.

Mary, he thought. Mary, who I should have married. Who I let go. He wondered where she was. He wondered if she were thinking about him at all.

Norman came trudging in, groggy with sleep and hangover. His mouth hung open. He looked dazed.

"Morning," he slurred.

"Good morning, merry sunshine," Richard said, without mirth.

Norman looked at him blankly. Then he went over to the sink and washed out his mouth. He spit the water down the drain.

"Charlie's dead," he said.

"I know," Richard said.

"Oh. When did it happen?"

"Last night," Richard told him. "You were unconscious. You remember how he kept saying he was going to shoot us all? Put us out of our misery?"

"Yeah," Norman said. "He put the muzzle against my head. He said feel how cool it is."

"Well, he got in a fight with Mort," Richard said. "The gun went off." He shrugged. "That was it."

They looked at each other without expression.

Then Norman turned his head and looked out the window. "It's still up there," he muttered.

They looked up at the great flaming ball in the sky that crowded out the sun, the moon, the stars.

Norman turned away, his throat moving. His lips trembled and he clamped them together.

"Jesus," he said. "It's *today*."

He looked up at the sky again.

"Today," he repeated. "*Everything*."

"Everything," said Richard.

Spencer got up and turned off the gas. He looked down at the eggs for a moment. Then he said,

"What the hell did I fry these for?"

He dumped them into the sink and they slid greasily over the white surface. The yolks burst and spurted smoking, yellow fluid over the enamel.

Spencer bit his lips. His face grew hard.

"I'm taking her again," he said, suddenly.

He pushed past Richard and dropped his shorts off as he turned the corner into the hallway.

"There goes Spencer," Richard said.

Norman sat down at the table. Richard stayed at the wall.

In the livingroom they heard Nancy suddenly call out at the top of her strident voice.

"Hey, wake up everybody! Watch me do it! Watch me everybody, *watch me!*"

Norman looked at the kitchen doorway for a moment. Then something gave inside of him and he slumped his head forward on his arms on the table. His thin shoulders shook.

"I did it too," he said brokenly. "I did it too. Oh God, what did I come here for?"

"Sex," Richard said. "Like all the rest of us. You thought you could end your life in carnal, drunken bliss."

Norman's voice was muffled.

"I can't die like that," he sobbed. "I can't."

"A couple of billion people are doing it," Richard said. "When the sun hits us, they'll still be at it. What a sight."

The thought of a world's people indulging themselves in one last orgy of animalism made him shudder. He closed his eyes and pressed his forehead against the wall and tried to forget.

But the wall was warm.

Norman looked up from the table.

"Let's go home," he said.

Richard looked at him. "Home?" he said.

"To our parents. My mother and father. Your mother."

Richard shook his head.

"I don't want to," he said.

"But I can't go alone."

"Why?"

"Because . . . I can't. You know how the streets are full of guys just *killing* everybody they meet."

Richard shrugged.

"Why don't you?" Norman asked.

"I don't want to see her."

"Your *mother*?"

"Yes."

"You're crazy," Norman said. "Who else is there to . . ."

"No."

He thought of his mother at home waiting for him. Waiting for him on the last day. And it made him ill to think of him delaying, of maybe never seeing her again.

But he kept thinking—How can I go home and have her try to make me pray? Try to make me read from the Bible, spend these last hours in a muddle of religious absorption?

He said it again for himself.

"No."

Norman looked lost. His chest shook with a swallowed sob.

"I want to see my mother," he said.

"Go ahead," Richard said, casually.

But his insides were twisting themselves into knots. To never see her again. Or his sister and her husband and her daughter.

Never to see any of them again.

He sighed. It was no use fighting it. In spite of everything, Norman was right. Who else was there in the world to turn to? In a wide world, about to be burned, was there any other person who loved him above all others?

"Oh . . . all right," he said. "Come on. Anything to get out of this place."

*   *   *   *

The apartment house hall smelled of vomit. They found the janitor dead drunk on the stairs. They found a dog in the foyer with its head kicked in.

They stopped as they came out the entrance of the building. Instinctively they looked up.

At the red sky, like molten slag. At the fiery wisps that fell like hot rain drops through the atmosphere. At the gigantic ball of flame that kept coming closer and closer that blotted out the universe.

They lowered their watering eyes. It hurt to look. They started walking along the street. It was very warm.

"December," Richard said. "It's like the tropics."

As they walked along in silence, he thought of the tropics, of the poles, of all the world's countries he would never see. Of all the things he would never do.

Like hold Mary in his arms and tell her, as the world was ending, that he loved her very much and was not afraid.

"Never," he said, feeling himself go rigid with frustration.

"What?" Norman said.

"Nothing. Nothing."

As they walked, Richard felt something heavy in his jacket pocket. It bumped against his side. He reached in and drew out the object.

"What's that?" Norman asked.

"Charlie's gun," Richard said. "I took it last night so nobody else would get hurt."

His laughter was harsh.

"So nobody else would get killed," he said bitterly. "Jesus, I ought to be on the stage."

He was about to throw it away when he changed his mind. He slid it back into his pocket.

"I may need it," he said.

Norman wasn't listening.

"Thank God nobody stole my car. Oh . . . !"

Somebody had thrown a rock through the windshield.

"What's the difference?" Richard said.

"I . . . none, I suppose."

They got into the front seat and brushed the glass off the

cushion. It was stuffy in the car. Richard pulled off his jacket and threw it out. He put the gun in his side pants pocket.

As Norman drove downtown, they passed people in the street.

Some were running around wildly, as if they were searching for something. Some were fighting with each other. Strewn all over the sidewalks were bodies of people who had leaped from windows and been struck down by speeding cars. Buildings were on fire, windows shattered from the explosions of unlit gas jets.

There were people looting stores.

"What's the matter with them?" Norman asked, miserably. "Is that how they want to spend their last day?"

"Maybe that's how they spent their whole life," Richard answered.

He leaned against the door and gazed at the people they passed. Some of them waved at him. Some cursed and spat. A few threw things at the speeding car.

"People die the way they lived," he said. "Some good, some bad."

"*Look out!*"

Norman cried out as a car came careening down the street on the wrong side. Men and women hung out of the window shouting and singing and waving bottles.

Norman twisted the wheel violently and they missed the car by inches.

"Are they crazy!" he said.

Richard looked out through the back window. He saw the car skid, saw it get out of control and go crashing into a store front and turn over on its side, the wheels spinning crazily.

He turned back front without speaking. Norman kept looking ahead grimly, his hands on the wheel, white and tense.

Another intersection.

A car came speeding across their path. Norman jammed on the brakes with a gasp. They crashed against the dashboard getting their breath knocked out.

Then, before Norman could get the car started again, a gang of teen-age boys with knives and clubs came dashing into the intersection. They'd been chasing the other car. Now they changed direction and flung themselves at the car that held Norman and Richard.

Norman threw the car into first and gunned across the street.

A boy jumped on the back of the car. Another tried for the running board, missed and went spinning over the street. Another jumped on the running board and grabbed the door handle. He slashed at Richard with a knife.

"Gonna kill ya bastids!" yelled the boy. "Sonsabitches!"

He slashed again and tore open the back of the seat as Richard jerked his shoulder to the side.

"Get out of here!" Norman screamed, trying to watch the boy and the street ahead at the same time.

The boy tried to open the door as the car wove wildly up Broadway. He slashed again but the car's motion made him miss.

"I'll get ya!" he screamed in a fury of brainless hate.

Richard tried to open the door and knock the boy off, but he couldn't. The boy's twisted white face thrust in through the window. He raised his knife.

Richard had the gun now. He shot the boy in the face.

The boy flung back from the car with a dying howl and landed like a sack of rocks. He bounced once, his left leg kicked and then he lay still.

Richard twisted around.

The boy on the back was still hanging on, his crazed face pressed against the back window. Richard saw his mouth moving as the boy cursed.

"Shake him off!" he said.

Norman headed for the sidewalk, then suddenly veered back into the street. The boy hung on. Norman did it again. The boy still clung to the back.

Then on the third time he lost his grip and went off. He tried to run along the street but his momentum was too great and he went leaping over the curb and crashing into a plate glass window, arms stuck up in front of him to ward off the blow.

They sat in the car, breathing heavily. They didn't talk for a long while. Richard flung the gun out the window and watched it clatter on the concrete and bounce off a hydrant. Norman started to say something about it, then stopped.

The car turned into Fifth Avenue and started downtown at sixty miles an hour. There weren't many cars.

They passed churches. People were packed inside them. They overflowed out onto the steps.

"Poor fools," Richard muttered, his hands still shaking.

Norman took a deep breath.

"I wish I was a poor fool," he said. "A poor fool who could believe in something."

"Maybe," Richard said. Then he added, "I'd rather spend the last day believing what I think is true."

"The last day," Norman said, "I . . ."

He shook his head. "I can't believe it," he said. "I read the papers. I see that . . . thing up there. I know it's going to happen. But, God! The end?"

He looked at Richard for a split second.

"Nothing afterward?" he said.

Richard said, "I don't know."

                    *   *   *   *

At 14th Street, Norman drove to the East Side, then sped across the Manhattan Bridge. He didn't stop for anything, driving around bodies and wrecked cars. Once he drove over a body and Richard saw his face twitch as the wheel rolled over the dead man's leg.

"They're all lucky," Richard said. "Luckier than we are."

They stopped in front of Norman's house in downtown Brooklyn. Some kids were playing ball in the street. They didn't seem to realize what was happening. Their shouts sounded very loud in the silent street. Richard wondered if their parents knew where the children were. Or cared.

Norman was looking at him.

"Well . . . ?" he started to say.

Richard felt his stomach muscles tightening. He couldn't answer.

"Would you . . . like to come in for a minute?" Norman asked.

Richard shook his head.

"No," he said. "I better get home. I . . . should see her. My mother, I mean."

"Oh."

Norman nodded. Then he straightened up. He forced a momentary calm over himself.

"For what it's worth, Dick," he said, "I consider you my best friend and . . ."

He faltered. He reached out and gripped Richard's hand.

Then he pushed out of the car, leaving the keys in the ignition.

"Solong," he said hurriedly.

Richard watched his friend run around the car and move for the apartment house. When he had almost reached the door, Richard called out.

"Norm!"

Norman stopped and turned. The two of them looked at each other. All the years they had known each other seemed to flicker between them.

Then Richard managed to smile. He touched his forehead in a last salute.

"Solong, Norm," he said.

Norman didn't smile. He pushed through the door and was gone.

Richard looked at the door for a long time. He started the motor. Then he turned it off again thinking that Norman's parents might not be home.

After a while he started it again and began the trip home. As he drove he kept thinking.

The closer he got to the end, the less he wanted to face it. He wanted to end it now. Before the hysterics started.

Sleeping pills, he decided. It was the best way. He had some at home. He hoped there were enough left. There might not be any left in the corner drug store. There'd been a rush for sleeping pills during those last few days. Entire families took them together.

He reached the house without event. Overhead the sky was an incandescent crimson. He felt the heat on his face like waves from a distant oven. He breathed in the heated air.

He unlocked the front door and walked in slowly.

I'll probably find her in the front room, he thought. Surrounded by her books, praying, exhorting invisible powers to succor her as the world prepared to fry itself.

She wasn't in the front room.

He searched the house. And, as he did so, his heart began to beat quickly and when he knew she really wasn't there he felt a great hollow feeling in his stomach. He knew that his talk about not wanting to see her had been just talk. He loved her. And she was the only one left now.

He searched for a note in her room, in his, in the livingroom.

"Mom," he said, "Mom, where are you?"

He found the note in the kitchen. He picked it up from the table.

Richard, Darling.

I'm at your sister's house. Please come there. Don't make me spend the last day without you. Don't make me leave this world without seeing your dear face again. Please.

The last day.

There it was in black and white. And, of all people, it had been his mother to write down the words. She who had always been so skeptical of his taste for material science. Now admitting that science's last prediction.

Because she couldn't doubt anymore. Because the sky was filled with flaming evidence and no one could doubt anymore.

The whole world going. The staggering detail of evolutions and revolutions, of strifes and clashes, of endless continuities of centuries streaming back into the clouded past, of rocks and trees and animals and men. All to pass. In a flash, in a moment. The pride, the vanity of man's world incinerated by a freak of astronomical disorder.

What point was there to all of it then? None, none at all. Because it was all ending.

He got sleeping pills from the medicine cabinet and left. He drove to his sister's house thinking about his mother as he passed through the streets littered with everything from empty bottles to dead people.

If only he didn't dread the thought of arguing with his mother on this last day. Of disputing with her about her God and her conviction.

He made up his mind not to argue. He'd force himself to make their last day a peaceful one. He would accept her simple devotion and not hack at her faith anymore.

The front door was locked at Grace's house. He rang the bell and, after a moment, heard hurried steps inside.

He heard Ray shout inside, "Don't open it Mom! It may be that gang again!"

"It's Richard, I know it is!" his mother called back.

Then the door was open and she was embracing him and crying happily.

He didn't speak. Finally he said softly,

"Hello Mom."

*   *   *   *

His niece Doris played all afternoon in the front room while Grace and Ray sat motionless in the livingroom looking at her.

If I were with Mary, Richard kept thinking. If only we were together today. Then he thought they might have had children. And he would have to sit like Grace and know that the few years his child had lived would be its only years.

The sky grew brighter as evening approached. It flowed with violent crimson currents. Doris stood quietly at the window and looked at it. She hadn't laughed all day or cried. And Richard thought to himself—she knows.

And thought too that at any moment his mother would ask them all to pray together. To sit and read the Bible and hope for divine charity.

But she didn't say anything. She smiled. She made supper. Richard stood with her in the kitchen as she made supper.

"I may not wait," he told her. "I . . . may take sleeping pills."

"Are you afraid, son?" she asked.

"Everybody is afraid," he said.

She shook her head. "Not everybody," she said.

Now, he thought, it's coming. That smug look, the opening line.

She gave him a dish with the vegetable and they all sat down to eat.

During supper none of them spoke except to ask for food. Doris never spoke once. Richard sat looking at her from across the table.

He thought about the night before. The crazy drinking, the fighting, the carnal abuses. He thought of Charlie dead in the bathtub. Of the apartment in Manhattan. Of Spencer driving himself into a frenzy of lust as the climax to his life. Of the boy lying dead in the New York gutter with a bullet in his brain.

They all seemed very far away. He could almost believe it had all never happened. Could almost believe that this was just another evening meal with his family.

Except for the cherry glow that filled the sky and flooded in through the windows like an aura from some fantastic fireplace.

Near the end of the meal Grace went and got a box. She

sat down at the table with it and opened it. She took out
white pills. Doris looked at her, her large eyes searching.

"This is dessert," Grace told her. "We're all going to have
white candy for dessert."

"Is it peppermint?" Doris asked.

"Yes," Grace said. "It's peppermint."

Richard felt his scalp crawling as Grace put pills in front
of Doris. In front of Ray.

"We haven't enough for all of us," she said to Richard.

"I have my own," he said.

"Have you enough for Mom?" she asked.

"I won't need any," her mother said.

In his tenseness, Richard almost shouted at her. Shouted—
Oh stop being so damned noble! But he held himself. He
stared in fascinated horror at Doris holding the pills in her
small hand.

"This isn't peppermint," she said. "Momma this isn't . . ."

"Yes it is." Grace took a deep breath. "Eat it, darling."

Doris put one in her mouth. She made a face. Then she spit
it into her palm.

"It isn't peppermint," she said, upset.

Grace threw up her hand and buried her teeth in the white
knuckles. Her eyes moved frantically to Ray.

"Eat it, Doris," Ray said. "Eat it, it's good."

Doris started to cry. "No, I don't like it."

"Eat it!"

Ray turned away suddenly, his body shaking. Richard tried
to think of some way to make her eat the pills but he couldn't.
Then his mother spoke.

"We'll play a game, Doris," she said. "We'll see if you
can swallow all the candy before I count ten. If you do I'll
give you a dollar."

Doris sniffed. "A dollar?" she said.

Richard's mother nodded.

"One," she said.

Doris didn't move.

"Two," said Richard's mother, "A dollar . . ."

Doris brushed aside a tear. "A . . . whole dollar?"

"Yes, darling. Three, four, hurry up."

Doris reached for the pills.

"Five . . . six . . . seven . . ."

Grace had her eyes shut tightly. Her cheeks were white.

"Nine . . . ten . . ."

Richard's mother smiled but her lips trembled and there was a glistening in her eyes.

"There," she said charfully. "You've won the game."

Grace suddenly put pills into her mouth and swallowed them in fast succession. She looked at Ray. He reached out one trembling hand and swallowed his pills. Richard put his hand in his pocket for his pills but took it out again. He didn't want his mother to watch him take them.

Doris got sleepy almost immediately. She yawned and couldn't keep her eyes open. Ray picked her up and she rested against his shoulder, her small arms around his neck. Grace got up and the three of them went back into the bedroom.

Richard sat there while his mother went back and said goodbye to them. He sat staring at the white table cloth and the remains of food.

When his mother came back she smiled at him.

"Help me with the dishes," she said.

"The . . . ?" he started. Then he stopped. What difference did it make what they did?

He stood with her in the redlit kitchen, feeling a sense of sharp unreality as he dried the dishes they would never use again and put them in the closet that would be no more in a matter of hours.

He kept thinking about Ray and Grace in the bedroom. Finally he left the kitchen without a word and went back. He opened the door and looked in. He looked at the three of them for a long time. Then he shut the door again and walked slowly back to the kitchen. He stared at his mother.

"They're . . ."

"All right," his mother said.

"Why didn't you say anything to them?" he asked her. "How come you let them do it without saying anything?"

"Richard," she said, "Everyone has to make his own way on this day. No one can tell others what to do. Doris was their child."

"And I'm yours . . . ?"

"You're not a child any longer," she said.

He finished up the dishes, his fingers numb and shaking.

"Mom, about last night," he said.

"I don't care about it," she said.

"But . . ."

"It doesn't matter," she said. "This part is ending."

Now, he thought, almost with pain. This part. Now she would talk about afterlife and heaven and reward for the just and eternal penitence for the sinning.

She said, "Let's go out and sit on the porch."

He didn't understand. He walked through the quiet house with her. He sat next to her on the porch steps and thought. I'll never see Grace again. Or Doris. Or Norman or Spencer or Mary or anybody . . .

He couldn't take it all in. It was too much. All he could do was sit there woodenly and look at the red sky and the huge sun about to swallow them. He couldn't even feel nervous any more. Fears were blunted by endless repetition.

"Mom," he said after a while, "Why . . . why haven't you spoken about religion to me? I know you must want to."

She looked at him and her face was very gentle in the red glow.

"I don't have to, darling," she said. "I know we'll be together when this is over. You don't have to believe it. I'll believe for both of us."

And that was all. He looked at her, marveling at her confidence and her strength.

"If you want to take those pills now," she said, "It's all right. You can go to sleep in my lap."

He felt himself tremble. "You wouldn't mind?"

"I want you to do what you think is best."

He didn't know what to do until he thought of her sitting there alone when the world ended.

"I'll stay with you," he said impulsively.

She smiled.

"If you change your mind," she said, "You can tell me."

They were quiet for a while. Then she said,

"It is pretty."

"Pretty?" he asked.

"Yes," she said, "God closes a bright curtain on our play."

He didn't know. But he put his arm around her shoulders and she leaned against him. And he did know one thing.

They sat there in the evening of the last day. And, though there was no actual point to it, they loved each other.

Little Girl Lost ◆◆◆◆◆◆◆◆◆◆◆◆◆◆◆◆◆◆◆◆◆◆

TINA'S crying woke me up in a second. It was pitch black, middle of the night. I heard Ruth stir beside me in bed. In the front room Tina caught her breath, then started in again, louder.

"Oh, gawd," I muttered groggily.

Ruth grunted and started to push back the covers.

"I'll get it," I said wearily and she slumped back on the pillow. We take turns when Tina has her nights; has a cold or a stomachache or just takes a flop out of bed.

I lifted up my legs and dropped them over the edge of the blankets. Then I squirmed myself down to the foot of the bed and slung my legs over the edge. I winced as my feet touched the icy floor boards. The apartment was arctic, it usually is these winter nights, even in California.

I padded across the cold floor threading my way between the chest, the bureau, the bookcase in the hall and then the edge of the TV set as I moved into the livingroom. Tina sleeps there because we could only get a one bedroom apartment. She sleeps on a couch that breaks down into a bed. And, at that moment, her crying was getting louder and she started calling for her mommy.

"All right. Tina. Daddy'll fix it all up," I told her.

She kept crying. Outside, on the balcony, I heard our collie Mack jump down from his bed on the camp chair.

I bent over the couch in the darkness. I could feel that the covers were lying flat. I backed away, squinting at the floor but I didn't see any Tina moving around.

"Oh, my God," I chuckled to myself, in spite of irritation, "the poor kid's under the couch."

I got down on my knees and looked, still chuckling at the thought of little Tina falling out of bed and crawling under the couch.

"Tina, where are you?" I said, trying not to laugh.

Her crying got louder but I couldn't see her under the couch. It was too dark to see clearly.

"Hey, where are you, kiddo?" I asked. "Come to papa."

Like a man looking for a collar button under the bureau I felt under the couch for my daughter, who was still crying and begging for mommy, mommy.

Came the first twist of surprise. I couldn't reach her no matter how hard I stretched.

"Come on, Tina," I said, amused no longer, "stop playing games with your old man."

She cried louder. My outstretched hand jumped back as it touched the cold wall.

"Daddy!" Tina cried.

"Oh for . . . !"

I stumbled up and jolted irritably across the rug. I turned on the lamp beside the record player and turned to get her, and was stopped dead in my tracks, held there, a half-asleep mute, gaping at the couch, ice water plaiting down my back.

Then, in a leap, I was on my knees by the couch and my eyes were searching frantically, my throat getting tighter and tighter. I heard her crying under the couch, but I couldn't see her.

My stomach muscles jerked in as the truth of it struck me. I ran my hands around wildly under the bed but they didn't touch a thing. I heard her crying and by God, she wasn't there!

"Ruth!" I yelled, "Come here."

I heard Ruth catch her breath in the bedroom and then there was a rustle of bedclothes and the sound of her feet rushing across the bedroom floor. Out of the side of my eyes I saw the light blue movement of her nightgown.

"What is it?" she gasped.

I backed to my feet, hardly able to breathe much less speak. I started to say something but the words choked up in my throat. My mouth hung open. All I could do was point a shaking finger at the couch.

"Where is she!" Ruth cried.

"I don't know!" I finally managed. "She . . ."

"What!"

Ruth dropped to her knees beside the couch and looked under.

"Tina!" she called.

"Mommy."

Ruth recoiled from the couch, color draining from her face. The eyes she turned to me were horrified. I suddenly heard the sound of Mack scratching wildly at the door.

"Where is she?" Ruth asked again, her voice hollow.

"I don't know," I said, feeling numb. I turned on the light and . . .

"But she's crying," Ruth said as if she felt the same distrust of sight that I did. "I . . . Chris, listen."

The sound of our daughter crying and sobbing in fright.

"Tina!" I called loudly, pointlessly, "where are you, angel?"

She just cried. "Mommy!" she said, "Mommy, pick me up!"

"No, no, this is crazy," Ruth said, her voice tautly held as she rose to her feet, "she's in the kitchen."

"But . . ."

I stood there dumbly as Ruth turned on the kitchen light and went in. The sound of her agonized voice made me shudder.

"Chris! She's not in here."

She came running in, her eyes stark with fear. She bit her teeth into her lip.

"But, where is . . .?" she started to say, then stopped.

Because we both heard Tina crying and the sound of it was coming from under the couch.

But there wasn't anything under the couch.

Still Ruth couldn't accept the crazy truth. She jerked open the hall closet and looked in it. She looked behind the TV set, even behind the record player, a space of maybe two inches.

"Honey, help me," she begged, "we can't just leave her this way."

I didn't move.

"Honey, she's under the couch," I said.

"But she's not!"

Once more, like the crazy, impossible dream it was, me on my knees on the cold floor, feeling under the couch. I got under the couch, I touched every inch of floor space there. But I couldn't touch her, even though I heard her crying— right in my ear.

I got up, shivering from the cold and something else. Ruth stood in the middle of the livingroom rug staring at me. Her voice was weak, almost inaudible.

"Chris," she said, "Chris, what is it?"

I shook my head. "Honey, I don't know," I said, "I don't know what it is."

Outside, Mack began to whine as he scratched. Ruth glanced at the balcony door, her face a white twist of fear. She was shivering now in her silk gown as she looked back at the couch. I stood there absolutely helpless, my mind racing a dozen different ways, none of them toward a solution, not even toward concrete thought.

"What are we going to do?" she asked, on the verge of a scream I knew was coming.

"Baby, I . . ."

I stopped short and suddenly we were both moving for the couch.

Tina's crying was fainter.

"Oh, no," Ruth whimpered, "No. Tina."

"Mommy," said Tina, further away. I could feel the chills lacing over my flesh.

"Tina, come back here!" I heard myself shouting, the father yelling at his disobedient child, who can't be seen.

"TINA!" Ruth screamed.

Then the apartment was dead silent and Ruth and I were kneeling by the couch looking at the emptiness underneath. Listening.

To the sound of our child, peacefully snoring.

"Bill, can you come right over?" I said frantically.

"What?" Bill's voice was thick and fuzzy.

"Bill, this is Chris. Tina has disappeared!"

He woke up.

"She's been kidnaped?" he asked.

"No," I said, "she's here but . . . she's not here."

He made a confused sound. I grabbed in a breath.

"Bill, for God's sake get over here!"

A pause.

"I'll be right over," he said. I knew from the way he said it he didn't know why he was coming.

I dropped the receiver and went over to where Ruth was sitting on the couch shivering and clasping her hands tightly in her lap.

"Hon, get your robe," I said. "You'll catch cold."

"Chris, I . . ." Tears running down her cheeks. "Chris, where is she?"

"Honey."

It was all I could say, hopelessly, weakly. I went into the bedroom and got her robe. On the way back I stooped over and twisted hard on the wall heater.

"There," I said, putting the robe over her back, "put it on."

She put her arms through the sleeves of the robe, her eyes pleading with me to do something. Knowing very well I couldn't do it, she was asking me to bring her baby back.

I got on my knees again, just to be doing something. I knew it wouldn't help any. I remained there a long time just staring at the floor under the couch. Completely in the dark.

"Chris, she's s-sleeping on the floor," Ruth said, her words faltering from colorless lips. "Won't . . . she catch cold?"

"I . . ."

That was all I could say. What could I tell her? No, she's not on the floor? How did I know? I could hear Tina breathing and snoring gently on the floor but she wasn't there to touch. She was gone but she wasn't gone. My brain twisted back and forth on itself trying to figure out that one. Try adjusting to something like that sometime. It's a fast way to breakdown.

"Honey, she's . . . she's not here," I said, "I mean . . . not on the floor."

"But . . ."

"I know, I know . . ." I raised my hands and shrugged in defeat. "I don't think she's cold, honey," I said as gently and persuasively as I could.

She started to say something too but then she stopped. There was nothing to say. It defied words.

We sat in the quiet room waiting for Bill to come. I'd called him because he's an engineering man, CalTech, top man with Lockheed over in the valley. I don't know why I thought that would help but I called him. I'd have called anyone just to have another mind to help. Parents are useless beings when they're afraid for their children.

Once, before Bill came, Ruth slipped to her knees by the couch and started slapping her hands over the floor.

"Tina, wake up!" she cried in newborn terror, "wake up!"

"Honey, what good is that going to do?" I asked.

She looked up at me blankly and knew. It wasn't going to do any good.

I heard Bill on the steps and reached the door before he

did. He came in quietly, looking around and giving Ruth a
brief smile. I took his coat. He was still in pajamas.

"What is it, kid?" he asked hurriedly.

I told him as briefly and as clearly as I could. He got down
on his knees and checked for himself. He felt around underneath the couch and I saw his brow knot into lines when
he heard Tina's calm and peaceful breathing.

He straightened up.

"Well?" I asked.

He shook his head. "My God," he muttered.

We both stared at him. Outside Mack was still scratching
and whining at the door.

"Where is she?" Ruth asked again, "Bill, I'm about to lose
my mind."

"Take it easy," he said. I moved beside her and put my
arm around her. She was trembling.

"You can hear her breathing," Bill said. "It's normal breathing. She must be all right."

"But where is she?" I asked, "you can't see her, you can't
even touch her."

"I don't know," Bill said and was on his knees by the
bed again.

"Chris, you'd better let Mack in," Ruth said, worried about
that for a moment, "he'll wake all the neighbors."

"All right, I will," I said and kept watching Bill.

"Should we call the police?" I asked. "Do you . . . ?"

"No, no, that wouldn't do any good," Bill said, "this
isn't . . ." He shook his head as if he were shaking away everything he'd ever accepted. "It's not a police job," he said.

"Chris, he'll wake up all the . . ."

I turned for the door to let Mack in.

"Wait a minute," Bill said and I was turned back, my heart
pounding again.

Bill was half under the couch, listening hard.

"Bill, what is . . . ?" I started.

"Shhh!"

We were both quiet. Bill stayed there a moment longer.
Then he straightened up and his face was blank.

"I can't hear her," he said.

"Oh, no!"

Ruth fell forward before the couch.

"Tina! Oh God, where is she!"

Bill was up on his feet, moving quickly around the room.
I watched him, then looked back at Ruth slumped over the
couch, sick with fear.

"Listen," Bill said, "do you hear anything?"

Ruth looked up. "Hear . . . anything?"

"Move around, move around," Bill said. "See what you
hear."

Like robots Ruth and I moved around the livingroom
having no idea what we were doing. Everything was quiet
except for the incessant whining and scratching of Mack.
I gritted my teeth and muttered a terse—"Shut up!"—as I
passed the balcony door. For a second the vague idea crossed
my mind that Mack knew about Tina. He'd always worshiped
her.

Then there was Bill standing in the corner where the closet
was, stretching up on his toes and listening. He noticed us
watching him and gestured quickly for us to come over. We
moved hurriedly across the rug and stood beside him.

"Listen," he whispered. We did.

At first there was nothing. Then Ruth gasped and none of
us were letting out the noise of breath.

Up in the corner, where the ceiling met the walls, we could
hear the sound of Tina sleeping.

Ruth stared up there, her face white, totally lost.

"Bill, what the . . ." I gave up.

Bill just shook his head slowly. Then suddenly he held up
his hand and we all froze, jolted again.

The sound was gone.

Ruth started to sob helplessly. "Tina."

She started out of the corner.

"We have to find her," she said despairingly. "Please."

We ran around the room in unorganized circles, trying to
hear Tina. Ruth's tear-streaked face was twisted into a mask of
fright.

I was the one who found her this time.

Under the television set.

We all knelt there and listened. As we did we heard her
murmur a little to herself and the sound of her stirring in
sleep.

"Want my dolly," she muttered.

"Tina!"

I held Ruth's shaking body in my arms and tried to stop her sobbing. Without success. I couldn't keep my own throat from tightening, my heart from pounding slow and hard in my chest. My hands shook on her back, slick with sweat.

"For God's sake, *what is it?*" Ruth said but she wasn't asking us.

Bill helped me take her to a chair by the record player. Then he stood restlessly on the rug, gnawing furiously on one knuckle, the way I'd seen him do so often when he was engrossed in a problem.

He looked up, started to say something then gave it up and turned for the door.

"I'll let the pooch in," he said. "He's making a hell of a racket."

"Don't you have any idea what might have happened to her? I asked.

"*Bill . . . ?*" Ruth begged.

Bill said. "I think she's in another dimension," and he opened the door.

What happened next came so fast we couldn't do a thing to stop it.

Mack came bounding in with a yelp and headed straight for the couch.

"He *knows!*" Bill yelled and dived for the dog.

Then happened the crazy part. One second Mack was sliding under the couch in a flurry of ears, paws and tail. Then he was gone—*just like that.* Blotted up. The three of us gaped.

Then I heard Bill say, "Yes. Yes."

"Yes, *what?*" I didn't know where *I* was by then.

"The kid's in another dimension."

"What are you talking about?" I said in worried, near-angry tones. You don't hear talk like that everyday.

"Sit down," he said.

"Sit down? Isn't there anything we can *do?*"

Bill looked hurriedly at Ruth. She seemed to know what he was going to say.

"I don't know if there is," was what he said.

I slumped back on the couch.

"Bill," I said. Just speaking his name.

He gestured helplessly.

"Kid," he said, "this has caught me as wide open as you. I don't even know if I'm right or not but I can't think of anything else. I think that in some way, she's gotten herself into another dimension, probably the fourth. Mack, sensing it, followed her there. But how did they get there?—I don't know. I was under that couch, so were you. Did you see anything?"

I looked at him and he knew the answer.

"Another . . . *dimension?*" Ruth said in a tight voice. The voice of a mother who has just been told her child is lost forever.

Bill started pacing, punching his right fist into his palm.

"Damn, damn," he muttered. "How do things like this happen?"

Then while we sat there numbly, half listening to him, half for the sound of our child, he spoke. Not to us really. To himself, to try and place the problem in the proper perspective.

"One dimensional space a line," he threw out the words quickly. "Two dimensional space an infinite number of lines—an infinite number of one dimensional spaces. Three dimensional space an infinite number of planes—an infinite number of two dimensional spaces. Now the basic factor . . . the *basic* factor . . ."

He slammed his palm and looked up at the ceiling. Then he started again, more slowly now.

"Every point in each dimension a *section* of a line in the next higher dimension. All points in line-*sections* of the perpendicular lines that make the line a plane. All points in plane are sections of perpendicular lines that make the plane a solid.

"That means that in the third dimension . . ."

"Bill, for God's sake!" Ruth burst out. "Can't we do something? My *baby* is in . . . in *there.*"

Bill lost his train of thought. He shook his head.

"Ruth, I don't . . ."

I got up then and was down on the floor again, climbing under the couch. I *had* to find it! I felt, I searched. I listened until the silence rang. Nothing.

Then I jerked up suddenly and hit my head as Mack barked loudly in my ear.

Bill rushed over and slid in beside me, his breath labored and quick.

"God's sake," he muttered, almost furiously. "Of all the damn places in the world . . ."

"If the . . . the entrance is here," I muttered, "why did we hear her voice and breathing all over the room?"

"Well, if she moved beyond the effect of the third dimension and was entirely in the fourth—then her movement, for us would seem to spread over all space. Actually she'd be in one spot in the fourth dimension but to us . . ."

He stopped.

Mack was whining. But more importantly Tina started in again. Right by our ears.

"He brought her back!" Bill said excitedly. "Man, what a mutt!"

He started twisting around, looking, touching, slapping at empty air.

"We've got to find it!" he said. "We've got to reach in and pull them out. God knows how long this dimension pocket will last."

"What?" I heard Ruth gasp, then suddenly cry, "Tina, where are you? This is mommy."

I was about to say something about it being no use but then Tina answered.

"Mommy, mommy! Where are you, mommy?"

Then the sound of Mack growling and Tina crying angrily.

"She's trying to run around and find Ruth," Bill said. "But Mack won't let her. I don't know *how* but he seems to know where the joining place is."

"Where are they for God's sake!" I said in a nervous fury. And backed right into the damn thing.

To my dying day I'll never really be able to describe what it was like. But here goes.

It was black, yes—to me. And yet there seemed to be a million lights. But as soon as I looked at one it disappeared and was gone. I saw them out of the sides of my eyes.

"Tina," I said, "where are you? Answer me! Please!"

And heard my voice echoing a million times, the words echoing endlessly, never ceasing but moving off as if they were alive and traveling. And when I moved my hand the motion made a whistling sound that echoed and re-echoed and moved away like a swarm of insects flowing into the night.

"Tina!"

The sound of the echoing hurt my ears.

"Chris, can you hear her?" I heard a voice. But was it a voice—or more like a thought?

Then something wet touched my hand and I jumped.

Mack.

I reached around furiously for them, every motion making whistling echoes in vibrating blackness until I felt as if I were surrounded by a multitude of birds flocking and beating insane wings around my head. The pressure pounded and heaved in my brain.

Then I felt Tina. I say I felt her but I think if she wasn't my daughter and if I didn't know somehow it was her, I would have thought I'd touched something else. Not a shape in the sense of third dimension shape. Let it go at that, I don't want to go into it.

"Tina," I whispered. "Tina, baby."

"Daddy, I'm scared of dark," she said in a thin voice and Mack whined.

Then I was scared of dark too, because a thought scared my mind.

How did I get us all out?

Then the other thought came—Chris, have you got them?

"I've got them!" I called.

And Bill grabbed my legs (which, I later learned, were still sticking out in the third dimension) and jerked me back to reality with an armful of daughter and dog and memories of something I'd prefer having no memories about.

We all came piling out under the couch and I hit my head on it and and almost knocked myself out. Then I was being alternately hugged by Ruth, kissed by the dog and helped to my feet by Bill. Mack was leaping on all of us, yelping and drooling.

When I was in talking shape again I noticed that Bill had blocked off the bottom of the couch with two card tables.

"Just to be safe," he said.

I nodded weakly. Ruth came in from the bedroom.

"Where's Tina?" I asked automaticaly, uneasy left-overs of memory still cooking in my brain.

"She's in our bed," she said. "I don't think we'll mind for one night."

I shook my head.

"I don't think so," I said.

Then I turned to Bill.

"Look," I said. "What the hell happened?"

"Well," he said, with a wry grin, "I told you. The third dimension is just a step below the fourth. In particular, every point in our space is a section of a perpendicular line in the fourth dimension."

"So?" I said.

"So, although the lines forming the fourth dimension would be perpendicular to every point in the third dimension, they wouldn't be parallel—to us. But if enough of them in one area happened to be parallel in *both* dimensions—it might form a connecting corridor."

"You mean . . . ?"

"That's the crazy part," he said. "Of all the places in the world—under the couch—there's an area of points that are sections of parallel lines—parallel in both dimensions. They make a corridor into the next space."

"Or a hole," I said.

Bill looked disgusted.

"Hell of a lot of good my reasoning did," he said. "It took a *dog* to get her out."

I groaned softly.

"You can have it," I said.

"Who wants it?" he answered.

"What about the sound?"

"You're asking me?" he said.

That's about it. Oh, naturally, Bill told his friends at CalTech, and the apartment was overrun with research physicists for a month. But they didn't find anything. They said the thing was gone. Some said worse things.

But, just the same, when we got back from my mother's house where we stayed during the scientific seige—we moved the couch across the room and stuck the television where the couch was.

So some night we may look up and hear Arthur Godfrey chuckling from another dimension. Maybe he belongs there.

The Doll That Does Everything ·······

THE poet screamed, "Devil spawn! Scrabbling lizard! Maniacal kangaroo!"

His scraggy frame went leaping through the doorway, then locked into paralysis. *"Fiend!"* he gagged.

The object of this mottled-faced abuse squatted oblivious in a snowbank of confettied manuscript. Manuscript delivered of sweaty gestation, typewritten in quivering agony.

"Foaming moonstruck *octopus! Shovel-handed ape!*" The blood-laced eyes of Ruthlen Beauson bagged gibbously behind their horn-rimmed lenses. At hipless sides, his fingers shook like leprous stringbeans in a gale. Ulcers within ulcers throbbed.

"Hun!" he raged anew, *"Goth! Apache!* Demented nihilist!"

Saliva dribbling from his teething maw, little Gardner Beauson bestowed a one-toothed grin upon his palsied sire. Shredded poetry filtered through his stubby fists as the semispheroid of his bottom hovered dampishly above each lacerated amphibrach with iambic variation.

Ruthlen Beauson groaned a soul-wracked groan. *"Confusion,"* he lamented in a trembling voice, "Untrammeled farrago."

Then, suddenly, his eyes embossed into metallic orbs, his fingers petrified into a strangler's pose. "I'll do him in," he gibbered faintly, "I'll snap his hyoid with a brace of thumbs."

Upon this juncture, Athene Beauson smock bespattered, hands adrip with soppy clay, swept into the room like a wraith of vengeance resurrected from the mud.

"What *now?"* she asked, acidulous through gritted teeth.

"Look! *Look!"* Ruthlen Beauson's forefinger jabbed fitfully as he pointed toward their sniggering child. "He's destroyed my *Songs of Sconce!"* His 20-90 eyes went bulgy mad. "I'll

177

carve him," he foreboded in a roupy whisper, "I'll carve the shriveled viper!"

"Oh . . . *look out*," Athene commanded, pulling back her butcher-bent spouse and dragging up her son by his drool-soaked undershirt.

Suspended over heaps of riven muse, he eyed his mother with a saucy aspect.

"*Whelp!*" she snapped, then let him have one, soundly, on his bulbous rump.

Gardner Beauson screeched in inflammatory protest, was shown the door and exited, his little brain already cocked for further action. A residue of clay upon his diaper, he waddled, saucer-eyed, into the plenitude of breakables which was the living room as Athene turned to see her husband on his knees, aghast, in the rubble of a decade's labor.

"I shall destroy myself," the poet mumbled, sagging shouldered. "I'll inject my veins with lethal juices."

"Get up, get up," said Athene crisply, face a sour mask. Ruthlen floundered to his feet. "I'll kill him, yes, I'll kill the wizened beast," he said in hollow-hearted shock.

"That's *no* solution," said his wife, "Even though . . ."

Her eyes grew soft a moment as she dreamed of nudging Gardner into a vat of alligators. Her full lips quivered on the brink of tremulous smiling.

Then her green eyes flinted. "That's *no* solution," she repeated, "and it's time we solved this goddam thing."

Ruthlen stared with dumb-struck eyes upon the ruins of his composition. "I'll kill him," he divulged to the scattered fragments, "I'll—"

"Ruthlen, *listen* to me," said his wife, clay-soaked fingers clenching into fists.

His spiritless gaze lifted for a moment.

"Gardner needs a playmate," she declared. "I read it in a book. He needs a playmate."

"I'll kill him," mumbled Ruthlen.

"Will you *listen!*"

"Kill him."

"I tell you Gardner has to have a playmate! I don't care whether we can afford it or not, he needs a playmate!"

"Kill," the poet hissed. "Kill."

"I don't care if we haven't got a cent! You want time for poetry and I want time for sculpturing!"

"My *Songs of Sconce.*"

"*Ruthlen Beauson!*" Athene screamed, a moment's time before the deafening shatter of a vase.

"Good God, what *now!*" Athene exclaimed.

They found him dangling from the mantelpiece, caterwauling for succor and immediate change of diaper . .

THE DOLL THAT DOES EVERYTHING!

Athene stood before the plate glass window, lips pursed in deep deliberation. In her mind, a vivid balance see-sawed—grave necessity on the one side, sterile income on the other. Implastic contemplation ridged her brow. They had no money, that was patent. Nursery school was out, a governess impossible. And yet, there had to be an answer; there *had* to be.

Athene braced herself and strode into the shop.

The man looked up, a kindly smile dimpling his apple cheeks, welcoming his customer.

"That doll," Athene inquired. "Does it really do the things your placard says it does?"

"That doll," the salesman beamed, "is quite without comparison, the nonpareil of toycraft. It walks, it talks, it eats and drinks, dispenses body wastes, snores while it sleeps, dances a jig, rides a seesaw and sings the choruses of seven childhood favorites." He caught his breath. "To name a few," he said "It sings 'Molly Andrews'—"

"What is the cost of—"

"It swims the crawl for fifty feet, it reads a book, plays thirteen simple etudes on the pianoforte, mows the lawn, changes its own diapers, climbs a tree and burps."

"What is the price of—"

"And it grows," the salesman said.

"It . . ."

"*Grows,*" the man reiterated, slit-eyed. "Within its plastic body are all the cells and protoplasms necessary for a cycle of maturation lasting up to twenty years."

Athene gaped.

"At one-oh-seven-fifty, an obvious bargain," the man concluded. "Shall I have it wrapped or would you rather walk it home?"

A swarm of eager hornets, each a thought, buzzed inside the head of Athene Beauson. It was the perfect playmate for

little Gardner. One-hundred-seven-fifty though! Ruthlen's
scream would shatter windows when he saw the tag.

"You can't go wrong," the salesman said.

He needs a playmate!

"Time payments can easily be arranged." The salesman
guessed her plight and fired his coup de grâce.

All thoughts disappeared like chips swept off a gambling
table. Athene's eyes caught fire; a sudden smile pulled up her
lip ends.

"A boy doll," she requested eagerly, "One year old."

The salesman hurried to his shelves . . .

No windows broke but Athene's ears rang for half an hour
after.

"Are you mad?" her husband's scream had plunged its
strident blades into her brain. "One-hundred-seven-fifty!"

"We can pay on time."

"With what?" he shrieked. "Rejection slips and clay!"

"Would you rather," Athene lashed out, "have your son
alone all day? Wandering through the house—tearing—
cracking—ripping—crushing?"

Ruthlen winced at every word as if they were spiked
shillelagh blows crushing in his head. His eyes fell shut behind
the quarter-inch lenses. He shuddered fitfully.

"Enough," he muttered, pale hand raised, surrendering.
"Enough, enough."

"Let's bring the doll to Gardner," Athene said excitedly.

They hurried to the little bedroom of their son and found
him tearing down the curtains. A hissing, taut-cheeked Ruthlen jerked him off the windowsill and knuckles rapped him
on the skull. Gardner blinked once his beady eyes.

"Put him down," Athene said quickly. "Let him see."

Gardner stared with one-toothed mouth ajar at the little
doll that stood so silently before him. The doll was just about
his size, dark-haired, blue-eyed, flesh-colored, diapered, exactly
like a real boy.

He blinked furiously.

"Activate the mechanism," Ruthlen whispered and Athene,
leaning over, pushed the tiny button.

Gardner toppled back in drooling consternation as the little
boy doll grinned at him. "Bah-bi-bah-bah!" Gardner cried
hysterically.

"Bah-bi-bah-bah," echoed the doll.

Gardner scuttled back, wild-eyed, and, from a wary crouch, observed the little boy doll waddling toward him. Restrained from further retreat by the wall, he cringed with tense astonishment until the doll clicked to a halt before him.

"Bah-bi-bah-bah." The boy doll grinned again, then burped a single time and started in to jig on the linoleum.

Gardner's pudgy lips spread out, abruptly, in an idiotic grin. He gurgled happily. His parents' eyes went shut as one, beatific smiles creasing their grateful faces, all thoughts of financial caviling vanished.

"*Oh,*" Athene whispered wonderingly.

"I can't believe it's true," her husband said, guttural with awe . . .

For weeks, they were inseparable, Gardner and his motor-driven friend. They squatted down together, exchanging moon-eyed glances, chuckling over intimate jollities and, in the general relishing to the full their drooly tête à têtes. Whatever Gardner did, the doll did too.

As for Ruthlen and Athene, they rejoiced in this advent of near-forgotten peace. Nerve-knotting screams no longer hammered malleus on incus and the sound of breaking things was not upon the air. Ruthlen poesied and Athene sculpted, all in a bliss of sabbath privacy.

"You see?" she said across the dinner table of an evening. "It was all he needed; a companion," and Ruthlen bowed his head in solemn tribute to his wife's perspicacity.

"True, 'tis true," he whispered happily.

A week, a month. Then gradually, the metamorphosis.

Ruthlen, bogged in sticky pentameter, looked up one morning, eyes marbleized. "Hark," he murmured.

The sound of dismemberment of plaything.

Ruthlen hastened to the nursery to find his only begotten ripping cotton entrails from a heretofore respected doll.

The gloom-eyed poet stood outside the room, his heartbeat dwindling to the sickening thud of old while, in the nursery, Gardner disemboweled and the doll sat on the floor, observing.

"No," the poet murmured, sensing it was yes. He crept away, somehow managing to convince himself it was an accident.

However, early the following afternoon at lunch, the fingers of both Ruthlen and his wife pressed in so sharply on their sandwiches that slices of tomato popped across the air and into the coffee.

"What," said Athene horribly, "is that?"

Gardner and his doll were found ensconced in the rubble of what had been, in happier times, a potted plant.

The doll was watching with a glassy interest as Gardner heaved up palmfuls of the blackish earth which rained in dirty crumbs upon the rug.

"No," the poet said, ulcers revivified and, "No," the echo fell from Athene's paling lips.

Their son was spanked and put to bed, the doll was barricaded in the closet. A wounded caterwauling in their ears, the wife and husband twitched through wordless lunch while acids bred viler acids in their spasmed stomachs.

One remark alone was spoken as they faltered to their separate works and Athene said it.

"It was an accident."

But, in the following week, they had to leave their work exactly eighty-seven times.

Once it was Gardner thrashing in pulled-down draperies in the living room. Another time it was Gardner playing piano with a hammer in respondence to the doll's performance of a Bach gavotte. Still another time and time after time it was a rash of knocked-down objects ranging from jam jars to chairs. In all, thirty breakables broke, the cat disappeared and the floor showed through the carpet where Gardner had been active with a scissors.

At the end of two days, the Beausons poesied and sculpted with eyes embossed and white lips rigid over grinding teeth. At the end of four, their bodies underwent a petrifying process, their brains began to ossify. By the week's end, after many a flirt and flutter of their viscera, they sat or stood in palsied silence, waiting for new outrages and dreaming of violent infanticide.

The end arrived.

One evening, suppering on a pitcherful of stomach-easing seltzers, Athene and her husband sat like rigor-mortised scarecrows in their chairs, their eyes four balls of blood-threaded stupor.

"What are we to do?" a spirit-broken Ruthlen muttered.

Athene's head moved side to side in negating jerks. "I thought the doll—" she started, then allowed her voice to drift away.

"The doll has done no good," lamented Ruthlen. "We're right back where we started. And deeper still by one-oh-seven-fifty, since you say the doll cannot be exchanged."

"It can't," said Athene, "It's—"

She was caught in mid-word by the noise.

It was a moist and slapping sound like someone heaving mud against a wall. Mud or—

"No." Athene raised her soul-bruised eyes. "Oh, no."

The sudden spastic flopping of her sandals on the floor syncopated with the blood-wild pounding of her heart.. Her husband followed on his broomstick legs, lips a trembling circle of misgiving.

"My figure!" Athene screamed, standing a stricken marble in the studio doorway, staring ashen-faced upon the ghastly sight.

Gardner and the doll were playing *Hit the Roses on the Wallpaper*, using for ammunition great doughy blobs of clay ripped from Athene's uncompleted statue.

Athene and Ruthlen stood in horror-struck dumbness staring at the doll who, in the metal doming of its skull had fashioned new synaptic joinings and, to the jigging and the climbing and the burping, added flinging of clay.

And, suddenly it was clear—the falling plant, the broken vases and jars on high shelves—*Gardner needed help for things like that!*

Ruthlen Beauson seered a grisly future: i.e., the grisly past times two; all the Guignol torments of living with Gardner but multiplied by the presence of the doll.

"Get that metal monster from this house," Ruthlen mumbled to his wife through concrete lips.

"But there's no exchange!" she cried hysterically.

"Then it's me for the can opener!" the poet rasped, backing away on rocklike legs.

"It's not the doll's fault!" Athene shouted. "What good will tearing up the doll do? It's Gardner. It's that horrid thing we made together!"

The poet's eyes clicked sharply in their sockets as he looked from doll to son and back again and knew the hideous truth

of her remark. It was their son. The doll just imitated, the
doll would do whatever it was—

—made to do.

That was, precisely, to the second, when the idea came and,
with it, peace unto the Beauson household.

From the next day forth, their Gardner was a model of
deportment, the house became a sanctuary for blessed crea-
tion.

Everything was perfect.

It was only twenty years later, when a college-going Gardner
Beauson met a wriggly sophomore and blew thirteen gaskets
and his generator that the ugly truth came out.